SURROUNDED

His words cut short as a rifle shot exploded from a ridgeline above them. The shot ricocheted off a rock and whined upward an inch from Jewel Higgs's ear. "Jesus!" Higgs shouted. His horse spooked and reared high as he ducked away from the whistling bullet.

Joe Poole snatched for his pistol with one hand as he tried to settle his horse with his other. Above them, a succession of rifle shots exploded, kicking up dirt and loose rock around the hooves of the already spooked horses.

"Run for it!" screamed Eddie Grafe. "They've got us surrounded!"

Twenty yards above the trail, Cray Dawson stood up, watching the gunmen race their terrified horses along the widening trail toward Somos Santos. Dust billowed high in their wake. Dawson raised his rifle to his shoulder. . . .

BETWEEN HELL AND TEXAS

Ralph Cotton

A SIGNET BOOK

SIGNET
Published by New American Library, a division of
Penguin Group (USA) Inc., 375 Hudson Street,
New York, New York 10014, U.S.A.
Penguin Books Ltd, 80 Strand,
London WC2R 0RL, England
Penguin Books Australia Ltd, 250 Camberwell Road,
Camberwell, Victoria 3124, Australia
Penguin Books Canada Ltd, 10 Alcorn Avenue,
Toronto, Ontario, Canada M4V 3B2
Penguin Books (N.Z.) Ltd, Cnr Rosedale and Airborne Roads,
Albany, Auckland 1310, New Zealand

Penguin Books Ltd, Registered Offices:
80 Strand, London WC2R 0RL, England

First published by Signet, an imprint of New American Library,
a division of Penguin Group (USA) Inc.

First Printing, March 2004
10 9 8 7 6 5

For Mary Lynn . . . *of course.*

PART 1

PART 1

Chapter 1

Cray Dawson had taken a partial load of buckshot in the back of his shoulder the day he and Lawrence Shaw killed Barton Talbert and his gang on the streets of Brakett Flats. But the pellets were small and it only took the town doctor a few minutes to remove them with a pair of long tweezers and the point of a sharp surgery blade. Within three days both Dawson and Shaw stepped up into their saddles, ready to ride away. The third man who had stood with them in the Talbert shootout, a young undertaker by the name of Jedson Caldwell, had already left town, headed for New Orleans he'd said. Lawrence Shaw hadn't made it clear where he might be headed, but for Dawson the decision came easy. He'd said all along that once the Talbert Gang had been taken down he would head back home. Home being Somos Santos, Texas.

"Tell anybody who needs to know that it'll be a while before I get back there," said Lawrence Shaw.

"I'll tell her," said Dawson, giving Shaw a look. He knew Shaw was referring to Carmelita, the sister of Shaw's dead wife, Rosa.

"She needs to go on back to her people," said Shaw.

"I'll tell her that too," said Dawson.

"Obliged. Watch your backside, Pard," Lawrence Shaw told him, the two of them stepping their mounts back from the hitch rail. "You're going to find life a little different now that you've gained a reputation as a big gun." Shaw gave him a flat smile.

"I'm not a *big gun*," said Dawson. "Gunfighting's over for me. All I want is a front porch facing south." He touched his fingers to his hat brim, watching Lawrence Shaw do the same, Shaw having to raise his arm slightly from a sling to do it.

"We'll see, *amigo*," Shaw said in parting. "Reputations are like guns; they're easier to pick up than they are to put down." Then he raised a glance to the southwest, where a black cloud boiled low on the distant horizon. "Got a storm coming . . . *un tormenta Mexicana*."

"It'll pass," said Dawson. "*Adios*, Shaw."

But for the rest of the day the storm pounded Dawson as he made his way toward the Quemado Valley, taking higher paths above rising creeks and run-off water. At a railroad settlement he stopped in the late afternoon and took dry shelter with a six-man survey crew that'd been mapping a route through the hillsides. After introducing himself to the surveyors he sat down with them and ate a plate of beans and salt pork. Then he sipped a steaming cup of coffee, feeling their questioning eyes upon him until finally he asked the leader, a fellow from Ohio named Robert Daniels, "Is there something on your mind, Mister Daniels?"

Daniels looked stunned at first, but then he let out a breath and said with a red face, "Well, yes, there is, if you don't mind me asking. Are you the Crayton Dawson who had the shootout with the Talberts in Brakett Flats?"

It had already started, Dawson reminded himself. "Yes, I am," he said reluctantly, going back to the coffee; raising it to his lips hoping the questions would stop there. But he knew that wouldn't be the case.

"My goodness, Mister Dawson!" said Daniels, pulling his wire-rim spectacles down the bridge of his nose, taking a closer look at Dawson above the thick lenses. "It certainly is an honor meeting you . . . we heard all about the fight. And we heard how you had also shot three gunmen over in Turkey Creek!"

Dawson said quietly, "Two of those men I shot in Turkey Creek weren't involved in the gunplay. One got shot by a secondhand bullet, the other was a pard of his who drew on me. I wish I hadn't shot him. But I can't change it."

"Well," said Daniels, as if he hadn't heard a word about the particulars surrounding the shooting, "it takes nerves of iron to face even *one* man with a gun, I'm sure, let alone *two or three*!" He nodded at the other surveyors for support.

They nodded in agreement. One asked, "What was it like standing side by side with Fast Larry Shaw?"

"I'd known Shaw for years," said Dawson. "We grew up together in Somos Santos, rode herd together soon as we were big enough to lift a rope. So I reckon I never gave it much thought, riding with him this time."

"My goodness," said Daniels, repeating himself, "you rode a vengeance trail with the fastest gun alive and thought nothing of it! That in itself says a lot about you. You are quite a gunman, sir, and I salute you. Indeed, we all salute you, right fellows?"

Heads nodded vigorously.

"With all respect, Mister Daniels," said Cray Dawson, "I'm no gunman. I'm just a regular fellow who joined a friend in search of the men who killed his wife. We found them, and we held them accountable for what they did. Now it's over and I'm headed home. This time next month I'll probably be sticking green horses or watching cattle swat flies off their rumps."

"Mister Dawson, I'm sure you are much too modest," said Daniels.

The surveyors nodded in unison again. This time their eyes fixed intently on Dawson, awaiting his response.

But Cray Dawson made no reply. He finished his coffee and sat in silence for a moment, staring into the empty cup. "Well . . ." Then he stood up, set the empty coffee cup on a shelf and said, "Much obliged for the coffee and food. I'll take my leave now."

"But, Mister Dawson," said Daniels, "it's still storming something awful out there. You're welcome to spend the night. We'd be greatly honored to say a famous gunman like you stayed here in the rail camp. You'll likely find nothing but floods and washouts twixt here and the Quemado Valley."

"Thanks all the same," said Dawson, "I best get on."

To avoid answering questions that held no meaning to him and discussing events he'd sooner forget, Cray Dawson rode his horse up a narrow, mud-slick path and made a camp in the deep shelter of a cliff overhang. At length, the fury of the storm passed, but in its wake heavy rain fell straight down with no sign of letup. Across the wide belly of the valley churning water rushed along filled with deadfall oak, scrub pine and mesquite brush. Twice in the night Dawson awakened to the unrelenting sound of water pounding the endless land, and twice in the night he again fell asleep to the explosion of gunfire in his memory, and to the sound of men dying.

By daylight the pounding rain had reduced itself to a thin, steady drizzle. Dawson rode high above the valley through a dull gray-copper morning. With the collar of his rain slicker turned high in back and his Stetson bowed low on his forehead, he kept to the higher ridges and broken hillsides until, by late afternoon, he put his big bay onto the wide, muddy trail leading into Eagle Pass. A half hour later he rode along the puddled street past the Desert Flower, where he and Lawrence Shaw had stayed, and where Lawrence Shaw had taken up with Della Starks, the recently widowed owner of the inn. Dawson started to turn his bay to the inn, but then, thinking better of it, he rode on down the empty, darkening street through a slow, cold drizzle to the hitch rail out front of the Big Spur Saloon.

Inside the saloon there were only five customers. Three of them were drovers who stood at the center of the bar. They wore long rain slickers and wet hats that drooped heavily. They stood, each in his own dark, wet circle on the wooden plank floor, two of them laughing quietly at something the other had said. A fourth man drank alone at the far end of the bar. The fifth man sat at a table dealing solitaire to himself, with a bottle of rye whiskey standing near his right hand. All five drinkers turned their eyes to the sound of the bat-wing doors creaking. Laughter fell away as Cray Dawson stepped inside and looked around before walking to the bar.

"Who's this?" one of the men at the bar asked his companions in a lowered voice, the three of them noting the rifle in Dawson's wet, gloved hand.

"Wants to dry his rifle," one of the men answered just above a whisper.

At the bar, Dawson laid the Winchester repeater up on his right atop the bar and took off his wet gloves. A young bartender appeared as if from out of nowhere and said, "What will you have, Mister?"

"Whiskey," said Dawson, taking a short look along the bar.

As the bartender reached for a shot glass and a bottle, Dawson took off his wet hat, shook it and placed it back on. At the end of the bar a pair of bloodshot eyes widened. "Lord, it's you ain't it?" said a shaky, whiskey-slurred voice.

Dawson just looked at the old man.

The old man pointed a trembling, weathered finger and said through a gray, whiskey-stained beard, "I saw what you did here! This is him!" he said to the other drinkers. "This is the man who stood with Lawrence Shaw, the day all the shooting took place!"

"Harve Bratcher, keep quiet! You don't know nothing," said the bartender, filling Dawson's shot glass. Then he said to Dawson, "Mister, that old teamster gets drunk, he thinks he knows everybody."

"No, wait, Dink," said one of the drovers to the young bartender, taking a closer look at Cray Dawson. "I believe Harve's right this time." He said to Cray Dawson, as if in awe, "You are the man who was here . . . the one who covered Fast Larry Shaw's back!"

"Yes, I am," said Dawson, raising his drink, hoping that would be the end of it but knowing it wouldn't. He chastised himself silently for coming here.

"All right, he was here with Shaw," the young bartender said quickly, seeing the look on Dawson's face. "Now he's here for a drink, and he doesn't need a bunch of questions thrown at him . . . am I right?"

"Obliged," said Dawson.

"I mean no offense, Mister," said the drover, "but it ain't every day a gunman like you shows up at the bar!" He almost took a step closer, but Dawson's eyes turned to him and seemed to hold him in place. "I'm Bud Emery, owner of the Emery Spread east of here near the Nueces," he said, touching his wet hat brim. "These two men ride for me, Emmet Crowder and Jake Laslow. Both good hands."

The two cowhands nodded, touching their hat brims.

Cray Dawson responded in kind, then raised his shot glass and tossed back the rest of his whiskey.

"And your name, Mister?" asked Bud Emery, raising his brow slightly as if he might have missed something.

Dawson replied, "I'm Crayton Dawson."

"From Somos Santos?" asked Emmet Crowder, an older cowhand with a scar showing through his chin whiskers, partially covered by the rise of his faded bandanna.

"Yes," said Dawson, turning to him now, wondering how he knew.

As if seeing the question in Dawson's eyes, Crowder said, "You wintered with Pearsall and his bunch up north above the Cimarron . . . the McAllister Spread? Before the English bought him out?"

"Yep." Dawson nodded in acknowledgment, feeling a little better knowing that somebody might see him as a drover rather than a gunman.

"We never met," said Crowder, "but I heard of you from Jimmie Pearsall. He said you was a top hand,"—he grinned—"but that you didn't like the cold."

"He was right about the cold," said Dawson, modestly sidestepping the complement of being a top hand.

"Hot dang!" said Crowder. "Wait till I tell Pearsall I seen you . . . you backing a big gunman like Fast Larry Shaw! He'll split something open and fall plumb through it. I'm betting!"

"Ole Jimmie Pearsall . . ." Dawson reflected. He eased down a bit, gesturing for the bartender to pour him another.

Jake Laslow, the youngest of the three drovers, looked at Dawson's glass as the bartender filled it. He blurted out mindlessly, "I'll pay for that drink, Mister Dawson, if you'll draw that Colt once, just as fast as you can!"

Dawson stared straight ahead across the bar as if his attention had just been riveted to the shelves of whiskey.

"Damn it, Jake, what's wrong with you?" asked Bud Emery, appearing shocked by his cowhand's remark. "You don't say something like that to a man!"

"I was just wanting to see how fast it is!" said Jake Laslow. Then, correcting himself, he added with a red face, "His *draw*, that is."

"Pay him no mind, Dawson," said Crowder. "He was kicked away from the teat too soon or something." He turned a cold gaze to Jake Laslow. "I hope I don't have to box his jaws before the day's over."

"Now wait a minute, old man," said Laslow to Emmet Crowder. "I might have spoken a little out of turn." He turned a nod of apology to Cray Dawson, then said to Crowder, "But don't go threatening to box my jaws unless you're ready to take it up!" He leaned toward Crowder, but Bud Emery held him back with a palm flat on his chest. As Laslow spoke, Dawson saw the old teamster at the end of the bar slip away and out the back door.

"Everybody settle down!" the young bartender shouted, slapping a hand down on the bar top, causing a stack of clean shot glasses to rattle. "Can't a man come in for a drink without a ruckus being raised?"

Cray Dawson pushed his empty glass back and picked up the rifle from the bar top. Silence fell almost with a gasp. "Got a towel?" he asked the bartender.

A towel came up from beneath the bar and dropped into Dawson's hand. He took his time wiping the Winchester dry. When he'd finished he dropped the towel on the bar. "Obliged," he said. He fished a coin from his pocket and flipped it to the bartender, who snatched it from midair.

"I'll tell Pearsall I seen ya," said Emmet Crowder in a guarded tone.

"*Adios,*" said Dawson.

On his way out of the Big Spur Saloon Dawson heard Bud Emery say to Jake Laslow in a low growl, "You stupid turd, he could've killed you."

On the boardwalk, Dawson came to an abrupt halt, looking at the five men spread in a half circle in the muddy street facing the saloon. Rain dripped from the shotgun and rifle barrels pointed at him from less than fifteen feet away. The man at the center of the half circle stood without a long gun, but with his right hand on the butt of a tied-down Colt .45. A sheriff's badge glinted in the wet evening gloom. "Cray Dawson," he said in a level, official-sounding voice, "Keep your gun hand away from that side-shooter and lay that rifle down, easy like."

"Sheriff Neff," said Cray Dawson, "what can I do for you?" Stooping straight down slowly, laying the Winchester down near his left boot, he kept his right hand raised chest high.

Sheriff Neff offered a flicker of a grin, rain running from his hat brim, from the sleeves of his long black linen duster. "Where is he, Dawson?" Neff's eyes glanced at the Desert Flower Inn, then snapped back to Cray Dawson.

"I have no idea, Sheriff," said Dawson. "Shaw and I broke away in Brakett Flats. I'm headed home to Somos Santos."

"Shaw's not down there?" Neff nodded at the Desert Flower.

"I told you, Sheriff, I'm alone, headed home," said Dawson with resolve.

"I heard the whole story about what happened in Brakett Flats," said Neff.

"Good," said Dawson. "Then you had to hear that Shaw and I acted in self-defense."

Neff brushed it aside. "I don't give a damn what you did. Anybody who killed the Talbert Gang ought to get a medal and a marching band."

Dawson just stared at him, knowing there was more to come. The other four men stood poised, rain running down them.

"But I told you and Shaw to stay out of my town. What are you doing back here?"

"I thought it would be all right, Sheriff," said Dawson, "since it's only me, and since all the trouble is over."

"Uh-uh," said Neff. "That went for you too. The trouble ain't over. Trouble is never over with you gunmen." He gestured to the old teamster standing in the rain near the edge of an alley. "Harve said you hadn't been in the Big Spur five minutes, you got Bud Emery's men at one another's throats."

"I had nothing to do with it, Sheriff. But I'm no gunman," Dawson said, correcting him. "I'm just a citizen like everybody else. . . . I'm headed home I told you."

"Not a gunman?" Neff grinned, bemused. "You sound like you really think that."

"I do think it," said Dawson.

"Suppose if I was to tie you to a hitch rail and horsewhip the piss out of you, you'd stay away from my town?" Neff asked.

Dawson bristled. His hand remained chest high, but it poised now. "If it comes to horsewhipping, Sheriff," he said in a tight, level voice, "I expect I'll die in your town." He looked from one pair of eyes to the next. "But not *alone*," he added.

"Easy now," said Sheriff Neff, seeing the look on Dawson's face. "See, that's what I'm talking about." He pointed his finger, keeping his hand away from his pistol butt. "You'd die before you'd take a whipping. That's what makes you different than a citizen like *anybody else*. You and Shaw and the rest of you live by your own law. I ain't blaming you. I'm just telling you. I don't want none of you here."

"Then I'll leave, Sheriff," said Dawson, seeing now that Neff was only making a point. "Let me get to my horse. I won't be back here, you've got my word."

Sheriff Neff looked him up and down; his wet, muddy boots, his wet hat and gloves. He looked at the bay standing soaked and shivering at the hitch rail. "Ah, hell," he growled, "I reckon one night won't hurt nothing . . . provided you stay out of the saloon, get you and your horse a dry spot and stay on it." He looked at the four men standing around him and said, "All right, lower them, boys."

"Much obliged, Sheriff," said Dawson, stooping down, picking up his rifle slowly and letting everybody see him place it up under his arm. "I'll clear out of here come first light, rain or no rain."

"See that you do," said Sheriff Neff. He pushed up his wet hat brim and said, "Right after you left here last time, that damned Sammy Boy White killed Fat Man Hughes and two other men right out here in the street."

"I thought Sammy Boy was dead," said Dawson.

Sheriff Neff gave him a look of warning. "First light, Dawson . . . I reckon I already *know* where you'll be staying the night." His eyes gestured toward the Desert Flower Inn then back to Dawson.

Dawson looked embarrassed. "Obliged, Sheriff. First light . . . my word on it."

As soon as the sheriff and his men had pulled back and walked away, Dawson let out a breath of relief, unhitched his bay and rode it around to the back door of the Desert Flower Inn. After knocking, then waiting, then knocking again, harder this time, and waiting another few minutes in the drizzling rain, Dawson had turned back to where the bay stood near the back porch. But before he could step into the saddle, a woman's voice called out from inside, "Who's there?"

Recognizing Della Starks's voice, Dawson replied, "Miss Della, it's me, Crayton Dawson, remember?"

"Crayton who?" said Della Starks.

"Crayton Dawson, Miss Della," said Dawson. "Shaw and I helped you get here after your wagon broke a wheel? We shot it out with a band of Comancheros?"

"Oh, *Cray* Dawson! Just a second." Following a silence, Della opened the door a crack and looked back and forth in eager expectation, hardly giving Dawson a glance until she saw he was alone. "What brings you here, Cray Dawson?" Her expression turned bland.

"I'm headed home to Somos Santos and I need a dry place to stay for the night," Dawson said, nodding toward the rain.

"And you figured you'd just drop by and spend the evening with me, the lonely widow Starks? No invitation, no nothing, just pop by?" She gave a toss of her hand and a sarcastic smile. "See if you can't throw my heels in the air, for free room and board? Is that what you thought?"

"Uh, ma'am," Dawson said, caught a bit off guard, "I'm not looking for a handout. I pay for my lodging. I just thought that . . ." His words trailed. Della gave him a knowing stare, crossing her arms across her large bosom, the low cut of her bodice showing plenty of rose-blushed flesh.

"Dawson, I see through you so easily," Della said, shaking her head slowly, long strands of fragrant blond hair brushing back and forth across her breasts. She gave him a long, harsh stare, but when Dawson retreated a step back as if he might excuse himself and leave, her expression softened until she smiled, batted her eyes and said, "All right, cowboy, come on in. Make yourself useful."

"Miss Della, I don't want to impose," said Dawson with hesitancy.

"Oh yes you do," Della said. She reached out, grabbed him by his gun belt buckle and pulled him forward. "So don't turn stubborn on me, Dawson. You talked me into it; now what are you going to do, make me beg?" She laughed playfully.

"No, ma'am!" said Dawson. "No begging needed here!" He stepped inside as she continued pulling him by his gun belt.

"I suppose you'll want something to eat before we settle in for the night?" Della asked.

"I could eat something," Dawson replied, "and the fact is I've got to see to my horse."

"No," said Della. "What you've got to do is get upstairs and into my bathing tub while the water is still warm and sudsy. I'll see to it that our town stable hostler takes care of your horse." Seeing the look of concern in Dawson's eyes, Della added, "Don't worry, once he hears that bay belongs to a famous gunman, he'll treat it better than he treats his children."

"I'm no *famous* gunman, Della," Dawson stated. "I'm not really a gunman at all. I'm just a working drover."

"You're not going to disappoint me are you?" Della asked coyly.

"No, ma'am, not if my life depended on it," said Dawson, feeling her fingernails dig against his belly behind his belt buckle.

"That's more like it," she whispered.

Dawson relaxed. Della turned his belt loose and

he pulled her to him, his arms encircling her, saying, "Miss Della, you just can't imagine how good it is to see you again."

"What's the quickest you've ever taken a bath, Cray?" she whispered into his ear, putting plenty of breath into her words.

"I don't know, but I've got a feeling I'm about to find out," Dawson said.

In moments he was in the small bathtub, lathered and rinsed, and out, standing on a soft braided rug in the glow of a lantern Della had lit and set on a soap stand. From her adjoining bedroom, Della purred softly, "Cray, are you ready yet? I'm getting all flushed in here just waiting for you."

Whew! Dawson hurried. "I won't be long, Della, I promise!" He dried himself frantically, then wrapped the towel around his waist and stepped through the open door into the glow of scented candlelight.

"Drop the damp towel," Della said, holding up the corner of the covers for him to slip into bed beside her. He saw her lying naked awaiting him.

"Yes, ma'am," he said, smiling, letting the towel fall to the floor. As he settled into the warm feather bed, he heard the slightest sound of a horse whinnying somewhere to the rear of the Desert Flower and he stopped and said, "Did the stable man take care of Stony?"

"Who?" said Della, sounding anxious, pulling him to her.

"Stony, my horse," said Dawson. "Did he get taken care of?"

"Yes, I'm sure he did," said Della, brushing the matter aside. Then she whispered, again drawing him to her, "Am I going to get *taken care* of?"

He felt her hands on him and gasped quietly. But as he once again tried to settle into the bed, feeling her warm and willing against him, he heard the same sound of a horse coming from the rear of the inn. "That's Stony," he said, this time rising halfway from the bed. "Didn't the stable man come get him? Didn't you tell him to?"

"I told him to," Della sighed in exasperation. "He said when he got time . . . he was busy. Don't worry, the horse will be all right. Come down here to me."

"I got to see about him," said Dawson, rising up from the bed, snatching the towel up off the floor and walking into the room where his clothes lay on a chair beside the tub.

"I can't believe this!" Della cried out. "A damn *horse!*"

"I'm sorry," said Dawson, with determination, "I can't leave him out there in weather like this. He's my horse for God sakes!" Heading down the stairs toward the back door, he called over his shoulder to her, "I'll be right back." He slipped his bib-front shirt over his shoulders and stuffed the tail down into his trousers.

"Like hell you will!" Della shouted.

Dawson heard the bedroom door slam hard enough to jar the long wooden handrail. He cursed under his breath and walked to the back door with his boots under his arm, his gun belt over his shoulder. Before stepping out into the rain, he put on his boots, strapped on his gun belt, and took down his slicker and wet hat from a peg on the wall.

Outside he heard the whinnying again and said aloud into the dark, drizzling gloom, "I'm coming Stony. I'll take care of you."

The big bay stood where Dawson had left him tied out back. "Don't worry, Stony, I'll take you to the stable," Dawson said, running a hand along the bay's wet muzzle. But as he unwrapped the horse's reins a voice called out above the sound of hurrying footsteps sloshing through the mud, "Here, I'll take him."

Dawson looked at the face of a young man coming toward him carrying a lantern. "I'm Vernon, from the livery barn. Sorry I'm late. I promised Miss Della I'd come get this horse and give him special treatment. I will, too, you can count on it. She told me who you are, Mister Dawson. Heck, this service is on the house!"

Dawson looked at Della's bedroom window in time to see the light go out. "That's all right, Vernon," he said, holding onto the reins. "I'll just walk along with you. How dry is that livery barn?"

Chapter 2

In the open doorway of the livery barn, Sheriff Neff stared at the endless gray morning in disgust. Then he turned and walked along the center of the barn to the darkened stall Vernon had pointed him to. The big bay made a low rumbling sound in his chest and stopped chewing his mouthful of hay as Neff approached the stall door. "Easy, boy," Neff said quietly. He heard a rustling sound in the hay inside the stall and said, "Crayton Dawson, it's me, Sheriff Neff. Are you awake?"

"I'm awake, Sheriff," Dawson said in a sleepy voice, grunting as he stood up and plucked a strand of hay from his hair.

Neff stifled a smile watching Dawson rub a hand across his face. "Looks like you didn't fair near as well as I thought you would, Dawson."

"Morning, Sheriff." Dawson looked at him, making no response. "Don't worry, I'll be leaving here as soon as I can get my horse under me," Dawson said.

"Good," said Neff. "I heard you was here. I just thought I'd drop by and tell you. The bartender said Mad Albert Ash rode into town about an hour ago. Said Ash knows you're here."

"He knows I'm here?" said Dawson. "Who told him?"

"Come on, Dawson," said the sheriff, "you know how word travels. He might have heard it in the last town you were in and just figured you'd be here. He could have happened by here and heard it from the bartender. It ain't no secret. Hell, from one of my men for that matter."

"Or you?" Dawson studied the sheriff's face.

"I'll pretend I didn't hear you say that," said the sheriff. "The point is he already asked the bartender over at the Big Spur where he might find you . . . said he might like to buy you a drink."

"At this hour of morning?" said Dawson.

Sheriff Neff shrugged. "Maybe he's one of them early drinkers. They don't call him *Mad* for nothing I reckon."

"Mad Albert Ash," said Dawson. "I've heard that name all my life, it seems like. I never thought there would be a day he'd be asking about me."

Neff looked at him. "It ain't like he wants to swap cowboy stories, Dawson. I expect he'll be wanting to kill you. You ought to know by now, it's a strange world these big guns live in. They ain't like the rest of us."

"Yeah, I learned that much riding with Shaw," said Dawson. "I've got to get myself away from all this, before I end up *becoming* what you say I already *am*."

"If you didn't realize you're a gunman already, this ought to sure enough cinch it for you," said Neff. "If I was you, I'd get on that horse and ride. Get on out of here . . . if you really ain't a gunman. If you really ain't out to carry a big reputation."

Dawson considered it for a moment, then said, "Sheriff, I ain't sneaking out of town like a cowed hound. I've wronged no one. It doesn't seem right, backing down from a fight I don't even *know* is coming."

"See?" said Neff, pointing a finger. "That's about what I figured you'd say. Like it or not, Dawson, that's about what you can count on *any* gunman saying. Maybe you better start to realizing what you are, before *not realizing* it gets you killed."

"Damn it, Sheriff, I can't just sneak out of town . . . and I can't just stay here knowing I could avoid killing a man or getting killed myself just by leaving." He ran his fingers back through his disheveled hair.

"Well, I'll leave you to ponder it," said Sheriff Neff. "And while you ponder it, remember this—I'm not standing for no more gunfighters disrupting my town. If the law means anything to you—which I doubt—you *will* sneak out of here like a *'cowed hound,'* or else in addition to carrying around a reputation, you'll also be carrying around a jail record." Sheriff Neff touched his fingers to his hat brim and gave a thin smile. "Morning then."

Before Neff stepped out the door, Dawson called out to him, "Sheriff, are you going to tell Mad Albert Ash the same thing when you see him?"

"Don't need to," said Neff, "he's known it for years."

When the sheriff had left, Vernon walked up quietly and said to Dawson, "I couldn't help but overhear. I can show you a back trail out to the main road if you want me to. It might be awful slick and deep with all this rain we've had."

"Obliged, Vernon," said Dawson, stepping into his damp, clammy boots. "But I don't reckon I'll be taking the back trail."

Vernon's attention perked. "Then you're going to stay and fight Albert Ash?"

"No," said Dawson, stepping his boots into place, "not if I can keep from it. But I'm leaving this town the way I came in. I ain't crawling out the back door on my belly."

Dawson reached around and took Stony's bridle from a peg on the outside of the stall. Vernon backed away quietly, leaving him to slip the bridle into the horse's mouth and lead the big bay outside the stall to prepare him for the trail. Stony stood still as Dawson smoothed a saddle blanket down and swung the saddle onto his back. When he'd drawn the cinch snug and laid the stirrups down the horse's sides, Dawson said, stepping around Stony and running a hand down his soft muzzle, "The accommodations might not have been the best, but we both kept dry, didn't we pard?"

The bay blew out a breath and scraped a hoof on the soft floor. Dawson made up his bedroll, wrapped it in a length of rubber-coated canvas, and tied it down behind his saddle. He took down his dry rain slicker and damp hat from the wall, put them on, and picked up his Winchester from where he'd leaned it inside the stall near his side. He stood checking his Colt as Vernon came back from the front of the barn carrying his stiff, but dry, leather gloves. "I shelved these above the wood stove for you, Mister Dawson."

"Obliged, Vernon." Dawson holstered his Colt and reached inside his trouser pocket for a coin, but Vernon stopped him, saying firmly, "No, sir, Mister Dawson, I told you last night, '*no charge*' for you, and I meant it."

Dawson started to protest, but realizing how little

money he had, he nodded and said "Obliged" again, reminding himself that this was one more thing he had said he wouldn't allow himself to do: accept free services, free goods, free *anything* just because he could draw a gun and kill a man with it. Well . . . it was easy to see how these things came about, he thought, seeing Vernon pull and stretch the stiffened leather gloves back into shape for him. People held gunmen in high regard, in fear, in awe. He couldn't say it was right, but he couldn't think of anything he could do or say that would change it. He nodded, taking the gloves and pulling them onto his hands and clenching his fists a few times to get them loosened up. Vernon watched as if entranced. Then he managed to say, "Mister Dawson, next time you're through here I'd give anything if I could introduce my oldest boy to you. It would be the biggest thing that ever happened to him!"

"Sure thing, Vernon," said Dawson, taking Stony's reins and leading him out through the front door, across a muddy corral, onto the muddy street.

Closing the livery corral gate behind him, Dawson led the bay along the edge of the boardwalk, keeping away from the middle of the street where water stood three inches deep. He wanted no trouble, yet he knew better than to allow himself to get caught on horseback in the rain on a muddy street, should a fight be forced upon him. With his Winchester rifle in hand he moved at a cautious pace, keeping his attention toward the Big Spur Saloon even as he appeared to stare straight ahead. He made it past the saloon by eight yards and thought he might ease out of town unnoticed, but then he heard a booming, gravelly voice call out, *"Mister Dalton!"* pronouncing his name incorrectly. "I have been hearing your name all across the hill country. I believe it's fitting time we said our *howdies*, don't you?"

Dawson stopped in his tracks and turned toward the Big Spur Saloon, across the street behind him. Raising the Winchester he cradled it in the crook of his left arm and kept his right hand around the stock, his thumb across the hammer. "I am Cray *Dawson*," he said, looking at the tall, lean man who stood with his weight shifted onto his right leg. "I take it you must be Mister Ash?"

"*Mad Albert* to be exact," the man said, wearing a wide, mirthless grin mantled by a thin black mustache. "Please call me Mad Albert." His eyes were hidden behind a pair of dark-tinted wire-rims in spite of the sunless morning. His wide-brimmed hat hung behind him on a leather strip. He wore a rawhide poncho, the right front of it flipped up over his left shoulder. His right hand rested on the bone handle of a big Colt similar to Dawson's. His black right glove was off, stuck down in his gun belt. "I would like to buy you a drink for breakfast, Mister *Dalton*," he said, again mispronouncing his name.

Realizing that Ash might be doing it deliberately, Dawson let it pass this time. "I'm on my way out of town, Mad Albert," said Dawson. "Another time perhaps?"

"In matters of both courtesy and killing, I always say '*no time like the present*,'" Ash said. He gestured with his free hand toward the gray sky and the rain. "It appears that all natural forces are against your departure anyway."

"I don't want any trouble with you, Mad Albert," Dawson said firmly, his voice carrying a warning tone.

Ash appeared to be taken aback by Dawson's

abruptness, but it was hard to tell if his gesture was sincere or feigned. "Nor I with you, sir!" he said as if surprised by such a thought. "I'm only suggesting a breakfast drink . . . call it one for the trail. I'm not used to having an invitation turned down. Do you rebuff me, sir?"

Dawson took a deep breath and considered his position: standing in the rain, the mud, his horse right behind him in the line of fire. Without answering, he nudged forward on Stony's reins and led the bay toward the Big Spur Saloon.

"There now, that's more like it, Mister *Dalton*," said Ash, grinning even more as Dawson walked the bay to the hitch rail out front of the saloon, hitched the reins, and shoved his Winchester into the saddle boot. Dawson noted that the gunman seemed sincere. Raising a long, gloved finger, Ash added, "I always say that a man who doesn't have his morning whiskey is an unenlightened soul." He stepped to the side and gestured Dawson to the bat-wing doors. "After you, sir!"

Dawson stepped inside the saloon and walked to the bar, feeling a bit uncomfortable with Mad Albert Ash behind him. But at the bar, Ash stood beside him, allowing three feet of space between them, and said to the young bartender, "Two tall ones if you will."

At the end of the bar, two men stood rigidly, wearing worried expressions. Two full glasses of whiskey stood in front of them. When the bartender had poured shots of rye for Ash and Dawson, Mad Albert said to the two other drinkers, "Well, gentlemen, you are both free to go now . . . I've found someone else to converse with."

"Thank you, Mister Ash," said one of the men in a shaky voice. They downed their drinks and hurried out the door.

It dawned on Dawson that Mad Albert Ash was slightly drunk, but doing a good job of keeping it hidden. "And then there were *only two*," said Ash, pulling his dark visor lens down enough to gaze at Dawson. A scar above his left eye caused a high arch in his black eyebrow, giving him an angry look. "Tell me the truth now, *Dalton*. You thought I came here to kill you, didn't you?"

Dawson wasn't going to allow himself to be intimidated. "I admit, I thought you might have come here to *try*," he said.

Ash chuckled. "Good answer, *Dalton*." He raised his drink and sipped it, then set it down and said, "I have to admit, when I heard what you did in Turkey Creek . . . then at Brakett Flats, I thought to myself, is this young man trying to outdo me?"

"It had nothing to do with you, Mad Albert," said Dawson. He took a short sip of whiskey, then set it down.

Ash shrugged. "I realized that of course, once I heard the whole story. But we are a vain lot, us rootin-tootin gunslingers." He grinned. "No matter what happens, we always wonder what it will have to do with us, our *reputations* that is." He gave Dawson a questioning look. "Tell me, *Dalton*, do you always wonder that way yourself . . . as if anything that happens in the world of guns and gunmen is all about *you*?"

"No," said Dawson, carefully considering his answer, already seeing how Albert Ash got his nickname. "But to tell you the truth I don't consider myself a gunman, at least not the way other people seem to."

"Oh really?" said Ash flatly. "Yet, the first thing that crossed your mind when you heard I was in town was whether or not I would *try* to kill you?"

"I wouldn't say it was the first thing," said Dawson, not giving in.

"Oh? Then what was?" Ash asked.

"All right," said Dawson, "you're right. I thought it."

"Ah! Yes, indeed," said Ash. "So you see, we all think the same way. If we hear that someone has come along and done something spectacular with a gun, we immediately think our position has been threatened. I'm certain we're all a pompous bunch of snobs. And, notice I don't judge myself any less guilty than the rest of you. I'm afraid that I too am hopelessly swollen on my own importance."

Dawson only nodded, not wanting to argue the point—or any other point—with Mad Albert Ash. He shoved the glass of unfinished whiskey back from him. "You've been at this business a long time, Mad Albert. I doubt anybody will ever take that away from you."

"Well, aren't you kind to say so," Ash said, his drunkenness becoming more apparent. Seeing that Dawson was getting ready to leave, he said, "What's your hurry, *Dalton?*"

"My horse is standing in the rain," said Dawson.

"Now that's admirable," said Ash. "I respect a man who will sacrifice his own comfort for that of a simple beast."

Thinking of the night before, Dawson replied, "You wouldn't believe what I've given up lately for that horse."

Ash only nodded. "*Dalton,* I'm glad we've had the opportunity to meet one another without guns in our hands."

"My pleasure," said Dawson, not sure what meaning this held for Mad Albert Ash, but glad that he wasn't going to have to fight the man.

Before Dawson could turn and leave, Ash said, "Tell me, *Dalton,* do you believe we are evil men?"

"I'm not the one to say," said Dawson. "Every man has to answer that sort of question for himself."

"Well spoken!" Ash grinned, raising his glass as if in a toast. "I, too, feel that way, most times. The problem is that sometimes I am haunted by the many ghosts inside my shirt. They cause me to doubt myself." He tossed back the drink and set the shot glass on the bar top, hard. Then, in reflection, he said, "We are all the terrible product of this unsettled time and place we live in, *Dalton.* We are civilized creatures . . . but *creatures* nonetheless. In Roman days there were mercenaries who hired their blades to the highest bidder. That's what we are, isn't it? Bold *mercenaries?*"

"I don't know," said Dawson. "I'm just on my way home."

Ash continued to speak as Dawson left. "We are all on our way *home,* aren't we?" He laughed aloud, then said, "*Dalton,* I've been at this for a long, *long* time! When I started, I took a bite out of the liver of the first man I ever killed. That was up in the high country! Can you imagine if I were to do that today? Stick a man in his gullet, rip out his liver, and take a big bite?" He hooted and laughed and raved. "Now that would most certainly raise some brows, wouldn't it? Wouldn't it! But see how civilized I've become? I don't do that anymore. No, sir!"

Leaving Mad Albert alone with his drunken rant-
ing and his shirt full of ghosts, Cray Dawson walked
through the bat-wing doors out onto the boardwalk,
only to be met by two men standing in the rain, one
with a shotgun, the other with a Spencer rifle, both
pointed at him. Raising his hands chest high, Dawson
said quietly and cautiously, "Every time I *leave* this
place, I get guns pointed at me. I'm getting tired of
it." Rain poured straight down.

"Then quit leaving," said the young man holding
the shotgun.

The other man lowered his rifle barrel an inch and
said in a hushed tone, nodding toward the sound of
Ash's voice, "You're with him, ain't you?"

"Do I look like I'm with him?" Dawson asked in
response.

"If you're with him, you're dead," said the man
with the shotgun.

"Then I'm for *damn*-sure not with him." Dawson
looked the two young men over, getting a picture of
what they were up to. He let his hands down
slightly.

"Keep 'em up, Mister!" growled the one with the
rifle. "I'll drop you deader than hell!"

"You're out to kill yourself a big gunman, huh?"
Dawson asked.

The young man gave him a look of bemused disbelief. "Now what would make you think a thing like
that?"

"So what if we are?" said the one with the shotgun, stepping closer. "Are you going to try to stop
us?"

"All I'm wanting to do is walk down to that big bay,
get on him, and ride out of here," Dawson replied.

"You won't try to warn him?" asked the one with the rifle.

"He don't need warning," said Dawson. "He'll know before you get to the doors.

"Yeah," said the one with the rifle, "how do you know he will?"

"He's been doing this longer than you two have been alive," said Dawson, hoping to dissuade them. "He'll know. Don't ask me how, but he'll know . . . and he'll kill you."

The two looked at one another. "Go on, Clifford," said the one with the shotgun. "This saddle tramp don't know nothing. He ain't no gunman! He ain't nobody!"

Clifford looked closer at Cray Dawson, at the big tied-down Colt and asked, "You ain't are you, Mister . . . nobody that is?"

"No," said Dawson. "I ain't nobody . . . nobody worth killing anyway. But I know something about how gunmen think, and how they sense things. He'll hear a board creak, a boot squeak. Hell, he might even just hear the difference in the sound of the rain once you both step out of it. But he'll kill you, that much I'm sure of."

"Clifford, are you going to do it or not?" the one with the shotgun asked, coming up onto the boardwalk, keeping Dawson covered.

"Damn it, Randall, yes! I'm going to do it," Clifford whispered harshly. "But I ain't going in there."

"What are you going to do then?" asked his companion.

Clifford bit his lip, thinking, then said, "Give me the shotgun. I'll nail him from over the doors."

"Hold it," said Dawson. "Don't ambush the man.

You get no reputation that way, unless you want to be known as cowards."

"Shut up," said Randall, poking the shotgun at Dawson's stomach. "I'm sick of your mouth!"

"Here, give it to me, Randall," said Clifford, grabbing the shotgun.

Seeing his chance as the shotgun changed hands, Dawson snatched the barrel and shoved it upward. A blaze of fire erupted, blowing a large hole in the boardwalk overhang. Randall fell back off the boardwalk into the mud, grabbing for the pistol he wore shoved down behind his belt. Dawson was too busy wrestling the shotgun from Clifford's hands to go for his Colt. Just as he managed to shove Clifford backward, Randall fired. Dawson buckled at the waist as the impact of the bullet lifted him slightly and tossed him sidelong against the front of the Big Spur Saloon. He tried reaching for his Colt but his hands seemed frozen in place, clutching his bloody stomach.

"You meddling son of a bit—" Clifford drew his pistol, leveled it at Dawson from less than ten feet, and cocked it quickly.

Dawson was coming back to himself now, getting his hand down to his Colt. But his hand was too bloody to get a grip on it. Shots from Randall's pistol hissed past his head. He could see almost in slow motion the fall of Clifford's gun hammer. Then everything seemed to stop and take off in a different direction. Clifford flew backward, a hole the size of a fist in his chest. In the mud, Randall had struggled upward onto his knees, but then he flew backward in a wide splash as a bullet nailed him between the eyes.

Dawson saw Mad Albert Ash step onto the boardwalk, his Colt up, cocked and smoking. He turned the barrel quickly in both directions. Then seeing Dawson slumped against the front of the building, he stepped over and stooped down, still keeping an eye on the street. "Damn, I expect you were right, *Dalton*," he said. "You really *aren't* much of a gunman. Are you?"

"That's what . . . I've been trying to tell . . . everybody," Dawson said, his bloody hands clutching his belly.

Chapter 3

—————

"You are one lucky fellow, Crayton Dawson," said Doctor Orville Peck, standing over Dawson's cot in the back room of the doctor's office.

Dawson raised his head off of the pillow enough to look down at the thick white bandage wrapped around his waist. He saw the wide pinkish circle where blood had begun to seep through the gauze. "Yeah?" said Dawson. "Then how come I don't feel real lucky from where I see it?"

The doctor smiled. "Because we're looking at it from two entirely different perspectives I suppose." He reached over and picked up Dawson's belt from a chair and held the buckle out for him to see. Part of the buckle had been flattened and mangled by Randall's bullet. "See? I call this a stroke of luck," he said. "You might call it just ruining your belt buckle. If this hadn't deflected the bullet and split it in two, it probably would have gone deeper into your belly and just cut everything you've got to pieces. Instead it only nicked your intestines a place or two. We'll talk about that later." He dismissed the matter, then went on. "As it is you're going to be pretty sore for awhile, but nothing inside your gut is damaged. I say you must have been born under a lucky star."

A deep, dull pain caused Dawson to collapse back onto the pillow with a moan. "That must be it," he rasped. "Where's Mad Albert Ash? I suppose he's all right?"

"Oh, yes, he's fine, discounting insanity of course," the doctor said. He shook his head. "Just listening to that man speak is unsettling."

"He saved my life," said Dawson, in Ash's defense.

"That doesn't mean he's sane . . . that just means he was present," said the doctor. "The fact is, he says *you* saved *his* life, warning him those two fools were out to kill him."

"I want to tell him I'm much obliged," said Dawson.

"Next time you see him maybe," said the doctor with a shrug. "He left town as soon as he heard you were going to live." Considering it, he rubbed his chin and said, "I shouldn't speak harshly about Mad Albert. He *did* pay your medical bill . . . in *full*. All in *cash*! Which must be some sort of record for any doctor in this town."

"Those two ambushers were nothing but kids," Dawson said with a tone of regret. "Ash killed them both without batting an eye."

"Mad Albert Ash would *never* bat an eye over something as trivial as killing a man," said Doctor Peck. "But under the circumstances, aren't you glad he did? And of course, now the big question, wouldn't you have done the same if you could have gotten a gun in your hand?"

"Yes, Doctor, I would have," said Dawson. "But it all just comes so easy, the killing, the justification for the killing. Where does a man lay it down and walk away? *How* does he walk away from it?"

"Mister Dawson, it seems to me you haven't been in this insane gunman world long enough to be asking those questions yet. Don't tell me you already want out?"

"I never wanted in, Doctor," said Dawson, feeling nausea deep down in his stomach, partly from the wound and partly from the conversation. "How soon can I ride?"

"If I tell you one week you'll likely leave tomorrow. So I'm going to say *two* weeks, on the outside chance you'll wait *one* week."

"The problem is, Doctor, Sheriff Neff wants me out of town, before somebody shows up wanting to do me the same way they wanted to do Mad Albert."

"I've already spoken to Sheriff Neff on your behalf," said Doctor Peck. "He said take a few days and get healed up, but get out as soon as you're up and around. Before the word gets out that you're here, is what I think he meant. But let's not worry about that right now. Get yourself some rest. If you think you're sore today, wait until tomorrow."

Stepping forward, the doctor held up a long steel syringe and examined it closely, then bent slightly and held it down toward Dawson's forearm.

"What's that, Doctor?" Dawson asked as the doctor held his arm in place.

"Just a little something to get rid of the pain and make you take a nice long sleep," said Doctor Peck. "You've lost a lot of blood. The best way to get it back is to rest, let it replenish itself. When you wake up we'll get some blood-rich food in you. But first, I want to put you to sleep."

Dawson protested as the sharp needle slid into his arm. "But I don't want to be knocked out, Doctor! I want to know what's going along around me."

"Oops, too late then," said the doctor, plunging the syringe. He smiled, pulling the needle from Dawson's arm and placing a short strip of gauze on the puncture. He patted Dawson's forearm. "Don't worry, I've never had a gunfight break out in here."

"That ain't the point, Doctor . . ." Dawson said, already feeling a silvery gray fur begin to engulf him.

"You'll have to tell me about it later," said Doctor Peck. He laid Dawson's limp arm across his chest, and stepped away from the bed and out of the room.

Dawson slept the rest of the day and most of the night, awakening only once for a few moments to the sound of the falling rain on the roof. He stared up at the ceiling, recounting the recent events that had so greatly changed his life. He'd come a long way, from breaking horses and driving cattle, to drinking morning whiskey with the likes of Mad Albert Ash. He pictured the two young men with guns in their hands, then he pictured them as he'd last seen them, both lying dead in pools of their own blood. Shaking his head slowly to put the picture out of his mind he murmured aloud to himself, "Lord, I've got to get home . . ." Then the gray-silver fur returned, taking him back into a mindless world of gentle darkness.

When Dawson awakened again it was to the feel of a cool, damp rag on his forehead, the same cool damp feeling he thought he'd felt on other parts of his body moments earlier, before the veil of sleep began to lift. Opening his eyes, he looked up at a young woman who stood over him, dutifully washing his face, his throat, his chest. "Who— Who are you?" he asked, coming more and more awake.

"I'm Suzzette," said a soft, melodious voice as she

continued washing him. "We met before, but you probably don't remember me."

Coming even more awake, it dawned on Dawson that he lay stark naked except for a bandage on his lower belly. His hands went to cover himself as he suddenly tensed up beneath the young woman's touch. "Ma'am, will you please throw that sheet over me?"

Suzzette laughed playfully. "Don't be embarrassed, Mister Dawson. It's okay. I'm a whore. I see naked men every night of my life."

"Still," said Dawson, reaching out with his right hand toward the sheet and blanket she'd pulled to one side.

"All right, lie still," said Suzzette. With her free hand she lifted the sheet and blanket as one and laid them gently over him, just high enough to cover him up to the bandage. "The doctor said for me to keep the dressing uncovered . . . 'to let it breathe,' he told me."

"Obliged," Dawson said. Growing more at ease, he looked closer at her face, then said, "Yes, I do remember you now. I met you and another lady at the Big Spur, my last time here."

"Yep." Suzzette smiled warmly. She stopped wiping his chest and said, "That was Lizzy. She and I worked our way here from Missouri. Now she's gone, and I miss her something awful."

Dawson just looked at her for a second, then said, "So, you work for the doctor, taking care of patients?"

"No, not exactly," said Suzzette. "I asked him if I could take care of you for a couple of days." She gave him a coy smile. "Is that all right?"

"It would be," said Dawson, "except I don't need any help, thank you all the same."

"Don't worry," said Suzzette, "you won't have to pay me anything." She shrugged. "I'm just doing this for you, to help you out."

"And . . . ?" Dawson asked, encouraging her to speak further on the matter.

"All right," she said in resignation. "I was hoping maybe when you leave here you might take me with you."

"I'm sorry," said Dawson. "I travel better alone."

She blurted out, "My friend Lizzy left here with Sammy Boy White, and I bet she's made him real happy he brought her along . . . that's what I would do for you, make you *real* happy, I mean any time you wanted me to. And it would be *free.* Just think, I'd be good company and a helping hand during the day, and someone you could have your way with of a night, *every* night for that matter."

"Suzzette," said Dawson, "I wouldn't envy your friend Lizzy if I were you. Living with a gunman ain't the kind of life you might imagine it to be."

"Oh, I don't envy her," said Suzzette. "I just want to be like her. When she said she was leaving with Sammy Boy, I told her she was crazy. But then I saw the way she looked up on that horse, waving back at everybody, the whole world before her. I decided I have to do that, first chance I get."

"And I'm that first chance," said Dawson.

"Well, is that wrong, for me to want that?" she asked. "All I'm asking for is just one man to sleep with who'll treat me kind, instead of wallowing with every man in town and having them treat me like dirt—most of them drunk half the time."

"If that's the way you feel, what you need to think about is changing your occupation," said Dawson. "But I can't take you with me."

"Am I not pretty enough for you?" Suzzette said, looking a bit hurt. "Everybody tells me I'm real pretty, especially with my clothes off." Her expression made it clear that she was willing to step out of her dress if Dawson so desired.

"Suzzette, you're a beautiful woman. A man would have to be blind not to see that, with or without your clothes on. But the answer is still no . . . and believe me, I'm doing you a kindness not taking you with me. I've gotten caught up in this gunman's world and it appears it'll take some doing for me to get myself out of it."

"Get out of it?" she asked in disbelief. "Why on earth would you want *out* of it? Most men would give anything to get *into* it!"

"Not once they saw it from inside, they wouldn't," said Dawson. He gestured with a hand at the bandage on his belly. "This is what it's gotten me so far. This and a peppering of buckshot back in Brakett Flats, and a bullet graze before that." He offered a smile of irony. "I'm beginning to think of bullet wounds as a way of remembering what day it is."

Suzzette smiled. "I heard what happened here," she said. "You wouldn't have had to warn Albert Ash. Not many gunmen would have. So, you took that on yourself."

Dawson nodded. "All right, you got me there. I've always had this problem of trying to do what's right, no matter what the cost. In this case it got me shot. Still, what was I supposed to do? Let a man get backshot? Then I'd have to live with that from now on."

Without realizing why, he began talking to Suzzette about things that had been on his mind. As he talked she nodded and sat down carefully on the side of his bed. Dawson caught himself and said, "Listen to me, going on this way. I reckon it's just having this belly wound and not being able to get around for awhile. I don't mean to take up all your time."

"Talk about whatever you want to, Cray Dawson," she said. "I'll be here for you . . . for as long as it takes."

There was comfort in her words. Dawson found himself relaxing, finding a peacefulness that he hadn't felt in years. He noted the gentleness of Suzzette as she laid a hand softly on his chest and idly drew circles with her fingertips.

The following week passed quickly for Cray Dawson. It took very little effort on the part of Suzzette Sherley to convince him he should move from the small room behind the doctor's office to her larger room in a two-story dwelling house, behind the Big Spur Saloon, that she had once shared with her friend Lizzy Carnes. "Don't worry," she'd assured Dawson the day she helped him walk up the stairs to her room. "We never brought any men up here . . . not customers anyway. This place is just for you and me. Our special place," she'd said, taking off her bonnet and shaking out her long auburn hair.

Two days later Doctor Peck stopped by to examine Dawson's wound and the incision he'd had to make to get in and remove the bullet fragments. Probing the tender flesh carefully with his fingertip, inspecting the thick black stitches where two incisions intersected below Dawson's navel, he said, "No sign of any infection sneaking up on you. How are you eating?"

"Good," said Dawson.

As if he couldn't take Dawson's word for it, the doctor looked for verification at Suzzette over the spectacles perched on his nose.

"He hasn't been eating heavy food, but he's been eating the soups and broths like you told him to," she said. "I don't think he's eating *enough* yet, but he's eating."

"I haven't been all that hungry, Doctor," said Dawson. "I'm not doing enough to give me an appetite."

"Oh, really?" This time Doctor Peck gave Dawson a skeptical look, shooting a quick glance toward Suzzette.

Dawson looked embarrassed. "You know what I mean, Doctor. I'm used to a day's work, or at least a day on the trail. I'm not used to laying around in a bed."

Again giving a quick summary glance at Suzzette, the doctor said, "I would think you might welcome such a change."

Letting it pass, Dawson said, "The thing is, Doctor, I'm feeling good. I just need to get up and around. There's no need in all this attention. It's a small wound."

Raising a finger for emphasis, Doctor Peck said, "Now here is where I can express my authority. It may be a small wound, but the damage it has done can be lethal, if you don't take care of yourself. This is the sort of wound that can linger for a long time, and even come back years later if you're not careful. The human intestines are not made up of hickory and rawhide, Mister Dawson."

"I'm doing everything you said, Doctor," Dawson replied. "I'm taking it easy, except for . . . well, you know." This time *he* gave a short glance in Suzzette's direction. She busied herself tucking up a loose strand of hair as if not hearing them.

"I'm not opposed to a man doing *that*," said the doctor, "although I can't see how, given the pain. But I suppose a man finds a way?"

Dawson let his question go. "I'm eating good enough for now, Doctor. That's all you wanted to know, wasn't it?"

"Yes, but appetite is no small thing. How you're eating is most important in keeping a check on these sort of wounds. Your damaged innards can fool you. A man loses his appetite, maybe it's from lack of activity, but maybe it's from this wound keeping his belly just enough upset that he doesn't have the desire to eat. Doesn't feel hungry. Has no taste for food, so to speak."

"I won't let that happen," said Dawson. "I promise, I'll eat, even if I'm not all that hungry at the time."

"Yes," Suzzette added, "and I'll be there to see that he does." She smiled and held her hand down to him. "Right, Cray?"

Doctor Peck noticed that Dawson didn't answer her, although he did take her hand and squeeze it firmly.

"Well, I'll be back in a couple of days to remove this bandage and take these stitches out," the doctor said, standing up to leave. "Then I want you to start getting up and around some."

When two more days had passed, Cray Dawson held Suzzette's hand mirror down and looked at the two healing incisions on his lower belly, and said,

"Look, it's a cross. Do you suppose the doctor intended it, or it just happened that he had to cut it this way?"

Suzzette studied the healing wound and said, "I don't know. Then, after consideration, she said quietly, "I've never been a very religious person, but the night I came to your room in the doctor's office, I prayed that you were going to be all right." She blushed slightly. "This might sound silly, but I think maybe this cross is a sign."

"A sign," said Dawson, with no expression.

"Yes, you know?" said Suzzette. "A sign that you were going to live and get well."

"Yes, I know what you mean by a sign," said Dawson. "But I don't think this wound was all that bad."

"Maybe, maybe not," said Suzzette. "You're alive though. I call that an answer to my prayer, don't you?"

"Yes, I suppose." Dawson felt uncomfortable. "I'm not an answer to anybody's prayer, Suzzette. I don't want to give you that impression."

"I can make my own impressions, thank you," Suzzette said, offering a smile. "The thing is, I prayed for you to live . . . and you did live. Now I have a special promise I have to keep because of that."

Dawson tried to let the conversation go, hoping she would do the same. "Suzzette, you don't need to keep any promises on my behalf."

Suzzette looked shocked. "But of course I do! I promised that if you lived I would find a way to quit doing what I do." She smiled again. "See? You've had a big influence on me, Crayton Dawson. Whether you meant to do it or not, you have come very close to making an honest woman out of me."

Dawson didn't know what to say. He'd made up his mind that he was leaving for Somos Santos in two more days. Now he had to figure the best way to tell her. He had made her no promises, yet it seemed that promises had been made; and though she would deny it if he brought it up, he knew she expected something from him, something he knew he couldn't give, even if he wanted to.

The conversation was stopped by the sound of a knock on the door, and the voice of Sheriff Neff saying from atop the stairs, "Suzzette, Dawson, it's me, Neff, open up, it's important I talk to you, Dawson."

Suzzette gave Dawson a questioning look. He nodded and said in a lowered voice, "Go on, let him in."

As soon as Suzzette opened the door Sheriff Neff stepped inside and turned, looking back over his shoulder toward the back of the Big Spur Saloon. Dawson stood up and looked past the sheriff to the alley below to see what held the sheriff's attention down there. "Well, just as I said, Dawson, having you around is drawing trouble," said the sheriff, finally closing the door after one last look along the dirt alley below. "There's a cousin and a half brother of one of those boys Mad Albert killed. They're here and they're out for blood."

Dawson stared at the floor letting out a tired breath. "There just ain't any end to it, is there, Sheriff?"

"None that I ever saw," said Neff. "One killing brings on another. Everybody has some kin or other who has to be as foolish as the one he's come to avenge."

"Do these men know it was Mad Albert who did

the killing? That those two were about to backshoot him, just to be able to say they *did it*?"

"I told them, or I tried to tell them," said Neff, "but it went straight through their ears, the shape they're in. They're both red-eyed drunk and armed to the teeth." He shook his head, then said, "Boy oh boy. I suppose you're starting to understand why I don't like having gunfighters around, ain't you?"

Before Dawson could reply, Sheriff Neff cut in, saying with a twist of sarcasm, "Of course, you're going to deny being a gunman, but just ask yourself: would these two be in town right now, had it not been for you and Mad Albert being here in the first place?"

"You don't have to hammer the point, Sheriff," said Dawson, standing up stiffly, and reaching for his gun belt.

"Where do you think you're going?" asked the sheriff.

"To straighten this out," said Dawson. "I'll get them to listen to reason on this thing before anybody else gets killed."

"Uh-uh," the sheriff said, "I came here to warn you, to keep down any more bloodshed, not to cause more of it!"

Dawson started to say more on the matter, but before he could a voice called out from the alley below. "Cray Dawson! We know you're up there with the whore! Come down and let's get settled up."

Sheriff Neff looked stunned and said, "I swear I was careful to make sure I wasn't followed here."

"It's like you said, Sheriff," Dawson commented, raising his Colt and checking it as he spoke. "Word travels."

"Let me try to talk them away from here," Neff offered.

"No," said Dawson. "It's my mess, whether I meant to make it or not. I'll clean it up."

"Sheriff Neff, stop him!" Suzzette pleaded, seeing Dawson step over to the door and start to open it. "He's in no shape for this!"

Dawson stepped out onto a small platform atop the wooden stairs and looked down at the two enraged faces staring up at him.

"Then I'll stop him!" Suzzette shouted.

"Hold it, Suzzette!" The sheriff grabbed her around the waist and held her back as she tried to run out onto the platform behind Dawson. "You can't go out there now. It's commenced."

With a firm grip on the long wooden banister, Dawson eased down one cautious step at a time, his right hand poised an inch from the butt of his Colt. "I didn't kill either one of those men," he said.

"You be Crayton Dawson?" one man asked, looking up at him.

"I wouldn't be here if I wasn't," said Dawson.

"I'm Bob Pulley," said the big, burly man wearing a long deerskin riding duster that hung to his boot heels and carried streaks of mud and other matter around its bottom edge. "Clifford Tillis was my beloved cousin."

"And my beloved brother," said the other man, thumbing himself on the chest. He was a shorter, slimmer version of one of the men Ash had dropped dead in the street. He wore a large gold earring that caused his earlobe to sag with the weight of it. "I'm Bennie Tillis."

"I want you to know the names of the men who killed you, Crayton Dawson," said Bob Pulley.

"If you want to know what happened, your brother and his friend got what they came here looking for," said Dawson to Bennie Tillis.

"Save it, Dawson," Pulley replied for both him and Tillis. "We already heard how it happened from the man at the livery barn. He told us we'd find you here, laid up with some whore while my poor cousin is stuck in the ground."

"Yeah, *my* brother!" Tillis repeated, once again thumbing himself on the chest.

"Vernon . . ." Dawson whispered to himself, disappointed. He stopped halfway down the stairs, noting the position of the sun. It stood high above, offering neither him nor the other two men an advantage. But standing above them forced them to raise their faces to him, letting more light beneath their hat brims. Was this his best position? he asked himself. He hoped so. Being on the narrow stairs offered him little room to maneuver out of the way if he had to. But it also forced the two men to fight upward, an unfamiliar position for them, he hoped. Seeing the men squint their eyes, he knew he had to make this happen quickly before they adjusted to the slight change of light.

"They're in the ground because they were back-shooting cowards. I have no more to say on the matter," said Dawson, knowing his words would either bring things to a quick outcome or send these two on their way.

"Backshooting cowards, *huh!*" shouted Pulley, grabbing for the pistol on his hip. "Then fill your hand you son of a—" His words stopped short.

Dawson's shot hit him high in the right shoulder, wounding him. The shot sent him backward, the gun falling from his hands. Dawson wasted no time swinging his Colt toward Bennie Tillis. But before he could get a shot off, the deafening sound of a shotgun blast from atop the stairs behind him caused both him and Tillis to flinch. Three feet in front of Tillis a large hole appeared in the ground, kicking a spray of dark earth up into the gunman's face. Bennie Tillis coughed and grabbed his eyes, his pistol waving back and forth aimlessly in front of him. "Don't shoot! I can't see! Don't shoot! It ain't fair!"

"Drop the gun, Tillis!" Dawson demanded.

"Okay! All right! Damn it, there, it's dropped!" Tillis shouted, half sobbing in his fear and frustration.

Seeing the gun hit the ground, Dawson ventured a look up the stairs and saw Suzzette standing with a long, double-barreled ten-gauge shotgun pointed down at the narrow alley. Dawson saw that the second hammer was cocked and ready to fire. He also saw Suzzette's arms tremble under the weight of the big gun and said in a firm, even tone, "Suzzette! Lower it toward the ground."

She did. Then she let out a long breath and said, "Cray, did I do good?"

Dawson kept his Colt cocked as he headed down to where Bob Pulley lay writhing on the muddy ground, holding his bloody shoulder. Ten feet away, Tillis stood digging dirt from his eyes, choking and cursing. Kicking Tillis's pistol aside, Dawson said to Suzzette, "Yes, you did real good! Now uncock that hammer before it goes off."

"All right," Suzzette said with uncertainty. "I'll try."

Dawson stood watching her as he kept his Colt pointed at the two beaten gunmen. It wasn't going to be easy telling her that she wasn't going with him . . . especially now.

Atop the stairs, Sheriff Neff stepped out beside Suzzette and took the shotgun from her. Then he looked down at Cray with a look that made Dawson feel ashamed for some reason.

Chapter 4

The next morning at dawn, Dawson had already gotten up and begun folding his belongings and placing them into his saddlebags when Suzzette sat up in bed, rubbed her eyes, and looked at him. Sleep cleared from her brow and she asked, "Cray, what are you doing?"

"I'm packing, Suzzette," he said gently but firmly. "It's time I get on to Somos Santos. I've been without work too long."

"You're leaving? Am I going?" she asked.

"No, Suzzette, I'm sorry," said Dawson, stopping, letting the flap fall on his saddlebags. "This is something we talked about, remember? I told you when it came time to go, I would have to go alone." He buckled the straps down on the saddlebags.

"I remember," said Suzzette, "but I thought you had changed your mind since then. We've gotten along so well. We've enjoyed each other's company . . . haven't we?"

"Yes, we have . . . I have," said Dawson. "I'm obliged for all you've done for me."

"You're obliged?" she asked flatly.

"That's all I can say," said Dawson. "You've taken good care of me. I'll never forget you for it."

"What have I done wrong?" Suzzette's voice sounded shaky and hurt.

"Nothing, Suzzette," said Dawson. "You've been perfect. It's not you, it's me. I've got things bothering me that I haven't settled inside myself. As long as they're still with me, I'm no good for a woman, I'm no good for myself. You deserve somebody better than me, Suzzette. And I hope you *get* somebody better than me."

She stood up and walked to him, putting her arms around him. "But we're so good together, everything about us, Cray. I love you. I'll do anything for you. Don't leave me. Tell me what you want, I can change!"

Dawson gently freed himself from her arms and held her hands in his as he said, "You're right, Suzzette, we're good together in every way. There's nothing about you that I would change. You're warm, you're kind, you're everything a man could ever want in a woman. The fact is, I just don't love you, Suzzette. I'm sorry, but there it is. I've tried to make myself love you. I watch you, the way you are, the way you do things, and I tell myself, 'Dawson, don't let this woman get away. Grab her and hold on and thank God for her.'" Standing close to her he saw a small tear form in her eye.

"Cray, please," she whispered.

"But it's just not there, and I don't think it ever will be, Suzzette," he whispered in reply.

"Give it time, Cray," she said. "Maybe after a while we'll—"

"No," Dawson said, cutting her off gently. "I'm in love with another woman, Suzzette. I can't seem to do anything about it."

"Who is she, Cray?" Suzzette asked. "Are you

going to her? Now? You're walking out of my arms, into hers?"

"No, Suzzette," Dawson said. "It's not the way you think it is. The woman I love, I can never have." He hesitated, then said, "She's dead, Suzzette. I love her . . . she's dead . . . and even still I can't seem to live without her."

Suzzette studied his eyes for a moment, trying to understand. Then she nodded and said in an accepting tone, "All right. I'll help you forget her, Cray. Just give me the chance. You'll see. I'll be so good for you, it will make you forget the past, I promise."

"It's no good, Suzzette, I'm sorry," he said, turning her hands loose slowly. "It's not fair to you, and it won't do me a bit of good. There are men who are born to only love one woman in their life. I'm one of those men." He offered a tired, hopeless smile. "And she was that kind of women. I'd give anything if I could spend the rest of my life with you, Suzzette, but it's not to be that way."

"Well then," Suzzette said, wiping her eyes on the back of her hand, "I can always say I tried. I saw my chance and I took a shot at it." She offered a weak smile herself. "You're *really* missing out on something good, Cray Dawson. You know what they say . . . if a whore loves a man she'll go all out for him."

"Don't Suzzette," said Dawson. "I don't like hearing you call yourself that."

"Well, it's what I am." She shrugged. "You would have been my move to respectability, Cray Dawson. But now I have to start all over."

"Being a gunman's woman isn't respectability, Suzzette," he said.

"It is from where I'm looking at it," she said.

"You're going to do something with yourself, Cray Dawson, I can see it. It shows in every way about you. I wouldn't be Suzzette the whore if I was with you. I would be somebody too."

"Suzzette, I ain't nothing but a drover . . . and it's all I'll ever be. It's all I even want to be," he said, returning her smile.

"Even that would have been all right by me," she said. "It just happens that I've fallen in love with you." She offered a sad laugh. "Sounds crazy doesn't it? A saloon whore like me, falling in love?"

"Suzzette, don't," said Dawson softly. "You're a good woman. Don't ever let anybody make you think otherwise."

"Sure," she said, passing it off, sniffling. "If I'm such a good woman, why is it I just keep on losing?"

Dawson offered no answer.

"Anyway, you've been good for me these past few days," she said. "I'm getting out of that business and I'm staying out of it."

"That's good to hear," said Dawson. "You can be more . . . I've seen that in you, Suzzette. I hope you will." He stepped back, picked up his saddlebags and laid them over his shoulder, feeling the motion of it down low in his belly. Then he picked up his rifle from where it leaned against a small table, and his hat from atop the table. "It's time I get back to my work."

"Watch yourself out there, Cray Dawson," she said. "I'll be thinking about you."

Dawson walked out, down the stair, and through the muddy alley to the main street. On his way to the livery barn he met Sheriff Neff, who stepped out of a small restaurant where he'd just finished his breakfast. "Morning, Sheriff," he said, slowing to a stop for a moment. "You'll be happy to know that I'm leaving."

Neff smiled, picking his teeth with a wooden matchstick. "You're right, Dawson, that's good news. Good for you because it means you're healing up . . . good for me because I won't have to worry about some fool wanting to kill you on my streets." He looked both ways along the street, then added, "Keep a wary eye for those two idiots you shot it out with. I run them out of here, but they could be anywhere along the trail."

"Obliged for the warning, Sheriff," said Dawson, "but I think they've had enough." He gave the sheriff a level gaze, saying, "For a man who doesn't care for gunfighters, you've treated me fairly."

"Yeah, well, maybe I was wrong about you, Dawson. You said you ain't a gunman, and I reckon you meant it. You could have killed those two fools but you didn't. I suppose that says something decent for you. Maybe you're all right, for a man tied down at the hip." His smile widened. "Now that you're leaving I wish you only the best." He touched his fingers to his wide Stetson brim. "In fact, since you're *leaving*, I wish you a good day."

Dawson left the sheriff, walked on to the livery barn and within moments had the big bay saddled and ready for the trail. Before leaving, he called Vernon forward from the rear of the barn. Vernon walked toward him hesitantly, his soft-billed cap in his hand. "Mister Dawson, I'm awfully sorry about what I done, telling them men where to find you. I reckon I just wasn't thinking. I meant you no harm though, I swear I didn't."

"Forget it, Vernon," Dawson said, "I know you didn't mean to cause me trouble. I just wanted to tell you 'no hard feelings,' before I left."

Vernon looked relieved. "Thank you kindly, Mister Dawson. I've been worried sick thinking you're mad at me." He offered a crooked grin. "Of course, I reckon if you'd truly been mad at me, I'd be dead by now, wouldn't I?"

Dawson saw that Vernon only saw him as a gunman and nothing else. There was respect in the stableman's eyes, and fear, and even envy. But there was nothing there to make Dawson think that Vernon considered him a man just like himself. To Vernon he was a larger-than-life killer of men. There was nothing he could say to change that. Instead of replying, he smiled and stepped up into his saddle. "You tell that boy of yours I'll meet him and shake his hand next time I'm through here."

"Will you?" Vernon followed along beside the big bay a few steps, excitedly. "Will you sure enough?" His face had lit up like a child's at Christmas. "I'll sure tell him! You can count on it! He'll be proud as a young rooster!"

Dawson put the bay forward onto the muddy street and rode south until Eagle Pass lay shimmering in the morning light behind him.

Dawson rode steadily throughout the day, feeling only the slightest discomfort in his lower belly. He stopped at noon only long enough to water Stony in a runoff stream of the Nueces before heading southeast in the direction of Somos Santos. While the healing stomach wound had not pained him, it had slowed him down. As the evening shadows drew long across the broken hillsides he realized it would take a hard push to get him to his weathered frame house, seven miles from town. Having brought no supplies, or even coffee for what he thought would be only a one-day ride, Dawson turned onto the old Missionary Trail toward the evening lights of the Bouchard Double D Spread, where he knew he would be welcome to share a meal and spend the night.

He followed a slim trail branching off to his right until, at the end of a narrowing valley, he stopped at the rail gates of the Double D, where he heard a voice call out from the shadow of a buckboard wagon, "Halt! Who are you and what's your business here?"

Surprised by such an encounter, Dawson called out in reply, "I'm Cray Dawson, your neighbor. My business is a hot meal and a bunk for the night."

"Cray?" said a familiar voice. "Is it really you?"

"Have I ever lied to you, Sonny?" said Dawson, recognizing the voice of his longtime trail partner, Sonny Wells.

"Not yet," said Sonny Wells, stepping up from beneath the buckboard wagon dusting his trousers with his left hand, his right holding a Henry rifle. "Crayton, we've heard many a tall tale about you lately. I hope you're here to clear them up."

"I'll do what I can," said Dawson, crossing his wrists on his saddle horn, looking down at the wide rail gate standing closed between them. "What's this all about? Last time I saw this gate closed was back when I was a kid . . . Gains Bouchard got wild-eyed drunk and chased his brother Gilbert off with a claw hammer."

Unlatching the gate, the slim, straight-shouldered cowboy looked up with a grin from beneath his sugar-loaf brim. "Them was good ole times." He gave the gate a hard shove and stepped to the side, allowing Dawson to ride through. Then, as he closed the gate he said, "Gains says there's too much meanness in the world these days. He told me to start pinning her down, so I do, every night at dark now."

"What kind of meanness is he talking about?" Dawson asked, stopping the bay and looking down at Sonny Wells.

Sonny shrugged. "Who knows? Most of it's in his head I reckon. But there has been lots more cattle rustled than usual, some killed, *some* for no reason. These days we find them butchered where they grazed, cooked and et and the biggest part of them left to waste. I expect that's the kind of meanness Gains can't abide."

"I expect so too," Dawson said quietly. He gave a look toward the main house and bunkhouses, where lanterns glowed through windows and open doors. "So, Gains Bouchard is closing his gate to it."

"Hard to believe, ain't it?" said Sonny, latching the gate. "Lately he walks like a man with a snake up his leg. Maybe you ought to talk to him, see if you can ease his mind some. You always could talk to him."

"I never could talk *to* him," said Dawson. "I could only talk in his direction. I don't know if anything I said ever stuck or not."

"It might now," said Sonny, grinning, "You being a big gunman and all."

"Don't start on me, Sonny," said Dawson. "I

thought if there was one place I wouldn't hear what a big gunman I am, it would be here."

"Then you thought wrong, *big gunman*," Sonny teased. "You've been the talk of the place ever since you rode with Shaw to avenge Rosa's death."

Dawson had mourned Rosa Shaw in silence so long that even the sound of her name palled his spirit. He felt his expression change and he was powerless to hide it.

Seeing the change sweep across Dawson's brow, Sonny said quickly, "We all thought highly of you for what you done, Crayton. It was a terrible thing what the Talbert Gang did to that poor, good woman."

"It's over now," said Dawson, not wanting to think about it . . . to talk about it.

"Yes it is." Sonny nodded as he continued, not taking Dawson's hint. "We all knew it took some nerves of steel, you backing a gunman like Fast Larry Shaw in the first place. Then when we heard about you gunning down three men at once! *Whooie!* You can bet we was all talking about that!"

Gesturing with a nod toward the glowing lantern lights at the house, Dawson asked, "Think I can get some grub before Shaney shuts the chuck wagon down?"

Sonny Wells gave him a look up and down. "From the looks of you I'd say you need to see Shaney as quick as you can."

"Good to see you again, Pard," said Dawson, turning his bay toward the house.

Giving Dawson a tip of his hat, Sonny said, "Aw . . . Get on out of here, then."

Dawson rode Stony up to the house and around it

to a wide backyard where a dozen drovers sat on the ground with tin plates and coffee cups in their hands. A large campfire crackled and glowed. Shaney the cook sat on the open tailgate of a small chuck wagon, drinking cool water from a long-handled dipper. But at the sight of Cray Dawson, the old cook stood up, spit a stream of water to the ground, then called out to him, "Crayton Dawson, what is wrong with Sonny Wells, letting the likes of you in here?"

"He took one look at me and said I'm an emergency case," said Dawson.

"Right he is," said Shaney, wiping his hands on his greasy apron. "Fall down off that horse and get your plate out. We'll soon have some meat on your bones."

"Obliged," said Dawson, "but I'm traveling light this evening."

"Traveling light?" The cook sounded surprised. "A man who don't carry his own eating tools, don't deserve to eat, I always said." But then he called out over his shoulder to his cook's helper, "Frenchy! Get Mister Dawson a plate and something to eat with. I want no man losing his fingers at my camp."

As the young helper hurried to get Dawson a plate, a cup, and eating utensils, Dawson stepped down from his saddle with a short wince, feeling the pain grow stronger in his stomach. Shaney noticed his expression but made no mention of it. Instead he took the reins to the bay and said to Dawson, "You grab yourself a piece of ground. Frenchy will load your plate."

"Obliged," said Dawson to the old cook, looking around at the faces in the shadowy glow of the campfire. "I'll need the loan of short supplies when I leave here in the morning, if you can spare it."

"Come morning I'll fix you up a poke—coffee, beans, and whatnot," said the cook, tossing the request aside for the time being. "I reckon you know everybody here, except Cleveland Ellis and Moon Braden."

"I'm Moon Braden," said a gruff voice from beneath a lowered hat brim.

"I'm Ellis," said another gruff voice, this one coming from a big man wearing a pair of studded stovepipe chaps, sitting to Braden's right.

Dawson gave them a nod.

"I reckon you remember Eldon and Max Furry?" said Shaney.

"The Furry boys, sure," said Dawson. "Howdy, boys."

Both the young drovers nodded, staring wide-eyed at Cray Dawson. He could tell by the look on their faces that they had both heard about what had happened in Brakett Flats and Turkey Creek.

"And Sandy Edelman, our ramrod?" said Shaney, pointing a finger as he spoke. "And Stanley Grubs . . . Jimmie Turner, Mike Cassidy . . . Broken Nose Simms?"

"Howdy all," said Dawson, nodding in turn at the men as they made short remarks, or gave a toss of a hand or a nod as they continued eating.

Then Shaney turned to three men on his other side. "And of course you know Decker, Barney and Slouch?"

"Indeed I do," said Dawson, touching his hat brim.

Frenchy Dupre hurried back with the eating utensils and a heaping plate full of beans and steaming salt pork with a chunk of bread on the side. "Here you are, Crayton, you eat right up," he said. "I'll fetch you some coffee now."

Dawson noted that Moon Braden nudged Cleveland Ellis. The two looked his way, said something in private, then chuckled under their breath.

Sandy Edelman, a seasoned drover and foreman for the Double D said, "Dawson, I know you probably don't want to talk about it, but I just want to say, 'Good job,' you and Shaw killing them dirty bastards. Hanging would have been too good for them."

Dawson nodded quietly as he ate.

Broken Nose Simms said in a nasal tone, "I knew you were pretty handy with a gun, but danged if I ever could see you riding side by side with the likes of Lawrence Shaw."

"Why don't you boys shut up and let Crayton eat. He's so skinny now if he lifted his feet his boots wouldn't follow."

"Sorry," said Broken Nose, going back to his plate of beans and pork.

"I always thought Shaw was a might bit overrated myself," said Cleveland Ellis. He stared at Cray Dawson.

The circle of eating men fell silent. Dawson knew that remark was meant to be a slight toward him. "We're all entitled to our own opinions, I reckon," he said.

"Yeah, I reckon we are," said Ellis, cold-staring Dawson with a look of thinly veiled contempt.

Dawson ignored the man, not wanting to ride into the Double D and have a disagreement with one of the cowhands. But Sandy Edelman saw the atmosphere starting to tense because of Cleveland Ellis, so he said, "Ellis, Braden, as soon as you two finish eating, go check on those new broncs that the Centrales Spread sent over today."

Realizing he had been singled out by the foreman, Cleveland Ellis stood up, slung the remains of his coffee from his tin cup and dusted his trouser seat. "Come on, Moon, looks like a man can't speak his mind around here without getting more work dumped on him."

"Yeah, let's go," said Moon Braden, standing up as well. "I'd just as soon be checking on broncs as sitting here. For two cents I'd take pay and ride."

Sandy Edelman started to speak, but before he could say a word, a voice resounded from the darkness on the rear porch of the house, saying, "That's the only thing you've said lately that I agree with." Gains Bouchard walked slowly down the wooden porch steps and over to where the cowboys sat in the glowing firelight. A scent of pipe smoke wafted on the air around his broad shoulders.

"Now, wait a minute, Mister Bouchard," said Cleveland Ellis. "I didn't know you was listening."

"I bet you didn't," said Bouchard. He turned a glance and a nod toward Cray Dawson and said through his walruslike gray mustache, "Howdy, Crayton."

"Howdy, Mister Bouchard," said Dawson.

Then Bouchard said to Ellis and Braden, "Roll your bunks and be out of here first thing in the morning. See me for your pay. Nobody treats a guest with rudeness around my fire."

Cleveland Ellis jutted his chin. "I don't have to wait till morning. I'll roll my bunk and take my pay tonight."

"That goes for me too," said Moon Braden.

"Shaney," said Bouchard, "go to the box . . . get both of them paid up through today."

"Yes, Mister Bouchard," said the old cook, hurrying away to the house.

While they stood waiting for Shaney to return, Cleveland Ellis said to Cray Dawson, "I'll run into you along the trail. Then I'll tell you what I think of you and your friend Shaw."

Dawson set his plate and coffee cup aside, and stood up facing Cleveland Ellis and Moon Braden with no more than ten feet between them in the flickering glow of firelight. "I ignored your mouth out of respect to Mister Bouchard and his spread. Now that you're not a part of the spread, say what you think you're able to back up." His hand poised near his Colt.

Cleveland Ellis thought about it. Dawson could see it in his eyes. He could also see in Moon Braden's eyes that he was ready to follow Ellis's lead. On the ground, cowboys scooted out of the line of fire, but most of them kept eating, their eyes riveted on Dawson and the other two men.

But then, instead of making a move, Cleveland Ellis eased down, raising his hand purposefully away from his tied-down pistol. "That's all right, Moon, let's let it go," he said over his shoulder to his companion. "We've got bigger fish to fry." He let himself offer a flat smile to Cray Dawson. "You and me will cross trail again. This can keep."

"Suit yourself," said Dawson. But he didn't sit down, nor did he turn his back on the pair. Instead he stood facing them until the old cook came trotting back from the house carrying money in both fists.

"Pay them," said Bouchard, keeping a steady gaze on Cleveland Ellis.

The cook handed each man a fistful of money. "Count it if you need to," he said.

"Don't worry, I *will* count it," said Cleveland Ellis. "It better all be there."

"Well, you insulting son of a—"

"That's enough, Shaney!" said Bouchard, cutting the cook off before his words sparked a gun battle. "If that money ain't right, you come see me," said Gains Bouchard. "I'll teach you how to count it."

"Come on, Moon," said Ellis. "I've been wanting to get shed of this bunch. This is a good time to do it." They both backed off a couple of steps, then turned and walked away toward the bunkhouse.

As soon as they were out of sight in the darkness, Bouchard turned to Cray Dawson and said in a gruff tone, "They're lucky this ain't the old days. We used to horsewhip a man for acting that way to somebody in off the trail at mealtime."

"I didn't mean to cause trouble," said Dawson.

"You didn't cause it. I've known you since you was too short to reach the stirrups. You always was too hard on yourself." Before Dawson could say another word, Bouchard said, "Come on, bring your grub up on the porch. I want to talk to you."

Picking up his plate and coffee, Dawson followed the broad-shouldered rancher and the smell of his pipe smoke across the dark yard to the house. Once they settled into two wooden porch chairs and Dawson set his coffee and food on a wicker table, Gains Bouchard said in a lowered tone of voice, "It's mighty good to see you, Crayton."

"Same here," said Dawson, "and I *do* apologize for

awhile ago. It seems like everywhere I go these days, trouble flares up."

Gains Bouchard's expression turned clouded. "Didn't you know it would before you strapped that gun on and went manhunting?"

"I never gave it any thought," said Dawson. "It had to be done. If I had to do it over, I'd do it the same way, whatever it cost me."

"I understand," said Bouchard. He took a long draw of smoke from his pipe and blew it out slowly. "I brought you up here on the porch so I wouldn't have to say this in front of the men." He hesitated for a moment, then said, "If you came here looking for work, I can't hire you right now, Crayton."

Dawson just looked at him.

"I can see what you're thinking," said Bouchard, "but it ain't because you've gone and got yourself a reputation." He pointed at Dawson with his pipe stem. "Although you don't make it easy on a fellow, coming back to Somos Santos with a string of shootings following you. You know how crazy these drovers get over something like that. Pretty soon they're all thinking they can do the same."

"Then what is it?" Dawson asked, sipping his coffee.

"I'm short of work and long on hands." Bouchard shrugged. "We just pushed a herd to Missouri for the army. Right now there's nothing else in sight. I can make a spot for you, but I know you don't want that."

"No," said Dawson, "I've never been hand-fed. I wouldn't know how to act."

"I knew that was how you'd feel," said Bouchard, settling back in his chair.

"Sonny Wells told me there's been more rustling going on than usual," said Dawson. "What's causing it?"

"More *people*, is what's causing it," said Bouchard. "It's no great surprise that where there's more people there's more stealing, is it?"

"I reckon not," said Dawson. "I was just curious, is all."

Realizing that Sonny Wells had said more on the matter, Bouchard gave Dawson a narrowed look and said, "But missing cattle ain't what's been bothering me. What's bothering me is seeing a good town like Somos Santos go to hell, and nobody there lifting a hand to stop it."

"Sonny never mentioned Somos Santos," said Dawson.

"He would have, if you'd gave him time," Bouchard replied. "Right after you left here, the town had an election and voted Sheriff Bratcher out of office." He sucked on the pipe, blew out a stream and said, "They voted in a fellow by the name of Martin Lematte. Since he took office the town has been turning into one big cesspool of crooked gambling, whoring, drinking, and opium smoking. Lematte is slicker than a bucket of eels. You watch your back if you spend any time in town. I figure he'll have to pin you down right away. He'll have to know right off whether you're with him or against him now that you're tied down at the hip."

"More gun trouble," said Dawson, shaking his head slowly. "That's exactly what I came back here to get away from."

"Good luck getting away from it." Bouchard smiled knowingly. "I just thought I better warn you before you ride in there and find you're not welcome anymore."

"I'm finding that most places I go," said Dawson. He sipped his coffee, ignoring the remaining food on his plate.

Chapter 5

Dawson rode out early the next morning, after scraping half of his breakfast off into the dirt for a couple of yard dogs to growl over. Shaney the cook looked at the dogs eating the discarded food and scratched his head. Then he watched the big bay trot out of sight onto the main trail toward Somos Santos as he said to his helper, "I reckon once a man gets himself a reputation he ain't required to eat the way the rest of us do, eh, Frenchy?"

Frenchy gave his boss a look and said, "I was giving it some thought this morning, and you know what? I believe I've known Crayton Dawson longer than *you* have."

"Like hell you have!" said Shaney, taken aback by such a claim. "Now get the rest of these drovers fed. We ain't letting them sit around all day doing nothing!"

Cray Dawson rode the main trail until midmorning, then turned off onto a weed-grown path and followed it to a clearing between two upthrusts of rock. In front of a sun-bleached plank line shack, he stepped down from his saddle at the hitch rail and shouldered his saddlebags and the poke bag Shaney had prepared for him. He drew his rifle from its boot and said under his breath, "Welcome home, Cray Dawson," as if his voice belonged to someone speaking to him from the rickety front porch. Then he walked up onto the porch and nudged the door open as it swung back and forth slowly on a hot breeze.

Inside, he saw the tail of a lizard disappear down off the top of an oaken table, then shoot down through a crack in the floor a second later. In the dust on the plank floor he saw where a snake had recently wound its way out the open back door. Leaning his rifle against a wall and dropping his saddlebags onto the table, he walked to a dust-covered broom standing in a rear corner and picked it up.

An hour later, he had swept the floor, dusted the few battered pieces of furniture, and gathered a pile of mesquite brush and oak kindling for a fire in the small hearth. He went outside and rolled a heavy rock off of the wooden well cover and pulled the cover off. He shook dust off of a small metal pail tied to the end of a coiled rope and let fifteen feet of the rope slide through his hands into the blackness, until he heard the pail splash quietly in the water. With the pail filled, he covered the well and walked back into the shack. He took a small bag of coffee beans from the poke sack Shaney had given him before he'd left the Double D Spread. He crushed enough beans with his pistol butt to boil a pot of coffee.

While the coffee heated, he took out a small bag of dried beans, considered cooking a pot, but then changed his mind and set the bag aside. He had no appetite. It wasn't food he needed, he told himself. He couldn't name what it *was* he needed, but he was certain it wasn't food. Waiting on the coffee, he walked out and led Stony out of the sun to a lean-to inside a small rail corral filled with clumps of wild grass that had grown all summer long.

"Graze it down," he told the bay. Lifting the saddle and bridle from the horse, he dropped them over a fence rail out of the sun. He picked up an oaken bucket, carried it to the well, and returned with it full of cool water. He set the bucket at the horse's hoofs, then walked back to the house.

When the coffee had boiled and he'd taken it off the fire and let it settle, he poured a cup and took it out on the front porch. He righted an overturned rocking chair with a busted cane bottom and sat on it sipping his coffee for a moment. Then, restless, he set the cup down, walked inside, and took out an old drawstring cloth pouch of smoking tobacco that had been in his saddlebags too long to remember. He carried the tobacco and some wrinkled rolling papers onto the porch and sat rolling and smoking cigarettes as the sun moved over into the western sky. He didn't realize he'd spent the afternoon thinking about Rosa Shaw until all of a sudden it was gone and there was nothing he could do about it. Looking down at the empty coffee pot and the stained cup sitting near his feet, he cursed silently and stood up.

"I can't stand this, Rosa," he said, not knowing if he'd said it aloud or only in his mind. Kicking his boot through a pile of crushed cigarette butts and the empty tobacco pouch, he stepped down off the porch, walked around the house, and came back moments later leading the bay by its reins, saddled and ready for the trail.

He rode into Somos Santos as evening stretched

long across the land and the sun set low and simmering in a sea of red fire. Stony cantered quarterwise the last few yards, as if knowing that cool shade awaited in the black slices of shadow reaching out from the rooftops of buildings to the wide street below.

"What have we here, Karl?" Sheriff Martin Lematte said to the man standing beside him on the boardwalk out front of the saloon.

"I don't know," said Karl Nolly. He spread a slight grin. "But if he's carrying any money, I think we better get a hold of it, before he wastes it on something foolish."

"There you go reading my mind again," said Lematte, smiling himself, working a thin cigar back and forth between his lips as the pair stood watching the big bay slow to a walk toward the hitch rail.

"Good evening to you, stranger," Lematte said, smiling affably, tipping his black flat-crowned hat. "Welcome to Somos Santos."

Cray Dawson remembered Bouchard's warning. But he returned Lematte's smile, and touched his fingertips to his hat brim. "Evening, Sheriff," he said, stepping down from his saddle and twirling Stony's reins around the hitch rail. He nodded at Karl Nolly. "Deputy."

"What brings you to Somos Santos, stranger?" asked Nolly, noting the big tied-down Colt on Dawson's hip.

Dawson stifled a short laugh and said, "It seems odd being called *stranger*." He looked back and forth along the nearly empty street, then said flatly, "I'm from here." He stared at them blankly until the two men felt compelled to reply.

Lematte squirmed slightly, then recovered and said with an even friendlier smile, "Well, then! Don't I feel foolish!" He showed Karl Nolly his smile to make sure the deputy saw how polite he wanted this to be. "I'm afraid I've only been the sheriff here a short while. Apparently you left Somos Santos before my time, *Mister* . . . ?" He left his words open, hoping they would be filled in.

"My name's Dawson . . . Crayton Dawson," he said, again touching his hat brim slightly.

"Mister Dawson," said Lematte, "I certainly hope you've taken no offense at my ignorance. I'm Sheriff Martin Lematte, at your service. . . . This is my most trusted deputy, Karl Nolly."

"Also at your service," said Nolly, but his eyes said otherwise as they studied Dawson curiously.

"We're both pleased to make your acquaintance," said Lematte. His smile seemed genuine, as did his eyes and expression. "I hope you'll find Somos Santos to be as enjoyable as you left it." He spread his arms as if to display the town with pride. "You'll notice there have been some changes, I'm sure."

Dawson looked up at the sign hanging above the saloon, and read aloud, "The Silver Seven Saloon." Then he cut his gaze back to Lematte and asked, "What happened to the Ace High? I always thought Ace High was a fine name."

"Indeed, so did I," said Lematte. "But since the Ace High fell on financial difficulty, and Karl and I had to bail it out, we thought it might be best to start with a clean slate so to speak, name and all." He looked up at the sign then back at Dawson. "I named her after a silver mine I used to own up in Colorado. I hope you like our decision, Mister Dawson."

"Just curious is all," said Dawson, stepping up onto the boardwalk. "What become of Nelson Hawkins, the Ace High owner?"

Lematte looked down and shook his head slowly with a sigh of regret. "That is not a happy story," he said. "It pains me to tell you, but poor Mister Hawkins took his business losses so personally that he went home one night and stared too long into his gun barrel, if you know what I mean."

Dawson didn't let the news move him one way or the other. "Nelson never struck me as that type."

"I know! Me neither," said Lematte, as if still stunned by the event. "But isn't that always the ones who do it? The ones you least suspect." He seemed to recover from his shock and regret and said, "But, Mister Dawson, let's not let this news spoil your evening. We have every game of chance you can imagine inside the Silver Seven!"

"Crayton *Daw*son?" said Karl Nolly, sounding amazed, as if his mind had just awakened to an important discovery.

"Yes, Crayton Dawson, wasn't it?" said Lematte, giving Nolly a bewildered look. "Did I miss something?" Saying Dawson's name again triggered Lematte's memory. His eyes widened the same as Nolly's.

"You're *the* Crayton Dawson?" asked Nolly. His hand crept instinctively closer to his Colt. But seeing Dawson look closely at his action, he raised his hand to the center of his chest and idly scratched himself, clearly showing he had no intention of reaching for his gun.

"Yes, I'm *the* Crayton Dawson. I just rode in for a drink," he said. "I heard there was a new sheriff here. What's become of Nate Bratcher?"

"Well, now, there is another sad story I'm afraid," said Lematte. "After the election, even though I made it perfectly clear that Bratcher could stay on as a deputy . . . he just started drinking more and more, then wandered off one night. Nobody has seen him since. I'm afraid something terrible has happened to him."

Dawson just looked at the two.

"Was Bratcher a friend of yours, Dawson?" Nolly asked, trying to get a feel for Dawson and where he stood.

"Not particularly," said Dawson, playing it down just to see if these men might reveal anything to him. "We weren't friends . . . we weren't enemies. I hate to hear about him being dead though."

"Well, yes," said Lematte, "and so do—"

"Nobody *said* he's dead," Nolly cut in. "He just wandered off, that's all." He gave Dawson a questioning look.

"Dead . . . wandered off. What's the difference?" Dawson shrugged. "Either way, I doubt if he'll be showing up for supper." He offered a thin smile.

Lematte and Nolly looked at one another, unsure how to take Dawson's words. But then Lematte gave a short, bemused chuckle and said, "Yes, come to think of it, Dawson, you're right; either way I doubt if he *will* be showing up for supper."

"Say, Dawson," Nolly commented, now that the air seemed calm between them, "we heard all about what you did up in Turkey Creek and Brakett Flats. That was some powerful account you gave of yourself. Feel like talking about it?"

"You mean over a drink?" Dawson implied.

Lematte smiled. "Bravo, Dawson! Of course he

meant over a drink. Come on, the drinks are on me."
He shook a finger. "But I better warn you, I intend
to win it all back from you at one of the gambling
tables."

"You're on," said Dawson, stepping toward the
doors of the Silver Seven Saloon. "But I better warn
you, Lematte . . . I don't plan on losing anything."

Two hours later, Cray Dawson stood at the roulette
table with a stack of chips in front of him. At the
bar, Martin Lematte and Karl Nolly stood watching
closely, each of them keeping a detached expression
on his face. When another round of hoots and ap-
plause went up around the roulette table, Karl said
under his breath, "I'd like to make him eat that gaming table, legs and all!"

"Believe me, Karl," said Martin Lematte, "if I
thought you were able to do something like that, we
wouldn't be letting him win. But I suggest you think
twice before you start any trouble with this gunman.
We're doing damn good here . . . let's not make a
foolish mistake and get ourselves killed in the
process."

"If I make a move on him, there won't be any
mistakes, Lematte," said Nolly. "You might be
smarter than me about lots of things, but not when
it comes to killing. When I make up my mind to kill
a man, he might just as well sell his horse . . . he
won't be needing it."

"That's all well and good," said Lematte. "But before we start burying men you've yet to kill, let me
see if I can get Dawson leaning our way. Give him
a taste of money. It wouldn't hurt to get a fast gun
like him on our side."

"I just hate seeing all this money going into his pocket instead of ours," said Nolly.

"So do I," Lematte said quietly, watching the roulette wheel from across the saloon. "But just call it seed money." Seeing Dawson look around toward them, Lematte raised his shot glass in friendly salute.

"Look at him," said Nolly when Dawson turned back toward the wheel. "It's almost like he knows we're letting him win . . . like he's rubbing our faces in something."

"He doesn't know a thing," said Lematte. "You're just letting your imagination run away with you. All these big, bold gunmen have a smugness to them. They're all arrogant sons-a-bitches. They all think they're smarter than they really are." He smiled. "But that's to our advantage if we get him on our side . . . and if he doesn't get on our side, that same arrogance will be his downfall, I'll wager."

As the two talked back and forth between themselves, the roulette table boss came walking over wiping sweat from his forehead and said to Lematte in a hoarse whisper, "Sheriff, this guy is killing us! What do you want me to do?"

"Keep doing what you've been doing, Ferguson, letting him win. Give him about ten more minutes, then start using the foot pedal. Start him losing slowly. We'll see if he's smart enough to know when to quit."

"Whatever you say, Sheriff," said Ferguson. "But this fellow is giving my table a beating." He backed up, turned, and hurried back to the table in time to see Cray Dawson rake in another tall stack of chips.

Martin Lematte saw a young tough named Henry Snead walking up to him and he said to Karl Nolly,

"Good, here comes Snead. Now we'll get a chance to see how Crayton Dawson handles himself."

Sliding in beside Lematte at the bar, Henry Snead said, "Collins told me to get right over here. Said there's some saddle tramp winning too much money."

Seeing sweat run down Snead's face, Lematte looked up and down at the dark circles on his shirt and asked, "Why are you so sweaty?"

Snead flexed his large arms and broadened his chest. "I was lifting nail kegs just for the fun of it," he said. "I like to keep myself ready for anything."

"Do you hear that, Karl?" Lematte beamed humorously at Nolly. "He lifts kegs of nails 'just for the fun of it.'"

"I heard," said Karl Nolly, sounding disinterested.

Henry Snead looked over at the roulette table, where the only player who seemed to be doing anything was the tall, thin cowboy with the tied-down Colt. "I guess that's him, huh?" Snead asked.

Lematte smiled at Nolly, then said to Snead, "Yes, that's the man." He drew on his cigar as if considering something. "Tell me, Snead, how would you like to earn yourself a deputy badge tonight?"

"Nothing would suit me better." Snead rubbed his fist into the palm of his hand. "Want me to go smack him around some . . . maybe drag him outside and stick his head down in a horse trough?"

"Now that would be interesting to watch." Again Lematte grinned at Nolly. "But use discretion, Snead."

"Use what?" Snead looked confused.

"What I mean is, Henry," said Lematte, "don't let

him know Nolly and I have anything to do with it. It will be our secret, yours and mine, all right?"

"Suits me," said Snead. "Can I go over there now?"

"Well, why not?" Lematte grinned. "But don't make a move for another ten minutes."

"I'm not carrying a watch," said Snead, looking concerned.

"Watch me for a nod. You can do that can't you?" Lematte asked with a note of sarcasm.

"Sure thing," said Snead.

At the table, Cray Dawson had not looked around during the time Henry Snead stood talking to Martin Lematte, so he had no warning of what was about to come. He'd been winning steadily from the time he started playing. But then his luck began to change slowly. Dawson realized right away that he'd been set up, first to win, now to lose. He didn't know why, but he did know that he wasn't about to give back any more money than he had to. If Lematte wanted to play games with him, Dawson would see to it that it cost him. After four bad spins in a row, Dawson drew his chips off into his hat and handed it to the table boss, saying, "Cash me in. Gentlemen, I'm calling it a night."

He watched Ferguson the table boss count the chips and place them to the side. Then he watched a large roll of bills come up from under the table near Ferguson's hand, and saw Ferguson quickly count out four hundred and eighty dollars and slide the money across the green felt tabletop to him. "Much obliged," said Dawson, folding the money and stuffing it down into his shirt pocket. He stepped back and turned to walk toward the bar, but from out of nowhere a thick fist hooked him low in the stomach and lifted him onto his toes. He jackknifed forward, bowed at the waist. The pain cutting into his tender, healing flesh paralyzed him for a moment, and dropped him to his knees. He rocked back and forth unsteadily, gasping for breath.

"Jeez!" said Henry Snead, looking surprised as he stepped back rubbing his fist. At first he'd been poised for a fight, but seeing no sign of one coming he shrugged and chuckled under his breath, looking around as if making sure everybody saw what he'd done. "This guy is really weak in the gut, huh?"

A few tense seconds passed as everybody in the Silver Seven seemed to hold their breath. Henry Snead, seeing that Dawson wasn't going to be doing anything in retaliation, finally reached down and dragged him to his feet and toward the front doors, saying, "Come on, cowboy . . . you can't sit there and get sick all over the floor. Then I'd *really* have to thump on you." Snead gave Lematte a triumphant look as he dragged Cray Dawson past him as if the man were a scarecrow.

Turning back to the bar, Lematte said to Nolly, "Well, I suppose that's that. Who would ever guess a man like Crayton Dawson would be such a pushover?"

"I always say they're all nothing without a gun in their hand," said Nolly.

"I have to say I am a little disappointed," said Lematte, raising a shot glass. "I had thought we might have a bit of sport here this evening. I always enjoy figuring a man out. I thought there would be more to Cray Dawson than *this*." He gestured toward the floor in disgust.

"Maybe you like to figure a gunman out," said Karl Nolly, standing beside Lematte at the bar but staring at the bat-wing doors. "Myself, I'm glad he's gone. I just hope we've seen the last of him."

"I don't think we need concern ourselves there," said Lematte. "I know a thing or two about people. He's not coming back. There's no fight in that man. You saw what he did as soon as the wheel stopped spinning his way—he quit! You saw what happened when he took a punch in the gut—he folded up!" He tossed back the shot of whiskey and let out a hiss. "Our boy Henry Snead has taken Dawson in front of everybody. These gunmen can't stand that sort of thing. He'll want to get as far from here as he can, I expect. He'll go somewhere and nurse his sore gut." He saluted Nolly with his empty whiskey glass and a smug grin. "So long, *Mister* Dawson!"

As they spoke, Henry Snead came back in and walked up beside Lematte, rolling his shirt sleeves down. "That didn't take long, did it?" he said with a cruel, flat smile.

"You didn't really dunk him in the horse trough, did you?" asked Lematte with a bemused expression.

"Naw," said Henry Snead with a swipe of a thick hand. "I could've, but the shape he was in, I figured why bother? Fact is, I even shoved him up onto his horse and slapped its rump to give him a send-off."

"How humane!" said Lematte, in feigned admiration.

"Did you happen to take his gun?" asked Nolly with a trace of warning in his voice.

"Naw," said Snead, brushing the question aside. "Oh!" Snead snapped his fingers. "Before I forget it—" He reached a thick hand into his trousers, took out the roll of money he'd lifted from Dawson's shirt pocket, and handed it to Lematte. "Here's your change. I thought you might want it back."

Lematte gave a dark little chuckle and said sidelong to Karl Nolly. "Do you see this, Karl? He brought me *change*."

Chapter 6

Cray Dawson had never experienced pain as severe and unrelenting in his life. It had left him helpless and broken. As the big bay carried him away from Somos Santos, he lay slumped forward, barely able to keep himself in the saddle. When the bay stopped out front of the shack, Dawson slid himself down the horse's side and limped inside, bowed at the waist. He dropped his gun belt and boots on the floor and lay in agony on the hard, flat bed, too tortured to sleep, too drained and exhausted to even undress himself. Come dawn he stood up in a half-conscious stupor, the pain having lessened only slightly during the night.

"Oh, God, Rosa," he moaned. Then, realizing he had called her name aloud and chastising himself for doing such a thing, he took a deep breath and forced himself to the front porch, where a half-filled bucket of water had sat since the day before. It took all of his strength to raise the bucket and pour it over his bowed head. He dropped the bucket and blew water from his lips, and stared blurry-eyed at the bay who'd spent the night in the yard still wearing its bridle and saddle. "Damn it, Stony, I'm sorry," he said in a raspy voice. Shoving his hand into his shirt pocket, he realized for the first time that his money was gone. He rubbed his hands up and down his face, drying himself. Then he walked inside, put on his boots, looped his gun belt over his shoulder, and made his way painfully to the front yard.

Picking his hat up from the dirt where it had fallen the night before, he dusted it against his leg and looked off along the trail leading toward Shaw's *hacienda*, where he knew Rosa's sister, Carmelita, still waited for Lawrence Shaw to return to her. "I said I'd tell her," he told the horse, as if the horse understood. He picked up the reins hanging in the dirt and struggled upward onto the horse's back. With a touch of his heels he sent the bay forward toward the Old Spanish Trail.

The ride should have taken less than an hour, yet by the time he topped the crest of a rise and looked down onto the house, the mid-morning sun beat down on him without mercy. Stopping the horse he waited for a moment, trying to force himself to sit straight up in his saddle. But, seeing the woman watch him from where she stood at the clothesline to the right of the house, Dawson adjusted the gun belt hanging from his shoulder and rode closer. When he stopped again he was no more than twenty yards from her. He did not hear her whisper, "Lawrence?" to herself. Nor could he see the look of disappointment appear, then disappear from her dark eyes when she realized it was only him. "Are you hurt?" she called out, using her hand as a visor against the sun's glare.

Feeling his voice was too weak to reach her, he nudged the bay forward, then stopped again fifteen feet from her. "He said to tell you he won't be coming back for a long while," Dawson said, his voice still sounding pained and shaky to himself.

"I did not think he would," she said flatly. She shrugged, holding a wicker basket of damp clothes resting against her hip.

"He might not be back at all," Dawson said.

"So?" she said, lowering her hand from over her eyes.

"So, I wanted you to know," Dawson said. His hand went to his stomach as he spoke.

"Are you hurt?" she asked again.

"No, I'm all right." A silence passed. "Yes, I am hurt," he corrected himself. "I'm healing from a wound . . . a bad one," he said. "It won't quit hurting."

Carmelita nodded and only stared at him.

"I better go," he said. Yet he continued to sit the horse, gazing off for a moment, then back at her.

"Are you hungry?" she asked.

"No," he said. "I haven't been eating. That is, I haven't wanted to." He shook his head and said quietly, "I mean, no, I'm not hungry."

She stared in silence.

"I never blamed you and Shaw for what you done that night," he blurted out.

"Oh? What night was this?" she asked.

"The night you slept together when he came home to visit Rosa's grave," Dawson said.

Carmelita shifted the wicker basket slightly on her hip. "I do not care whether you blamed me or not," she said.

"I didn't, anyway," he said.

She stared at him.

"Well, I better go," he said. Still he made no effort to do so. Instead he nudged the bay forward a step and looked at her, seeing how much she resembled Rosa—her hair, her eyes, the turn of her mouth when she spoke. Seeing her, he could almost smell Rosa's scent, almost taste Rosa's mouth. He felt a sudden dull ache inside him that was as real, if not as intense, as the pain in his tender, healing stomach. Seeing Carmelita look at him curiously, he shoved his hand down slightly into his waist belt and said, "It hurts something awful."

"*Si*," she said, "I understand."

He wasn't sure what it was she understood, whether she referred to the apparent pain he felt in his wounded stomach, or to some deeper pain she sensed in his spirit. But looking into her dark eyes he realized that she did indeed understand things about him, things that he would never even have to mention. Looking away from her he asked quickly, as if to hesitate a second longer would keep him from asking at all, "Can I stay here with you?"

A silence seemed to engulf the land as he waited for her answer. After a moment of thoughtful pause, Carmelita said, "There is plenty of room. *Si*, you can stay here."

"No," he said, I mean *with you*. Can I stay here *with you*?"

Carmelita gazed off along the Old Spanish Trail as if considering it further. A hot breeze swept a strand of dark hair across her face. She pushed it back with her fingertips. "*Si*," she said at length, "You can stay here . . . *with me*."

After the incident with Cray Dawson in the Silver Seven Saloon, Henry Snead spent the next week recounting the story for anyone who would still listen.

Martin Lematte had given the bartender a nod, letting him know that Snead's drinks were on the house. Having Snead around telling his fight story was good for business, Lematte thought, whether Karl Nolly agreed with him or not. Lematte and Nolly noted that the story had changed some over the past few days. Now Henry had actually found a way to make it sound like Dawson had made the first move. No one could dispute Snead's version, not even the ones who had been there the night it happened. It had happened so quickly, the only one who could give the details was Henry himself. And with Lematte backing his every word, Snead's story became more and more daring each time he repeated it.

"I can't listen to any more of this," Nolly said to Lematte, the two of them standing at the bar only a few feet away from Snead and a gathering of thirsty miners.

"Stick around," Lematte chuckled, rolling the black cigar in his mouth, taking a long draw on it. "He's getting to the part where he saw Dawson going for his gun, but he knocked it out of his hand before he could get it cocked and aimed."

"No, thanks," said Nolly. "I've got better things to do than listen to a rooster crowing over his own comb."

"The trouble with you, Nolly," said Lematte, grinning, "is that you never look at the full line of possibilities life has to offer."

"I look at things for what they are," said Nolly, half turning from the bar as he tossed back his drink and set the empty glass on the bar top. Nodding toward Henry Snead, he said to Lematte in a lowered voice, "That thick-headed fool better hope Cray Dawson doesn't come back here and make him eat all his lies one word at a time." He gave Lematte a quick look up and down, saying, "And you better hope Dawson doesn't connect us to what happened here. I ain't writing the man off. It wasn't no small thing he did taking down the Talbert Gang. He ain't to be taken lightly."

"You're worrying too much, Nolly," said Lematte with confidence, puffing his cigar. "But if it makes you feel any better, I'll send out a couple of the boys to check on him. Word has it he's staying at a shack north of here . . . the place used to belong to his family."

"As far as I'm concerned, send them on," said Nolly. "I'd like to know what his moves are before he makes them. Just tell whoever you send not to go stirring things up any more than they already are."

"Consider it done," said Lematte, dismissing the subject with the toss of a hand.

"Good." Nolly stepped away. As he raised his hat to put it on, he saw three men in black linen suits walk into the saloon and look around at the gambling and drinking with an expression of disgust. "Here comes the town council again," he said sidelong to Lematte.

"Yes, I see them. Let me handle them. It's time I crack the whip on this bunch of *town* sheep . . . show them who's running things now."

"Yeah," said Nolly, settling back beside Lematte now that it looked like they might have some business to attend to. "I'll just hang around here in case they decide to get hardheaded."

The three men stopped a few feet back from the

bar as if coming any closer might distract them from their task at hand. "Sheriff Lematte, we need to talk to you," said a tall, thin councilman with bushy gray hair and a wide handlebar mustache.

"Well, of course, Councilman Freedman," said Lematte with a broad smile, taking his time. He nodded at the other two councilmen, saying, "Howdy Councilman Deavers . . . Councilman Tinsdale. Step up to the bar, let me buy you gentlemen a drink."

"Naw-sir," said Councilman Freedman, "we didn't come here to socialize. We came here to straighten a few things out."

"Really now?" said Lematte, his smile fading, his expression turning harsh. "And just what things are there that need to be *straightened out*?" Lematte looked around the large saloon, spotting two of his deputies.

"There's plenty that has to be talked about," said Alex Freedman. "This town is being turned into a cesspool of gambling, whoring and crime! You were elected to uphold the laws of this town . . . not twist them into a way of fleecing honest citizens and keeping our modest womenfolk too frightened and ashamed to walk the streets!"

"Is that so?" Lematte asked absently.

"Damn right, that's so!" said the enraged councilman. "And that's just the half of it! I've found out about you, about what you tried to pull in Hide City! You didn't get away with it there and you're not getting away with it here! You're not taking over Somos Santos!"

"Is that a fact?" said Lematte, appearing a bit stung by the councilman's words. "Let me get you to repeat all that to my deputies." He raised a hand

and drew three of his deputies toward the bar from amid the gambling crowd.

One of the deputies, a young Arkansan named Joe Poole, carried a long black bullwhip coiled on his shoulder. A crooked cigarette dangled from his lips. On his wrists he wore leather riding gauntlets trimmed with silver studs. "What's the problem, Sheriff?" Poole asked Lematte.

"No problem, Deputy," Lematte answered Poole, staring into the councilman's eyes. "But hand me that whip and stand by. The good councilman here wants to tell you and *everybody* else what I *can* and *can't* do in Somos Santos." He gave Freedman a tight scowl, then said to Poole, "I might have some cleanup work that needs doing later."

"Sure thing," said Poole, slipping the whip from his shoulder and pitching it onto the bar near Lematte's right arm.

"Now see here, Sheriff!" said Councilman Freedman. "I won't be frightened off by you and your monkeys!"

"Who you calling a monkey?" said Poole, adjusting the gauntlets on his wrists, taking a step toward Freedman.

"Take it easy, Deputy," said Lematte, picking up the bullwhip and letting it uncoil down to the floor. "I'm certain our good Councilman Freedman meant no offense. He's simply gotten himself caught up in the fervor of the moment . . . wanting to reveal my failings in Hide City." He shook the whip out loosely, giving the councilmen a flat, menacing grin. "Isn't that right, Freedman?"

"Well, I—" Freedman's words cut short as he glanced around and saw the other two councilmen shy back away from him, leaving him standing on a small clearing of floor as a crowd began to gather around. "I did hear some things . . ." He swallowed a knot in his throat and continued, his voice having lost most of its strength and determination. "Enough to know that we won't tolerate such a thing happening here."

Lematte stood puffing his cigar, letting Freedman talk while the other two deputies slipped up behind him. When they were in position, Lematte shouted quickly, "Grab him, Deputies!"

The deputies, Hogo Metacino and Eddie Grafe, grabbed Freedman by his arms and held him. He struggled in an effort to resist their grasp. But only for a moment. Then, seeing he was powerless against the two men, he turned to Lematte and said, "You won't get away with this! I'll see to it you face charges for this if it's the last thing I do!"

"Careful now," Lematte warned, "it just might be." To Joe Poole he said, "Get a rope." Turning to the two deputies holding Freedman, he said, "Tie his arms out along the bar." He cracked the whip again as if loosening it up.

"Sheriff, please, for God sakes!" said one of the other councilmen. "You can't do this! Freedman is the head councilman for this town!"

"Oh, I see. Then perhaps you'd like to take his place?" Lematte asked.

The two councilmen stepped back, a look of terror on their faces. They watched the deputies press Freedman against the bar and stretch his arms out along the edge. Deputy Hogo Metacino laughed and hooted aloud as he grabbed both tails of the councilman's linen swallowtail coat and ripped the back open all the way up to the collar. He did the same with Freedman's white shirt. "Somebody do something, please!" Freedman pleaded, trying to glance over his shoulder at the other councilmen.

"Just to clear up any further misunderstanding about whether or not I already *have* taken over this town," said Lematte, disregarding Freedman and cracking the whip again in the air beside him. "I want everybody here to see that *I* and *I alone* crack the whip in this town from now on!" As the deputies tied ropes around Freedman's wrists and stretched his arms out along the bar, Lematte stepped in close to the trembling man's face and said, "You want to know what went wrong for me in Hide City? I'll tell you what went wrong! I was too damn easy on the town leaders. But I'm not making that mistake again, no *sir*!"

Lematte stepped back ten feet and, without another word, unleashed a vicious lash of the long bullwhip. Freedman screamed long and loud as the whip cracked against the pale flesh on his back.

A few feet from the bar, Karl Nolly said to Henry Snead, "Come on, let's gather the rest of the deputies."

"Right now?" Snead asked, as if stunned by such a suggestion. Nodding toward the gruesome exhibition going on before him, Snead said, "I don't want to miss any of this! I love this kind of stuff!"

"I said, come on, Snead!" This time Nolly put more force in his words. Snead tore his eyes away from the spectacle just as another loud crack of the whip resounded above the councilman's screams. "We need to get our other three men here in case somebody in this town decides to be a hero." He looked back at the whip flashing through the air as they headed out the door. "Damn it, Lematte," he said to himself. Then to Henry Snead he said, "Don't worry, I expect you'll be getting your fair share of *this kind of stuff* if Martin Lematte has any say in it."

On the boardwalk out front of the Silver Seven Saloon, Karl Nolly looked both ways along the dirt street and saw the other three deputies walking quickly toward the saloon. Two of the deputies, Delbert Collins and Jewel Higgs, carried sawed-off shotguns. The third deputy, Rowland Lenz, held a pistol cocked in his hand. As they approached the boardwalk where Nolly and Snead stood waiting, they had to walk wide of two horsemen who had ridden up to the hitch rail. The two horsemen, Moon Braden and Cleveland Ellis, watched the gathering of deputies with curiosity as they listened to the sound of the bullwhip and the screams it evoked.

"What's going on in there?" Delbert Collins asked Karl Nolly, nodding at the doors of the saloon.

"Aw," said Nolly with a trace of a cruel grin. "Our *sheriff* needed to teach a councilman a lesson in manners I reckon. You three get on in there and see to it no townsman gets out of control."

The three deputies walked inside as the two horsemen sat staring in astonishment. Finally Nolly asked in an impatient tone, "Is there something we can do for you?"

"If the sheriff of this town is Martin Lematte," said Cleveland Ellis, "I believe there is something you can do for us." He nodded to his side, saying, "This is Moon Braden . . . I'm Cleveland Ellis. We heard Lematte was getting together some deputies to keep peace here in Somos Santos." A dark grin crept onto Ellis's face.

"Yeah," said Nolly, his voice becoming more

friendly. "I've heard Lematte talk about you two. Step down and make yourselves at home. The sheriff is straightening out a councilman right now, but he won't be a minute."

"Sounds like some serious *straightening*," said Moon Braden. "We heard the screaming all the way from the edge of town." The two stepped down, twirled their reins around the hitch rail, and stepped up onto the boardwalk.

"Anything we can do to help?" asked Ellis.

"Obliged, but no thanks. I believe we've got things covered pretty good," said Nolly. "Who have you boys been working for lately?"

"We just left a job poking steers for the Double D Spread," said Moon. "The fact is, we got run off over some trouble we had with a big gunman named Crayton Dawson. Have you ever heard of him?"

Nolly and Snead both grinned. "Yeah, I'll say we've heard of him," said Karl Nolly. He pointed at Henry Snead. "This man just beat the blue living hell out of him a week back, sent him crawling in the dirt."

Braden and Ellis looked Snead up and down, then Ellis gave Nolly a skeptical look. "*This* man?"

Henry Snead gave Ellis a harsh stare.

"Yes, this man," said Nolly, dropping a palm firmly on Snead's broad, powerful shoulder. "Meet Henry Snead, gentlemen. Mister Snead here spends his time lifting nail kegs just for the fun of it."

"The fun of it?" Moon gave a bemused look.

"*This* man?" Cleveland Ellis repeated, pointing at Snead as if no one had adequately answered him before.

Henry Snead wasn't about to let the insult go twice

unattended. "Damn right, *this man*," he said, stepping forward in his own defense. "What of it?"

"Whoa now," said Ellis. "No offense intended. I was just making sure I got all the particulars right."

"I can make it more clear to you." Snead expanded his chest like a game rooster.

"Well, you sure have got all the particulars right." Nolly grinned broadly, cutting in on Henry Snead before things got out of hand. "Snead here made him look bad in front of the whole saloon."

"Anybody who put a hurting on Crayton Dawson is A-OK in my book," Moon Braden offered, hoping to smooth over anybody's injured pride. "I'll be glad to hook up with Lematte again. I've stared up a steer's ass so long I was starting to worry about myself. It'll be good to get back to some decent work. I just hope it goes well this time . . . not like it went for us over in Hide City."

"Don't worry," said Nolly. This time is different. Lematte even has a big hired gun coming to town to keep things pinned down for us, in case anybody tries to muscle in after we get this town going the way we want it to."

"A big gun, huh?" said Cleveland Ellis. "Who is it?"

"It's a big secret," said Nolly. Lematte hasn't even told *me* yet. But it will be somebody good, you can bet on it." He pointed a finger at the two and added, "But I can tell you one thing; you don't have to worry about Crayton Dawson any more. He don't want to tangle with us."

Moon Braden and Cleveland Ellis looked at one another, then back at Karl Nolly. "Who said we was *worried* about Dawson?" asked Ellis. He patted the

Colt on his hip. "The fact is, we plan on killing him, first chance we get. Ain't that right Moon?"

"Sure is right," said Moon, a grin coming across his whisker-stubbled face. "First chance we get, he's graveyard dead."

"Graveyard dead," Nolly chuckled. "I admire a man with confidence." Looking them up and down, he wondered if their confidence was founded on anything more than tough talk. "It doesn't bother either of you, the things folks are saying about Dawson killing three men at Turkey Creek?"

"I'd have to see the *three men* before I'd be greatly impressed," said Cleveland Ellis. "I heard one was an idiot who stumbled into the wrong place at the wrong time."

As they spoke, the two councilmen came dragging Freedman out of the saloon between them, his arms draped limply over their shoulders. Freedman moaned pitifully, his head bobbing slightly on his chest. His back was a glistening pulp of blood and tortured flesh. "Lord!" said Moon Braden, "He looks like a skinned possum!"

"I heard how things went wrong for Lematte in Hide City," said Nolly. "He doesn't intend to let the same thing happen here. We're keeping this town under our thumbs."

"I'm glad to hear it," said Ellis. "Suppose we can buy ourselves a drink now that all the bullwhipping is over?"

"Not if I can help it," said Martin Lematte, stepping out onto the boardwalk straightening his coat sleeves. He offered the two newcomers a friendly smile as he pulled out a handkerchief and blotted his sweat-beaded brow. "Your money is no good here today. Drinks are on the house."

"Howdy, Lematte," said Cleveland Ellis, returning Lematte's grin. "It's about damn time somebody bought me a drink. I was beginning to think me and Moon smelled bad."

"Nonsense!" said Lematte, "You smell no worse than you ever did. Come on inside, take a look at our setup . . . I might even manage to round you up a couple of women to straighten the kinks out of your backs."

"Moon," said Ellis as they walked into the saloon, "I like this place already."

PART 2

PART 2

Chapter 7

———————

Cray Dawson watched Carmelita stand up from the bed naked and not bother to pick up a robe, or a sheet, or anything else to cover herself. For some reason that bothered him. He had no idea why, since there was no one within miles and there were no secrets their bodies had held back from one another. The first two days he'd been here had been little more than blur. He recalled her washing him with a cool, wet cloth. He had glimpses of her spoon-feeding him warm broth and soup and raw eggs and goat milk until his stomach grew more acceptable to holding down solid food. He had been like a man with a terrible fever, and he could not accurately say when that fever had broken.

But in the middle of the third night, as his strength and his senses came back to him, she had slipped into the bed beside him, naked, and held him against the length of her until she felt his needs awaken and press against her warm flesh. "Rest, relax, I will be gentle," she had whispered warmly into his ear. And so she was . . .

Now he watched her pad barefoot across the stone floor through the early morning shadows of the *hacienda*. When she was no longer in sight he waited for a moment, listening until he heard the slight creak of the front door closing. Then he looked out the half-raised window of the bedroom and saw her in the side yard. First he saw her through wavering panes of glass, then more clearly when he lowered his level of vision and saw her beneath the raised window edge.

Rosa . . . he murmured silently to himself.

In the thin dawn light she became ghostlike, still naked but wearing his tall boots. Dawson thought of her sister as he watched her gather mesquite twigs and oak kindling and strike up a small fire in the *chimnea*. It troubled him that he thought so often of Rosa as he held Carmelita, that he smelled the scent of Rosa even as he pressed his face into Carmelita's hair. In the height of his passion it was nonetheless Rosa he tasted, Rosa he caressed. And it was Rosa whose body surrendered, and shuddered, and received him without hesitance, without question.

Stop it, he told himself.

The woman he saw in the soft glow of firelight from the *chimnea* needn't be held in second place to any woman, living or dead. Yet, being honest to himself, he knew it was her likeness to her sister that had drawn him here. It was some crazed hope that he might lose himself in Carmelita, at least until the pain of losing Rosa became more bearable. How wrong was it, he asked himself, his hand falling idly to the mending incisions on his lower belly. Carmelita knew nothing of his loving her sister. So if he treated her right, if he gave back to her as much as he took, if he held her special . . . if she never knew otherwise, was that so wrong?

He did not attempt to answer the question he

asked himself, because he knew an honest answer
would not suit him. Instead, he relaxed on his side,
watching her through the waver of glass and silver
morning air as she picked up the metal coffeepot
from a row of pegs on the weathered sideboard and
stepped out of sight toward the well. He saw her
return moments later and place the filled pot atop the
fire. Dawson marveled how, at any particular time,
Carmelita might appear and suddenly remind him
so much of Rosa that it would almost take his breath.

Stoking the small fire with a stick, Carmelita pre-
tended not to know he was watching her until she
had picked up a tiny twig with her free hand and
quickly threw it against the window. Then she smiled
and faced him from where she sat stooped in front
of the *chimnea* in his tall, brush-scarred boots, her
skin aglow in the firelight. "It is not polite to watch
someone when they do not know it."

"Sorry," said Dawson.

Carmelita shrugged. "You should get up and come
join me," she said. "Sometimes coffee boils quicker
when two people are watching it."

Standing up from the bed, Dawson picked up his
trousers from a chair back and said, "I believe I will
then. It's time I start earning my keep here."

She looked around and saw him step into his trousers. She smiled softly to herself and gazed into the
fire until she heard him close the front door behind
himself. This was the first time in a week that he had
gotten up as early as she did. She knew that for a
man to grow restless of recuperating was a good
sign. Cray Dawson had come to her very near death,
over a week ago, she reminded herself. She had done
all that was in her power to save him. She had fed

and nursed him, and teased and seduced. She had brought to him all a woman could bring to a wounded man, to help heal both his body and his spirit. "Be careful you do not step on a scorpion or a snake," she said over her bare shoulder to him as he walked barefoot across the yard.

"Any snake or scorpion out at this time of morning is looking to get stepped on," he said, his voice stronger than it had been since he'd arrived.

He stooped down beside her and spread a blanket over her bare back. "There," he said. "The morning air is still cold, I thought you might want this."

She could have told him that the heat of the fire was more than enough, and that she enjoyed being naked at this time of morning, aglow in firelight, and that yes, she enjoyed his eyes upon her. But she knew by now that Cray Dawon was a modest man, as most men were when they were sober, when they were wounded, or when they were in some other sense vulnerable. She smiled patiently into the fire and said *"Si, gracias,"* gathering the blanket across her breasts.

A moment of silence passed, then Dawson said, "I think I ought to take the buckboard up into the hills and chop some firewood this morning."

"If you feel like it." She nodded.

"We'll be needing it before long," he said.

"Si, before long," she said, realizing that this was his way of saying he would not be leaving her, at least not for a while longer.

She noted to herself that the amount of firewood he brought back today would be significant in measuring what time they had left together. *Men . . .* She knew that leaving had already crossed his mind, and she knew that being the kind of man he was he would be wondering how she would take it when it came time for him to tell her good-bye. She'd only been with him a week, yet that was long enough for her to know that he was a good man. He would feel guilty leaving her, although he had never said that he loved her, nor had she said such a thing to him. Even if they had spoken such words to one another, she would have realized it was only in their passion, or perhaps in his pain. She would not hold him accountable to anything when it came time for him to leave.

She gazed into the fire until at length he cupped her cheek in his hand and said, as if having heard her thoughts, "I can't tell you how much it means to me being here with you." He looked into her eyes as if seeing in them a familiarity that was puzzling to her. "I don't think I could have gone much longer the shape I was in. I don't think I even *wanted* to go on much longer."

"But you are stronger now, *si?*" she asked, leaning back slightly, letting the blanket slip down below her shoulders.

"*Si*—Yes," he said, "I am stronger now. I have you to thank for it."

Carmelita shrugged it off. "You feel well enough to chop wood all morning?" she asked, a smile forming on her face as she let the blanket fall farther down her back, the glow of the firelight dancing on her skin and glistening in her raven hair.

Dawson sensed what she was up to, returning her smile. "Yes, I feel like I could do most anything today," he said.

"Good." Carmelita let the blanket fall and she hiked herself up and spread it loosely beneath her

on the ground. She lay back onto her elbows and
kept her knees bent and spread, the heels of the boots
rocking back and forth slowly, invitingly. "Then now
it is *my* turn."

"Lord, yes, Carmelita!" Cray Dawson gasped, "I'd
say it *is*."

In the crackling glow of firelight they made love
until daylight spilled bright and clear over the east-
ern edge of the earth. When they had finished with
one another, they lay sated on the blanket catching
the last cool, lingering breeze off of the hills north of
the *hacienda*. Dawson in his modesty slipped his trousers back on, but Carmelita seemed to take great
pleasure in lying naked in the heat of the fire and
the first rays of morning sunlight. On his side facing
her, Dawson caressed her stomach gently and said,
"I will never doubt the healing properties of sleeping
with a beautiful woman."

She smiled with her eyes closed, luxuriating beneath his warm touch. "Oh, you think I am beautiful? Really beautiful?" she said.

"I think you are about one of the most beautiful
women I have ever seen," Dawson said, knowing in
his heart that while his words were true, the image
of Rosa loomed near.

"*One* of the most . . ." said Carmelita, dreamily,
with her eyes still closed. She let her words trail, not
pursuing any more on the matter. Cray Dawson fell
silent for a moment until Carmelita asked, "Should
I prepare something for you to take with you to eat?"

"No," said Dawson, letting his hand lie still on her
flat stomach. "I won't be gone over a few hours. I'll
eat when I get back."

"Then you must eat before you leave," she said.

"I'm not hungry right now," Dawson replied.

"Still, I will fix you something from the cupboard while the fire is still burning," she said, standing and stepping out of his tall boots before turning and walking toward the *hacienda*. Dawson sat up and watched her, enjoying the sight of her, naked in the morning light.

Before she returned, Dawson had stood up and pulled on his boots and fastened the loose waist of his trousers. As he did so he caught the sharp glint of sunlight on metal coming from the nearby line of low, jagged hills. For a second he felt himself tense up, wondering if he had just stood in somebody's gun sight.

Then, without hurrying or turning his eyes in that direction, he walked to the *hacienda* and met Carmelita as she came out the door carrying a bowl of fresh corn tortillas and beans to be reheated from the night before. She had slipped on a thin cotton dress and pulled her hair back with a ribbon tie. Seeing the look on Dawson's face, she asked, "What is wrong?" as he guided her back inside.

"Probably nothing," Dawson said, closing the door, but leaving it slightly cracked, enough for him to look through and scan the hillsides. "I caught a flash of something from up there. Let's just play it safe."

"Play it safe how?" Carmelita said, closing the thin cotton dress at her throat.

"By going on with what we were doing," said Dawson. "Only I'm going to circle around the trail on horseback instead of taking the wagon. "If someone has been watching us, maybe I can catch them by surprise."

"Someone been *watching* us?" Carmelita's expression turned concerned at the possibility of what someone might have seen them doing in the earlier hour of morning. "How— How long?"

"I don't know," said Dawson. "There might be nothing to it. But that's what I intend to find out."

On a flat terrace of rock, partially hidden by a pile of broken boulders and scrub juniper, Jewel Higgs lowered his battered army telescope and closed it between his gloved hands. With a sigh he said, "Looks like the show is over, boys. It's been almost an hour. She ain't come out since Dawson left."

"Damn it," said Eddie Grafe, the youngest of the three gunmen. He stood high in his stirrups and squinted toward the distant *hacienda* below. "I didn't get to see near enough!"

"Hummph." Joe Poole spit and ran a hand across his mouth. "If you saw any more, it could cause you to do something to embarrass yourself." He and Jewel Higgs laughed in unison.

Eddie Grafe scowled at them. "What's so damn funny? I don't get it!"

"Think about it for a while," said Joe Poole. "It'll come to you."

"I've got no time for figuring out what you two gun buzzards think is *funny*," said Grafe. Looking down at the empty yard of the *hacienda*, he changed the subject by saying, "Man, I ain't never seen a woman look that good, straight-up naked in my whole life! Now that he's rode off, it wouldn't take much for me to trot down, snatch that woman up under my arm, and take off with her."

"If I was a few years younger I might join you," said Jewel Higgs, staring down at the *hacienda*.

"Let's not get sidetracked, boys," said Joe Poole. "Don't forget, we was sent to check on Crayton Dawson . . . see what he's up to."

"Well, we sure as hell seen *that*," Jewel Higgs chuckled. "He's up to his neck in *warm woman*! By God! What does a man have to do to deserve something like that?"

"I never seen a big gun yet who didn't have women falling all over him," said Poole. "It's enough to make me sick." He backed his horse a step and turned it. "I guess we just as well get on back to town. Hell, we spent all day yesterday and last night looking for Dawson. I reckon Lematte ought to show us some gratitude." He rubbed his thumb and finger together in the universal sign of greed. "Maybe a little special bonus, since we had to track him all the way from that shack to here."

"Good luck getting a bonus from Lematte," Eddie Grafe said sullenly, jerking his horse around beside Poole.

The three rode a rough switchback trail seventy-five yards around the hillside until they came to a larger trail that meandered down toward a stretch of flatlands. After a contemplative silence Eddie Grafe said, "I don't know about you two, but I'm coming back to see more of that woman, first chance I get. Do you suppose she runs around naked like that all the time? Because if she does, I'm half of a mind to bring Lenz and Collins and charge them a dollar or two just to—"

His words cut short as a rifle shot exploded from a ridgeline above them. The shot ricocheted off of a rock and whined upward an inch from Jewel Higgs's ear. "Jesus!" Higgs shouted. His horse spooked and reared high as he ducked away from the whistling bullet. As the horse touched down, Higgs flew forward, headlong out of his saddle onto the hard rocky ground, his forehead slamming hard against the earth.

"Jewel is shot dead!" shouted Joe Poole, snatching for his pistol with one hand as he tried to settle his horse with his other. Above them a succession of rifle shots exploded, kicking up dirt and loose rock around the hooves of the already spooked horses.

"Run for it!" screamed Eddie Grafe. "They've got us surrounded!"

Twenty yards above the trail, Cray Dawson stood up, watching the two gunmen race their terrified horses along the widening trail toward Somos Santos. Dust billowed high in their wake. Looking almost straight down, Dawson saw Jewel Higgs's horse making a wild run for the flatlands. He raised his rifle to his shoulder and sent a bullet pounding into the dirt in front of the horse, causing it to spin and run back and forth aimlessly along the switchback trail past its downed rider. Dawson watched and waited until the horse settled into a restless trot. Then Dawson cradled his rifle in his arm, walked back to where he'd left his horse, and rode it down to the lower trail.

Chapter 8

Twenty minutes had passed before Jewel Higgs responded to the persistent nudge of Cray Dawson's rifle barrel in his ribs. Having caught the loose horse and hitched it to a rock spur, Dawson had rolled the unconscious man onto his back with the toe of his boot and winced at the large goose-egg knot on his forehead. He'd lifted the pistol from Higgs's holster and shoved it down inside his belt. By the time Higgs groaned in acknowledgment of Dawson's rifle barrel, Dawson had untied the man's bandanna, soaked it with water from a canteen, and held it ready for when he awakened.

"Jesus, God almighty, what hit me?" Higgs moaned as the pain sliced through his head. He raised a dirt-streaked hand to his forehead, but upon touching the knot his eyes rolled up into his head in agony. "It's like . . . a hammer striking an anvil in my head."

Dawson could see that it pained him to even talk. "Here, put this on it," he said, holding the wet rag down to him without taking the tip of the rifle barrel away from his chest.

Jewel Higgs looked first at the rifle barrel, then up at Dawson's face. "Obliged, Mister," he said. Then as recollection caught up to him he asked in a strained, halting voice, "You— You didn't kill Joe Poole and Eddie Grafe, did you?"

Dawson noted the two names for future reference. "If you mean the two men riding with you, no," said Dawson. "They lit out and left you laying in the dirt."

Higgs took the wet rag and touched it carefully to his forehead. "That figures," he said flatly, the pain in his forehead throbbing with no letup. "I never . . . left a pal behind in my life. First time something . . . like this happens to me, there they go." He looked hurt and disgusted. "It's a wonder they didn't steal my boots, I reckon. If you hadn't been up there shooting at us . . . I expect they would have."

"What were you doing up here, anyway?" asked Dawson. "I mean, besides watching something that was none of your business."

"We was looking down that way . . . but we never saw nothing, Mister," said Higgs, his face reddening. "I swear we never. It's too far away."

"Even with this?" asked Dawson, taking the dusty telescope from inside his shirt and wagging it back and forth.

"Well, hell, all right. You got me straight up," said Higgs, holding the wet rag to his forehead as he spoke. "It ain't something worth killing a man over, is it?"

"No," said Dawson, "it's not."

"I mean . . . if you two hadn't been doing it, we couldn't have been watching. Any red-blooded man sees something like that going on, Lord!" said Higgs, shaking his head carefully. "I reckon he's bound to watch for a little while. Just long enough to see what's—"

"That's enough," said Dawson, cutting him off. Now it was his face that reddened. "I told you it's not worth killing a man over." He stuck the telescope back inside his shirt. "But that wasn't what you came here to see. Who are you? What were you doing here?"

"All right, I'm going to be honest with you, Mister Dawson," Higgs said, wincing slightly from the pain. "We knew who you are. Martin Lematte sent us to check up on you. He was worried that you might be coming back to Somos Santos to even the score for what Henry Snead did to you."

"Henry Snead?" Dawson asked. "Is that the name of the man who hit me?"

"Are you going to tell anybody I told you?" Higgs asked, slipping a glance back and forth as if someone might be listening.

"No, I won't tell," said Dawson.

"All right then, yes, it was Henry Snead who hit you. He's a tough *hombre* . . . it's nothing to be ashamed of, being beaten up by Snead." He looked Dawson up and down, appraising him, then asked, "What was wrong with you anyway? You don't look like a weakling. One punch in the gut and you folded like a busted army tent."

Dawson wasn't about to tell him about his stomach wound. Instead he said, "I was just caught off guard, that's all. It never happened before. It won't happen again."

"Can I have a drink of that water?" asked Higgs, pointing his free hand toward the canteen hanging by its strap from Dawson's shoulder.

"Sure," said Dawson, dropping it off his shoulder and handing it down to him. "Why did Lematte think I would blame him? Does this Snead fellow work for him?"

"Yep, Henry is one of the deputies in Somos Santos," said Higgs. "Lematte didn't want a big gunman like you carrying a mad-on at him. So he sent us to see if you was still around."

"That's all? Just check on me?" Dawson asked.

"Yes, so help me that was all," said Higgs. "Me and those other two ain't fools. We wasn't about to try and do you any harm."

"And you three came straight here?" asked Dawson, just to see how persistent they had been in their search.

"No, we started at the old house where he heard you'd be staying. We followed your tracks from there toward here, what was left of them anyway."

"This Snead, what does he look like?" asked Dawson, already having a pretty good picture of the broad, powerful young man who'd dragged him outside the saloon and shoved him up into his saddle.

"He's your height, or thereabout," said Higgs. "He's got a big old gold tooth right up in front of his mouth." He took a drink of tepid water and poured a thin trickle onto the wet bandanna. "Strong as an ox, he is. Got broad shoulders like a bare-knuckle fighter. He lifts nail kegs, whiskey barrels, and such . . . just to keep himself strong." He looked Dawson up and down. "That's why I say, it's nothing to be ashamed of, him knocking you down that way."

"I'm not ashamed of it," said Dawson. He considered it for a moment then said, "A gold tooth, eh?" He pulled up a vague image of Henry Snead's smirking face standing above him while he lay on the ground wracked by pain.

"Yep," said Higgs, dabbing the wet bandanna to his swollen forehead. "The word is he didn't even have a missing tooth there. He just wanted to wear a shiny gold tooth . . . had the dentist yank one out and replace it."

Higgs eyed him closely. "I reckon you'll be calling on him now that you know who to look for?"

"I'm not looking to even the score," said Dawson.

"You're not, sure enough?" Higgs asked, giving him a dubious look.

"No, I'm not," said Dawson. "If I send you back to Somos Santos, will you tell him so? Tell him and Lematte both that as far as I'm concerned it's over. I don't want any trouble."

Higgs's look turned to one of disbelief. "You *are* Crayton Dawson, ain't you? The man who helped bring down the Talbert Gang?"

"That's right, I am," said Dawson. "And if I wanted to even any scores, I could have killed all three of you men up here. But I didn't, did I?"

"No, and I'm obliged for that," said Higgs.

"Then tell Lematte and Snead that all I want is to be left alone. Can you make them understand that for me?"

"I'll try my best," said Higgs. "Can I walk on back to town now?"

"You're free to leave here when you feel like it," said Dawson. "But you don't have to walk to Somos Santos." He nodded over his shoulder. "There stands your horse. I caught him for you."

Higgs squinted as if there might be some trick. "Alls I got to do is get on my horse and ride?"

"That's all," said Dawson. "But don't let me catch you snooping around spying on me and the woman again." He looked embarrassed. "Now get up and go." He raised Higgs's pistol from behind his gun belt, unloaded it into the dirt and pitched it to him. "Here's your side arm."

"Obliged," Higgs said, struggling to his feet, still looking suspicious. "How come you're being so good to get along with, if you don't mind me asking?"

"I want to be able to ride into Somos Santos when I feel like it and not have to be looking over my shoulder," said Dawson.

"No kidding?" Jewel Higgs chuckled, dusting the seat of his trousers and shoving his pistol into his holster.

"That's right," said Cray Dawson, ignoring Higgs's bemused laugh. "Is that going to be a problem?"

"Not to me it ain't," said Higgs, walking toward his horse, still holding the wet bandanna to his swollen forehead. He unhitched his horse and climbed up into his saddle. "I can see where Henry Snead might have a hard time with it."

"Then I'll have to deal with that when the time comes," said Dawson. He watched Higgs turn his horse and ride away. Before Higgs's dust had settled on the trail, Dawson raised himself into his saddle and said to his horse, "Come on, Stony. Let's hope that's the end of it."

Dawson rode back to the *hacienda* and found Carmelita watching for him through the front window. She hurried out to him carrying a rifle, but then she dropped it on the ground and threw her arms around him as he stepped down from Stony's back. Dawson felt her trembling against him. "Take it easy," he said, hoping to soothe her. "Everything's all right, see?" He held her back for a second at arm's length, letting her get a reassuring look at him.

But she only looked him up and down quickly,

then pressed herself back against him, saying close to his chest, "I heard shooting! I was afraid you had been killed!"

"Those were *my* shots, Carmelita," he said, holding her, letting her settle down in her own time. "I fired those shots to scare them away. We're all right. They're gone." He stroked her dark hair.

"They?" she asked. "How many were there?"

"Three of them," he said. "But don't worry, they're gone now."

"Three of them, and they were watching us?" she said, trembling again. "I can't stand thinking that their eyes were on us while we—"

"No, no," said Dawson, "put it out of your mind. They were too far up to see anything if they'd wanted to. But they weren't watching us," he lied. "They had only gotten there about the time I saw the flash of the sunlight off of a canteen." He wasn't about to mention the telescope he'd kept and shoved down into his saddlebags on his way back.

"Oh?" She seemed to ease down. She looked up into his eyes, saying, "They were not watching us?"

"No," said Dawson.

"But how do you know if you scared them away?" she asked.

"Because I caught one of them," Dawson said, seeing that he would have to tell her the whole story, except for the part where the three men had been taking turns staring at them through the telescope. "They're deputies for Martin Lematte, the new sheriff in Somos Santos. The one I caught told me that Lematte sent them to check up on me. They tracked me all the way here from my place."

"Check up on you?" Carmelita drew back from

against his chest and looked up into his eyes. "Check on you? How? Why? Haven't they done enough to you already?"

"It sounds like Lematte mostly just wanted to know my whereabouts," said Dawson. "The man who hit me works for him. A tough fellow by the name of Henry Snead. Lematte is afraid I'll think he was behind this."

"And *was* this Sheriff Lematte behind this?" Carmelita asked.

"That's a good question. I don't know." Dawson looked away from her for a moment. She saw something cross his mind. Then he said, "Snead is no doubt wondering if I'm going to come looking for him, to even the score."

"Are you?" Carmelita asked.

"That's not the message I sent to him," said Dawson, appearing to not want to give her a straightforward answer.

"Yes, I understand that it is not the message you sent. But are you?" she asked pointedly.

"I think I'm going to have to," Dawson said grudgingly.

Carmelita shook her head. "Even though you have told his man that you want no trouble with him?"

"I'll give this man no better than he gave me, Carmelita," said Dawson. "He hit me without warning. When and if I hit him, I'll do it the same way. He didn't try to kill me, so I won't try to kill him, unless he brings it to that level."

"Listen to yourself! You say you want to put an end to this thing," said Carmelita. "There will be no end to it until somebody is willing to take their loss in order to stop the violence."

"I thought that was what I did," said Dawson. "I took my loss. I came here and tried to put it behind me." He shrugged. "After all, except for the pain it caused me, it was only a punch in the gut." A silence passed as he seemed to run it all through his mind. "Had this happened to me a year or two ago, it would have been over before I rode out of town. Now, because I'm thought of as a *big gun*, this thing is going to keep on going whether I want it to or not."

"Then you will soon be going to Somos Santos looking for trouble?" Carmelita asked.

"No," said Dawson, "I won't go *looking* for trouble. But I'd be a fool not to go *prepared* for it."

"Why go at all?" she asked.

"Because it's my home town. It's the only place to go for supplies in forty miles," Dawson said. "How would it look, riding forty miles out of my way over somebody punching me in the stomach."

"Oh, I see," said Carmelita. "So it is a matter of your pride, and of *appearance*. You are concerned with what others will think of you."

"If you think that, you don't know me as well as I thought you did," said Dawson. "I've never cared about pride, or what kind of showing I make to the rest of the world, Carmelita. But folks call me a gunman now. Whether I want to be one or not, it doesn't matter. That's how folks are seeing me and that's how it is, I reckon. It's bad enough that other gunmen want to try me on. If the word gets out that I'm ducking a man who has already made me crawl in the dirt, even saddle tramps and backshooting cowards will want to try to put a bullet in me, just to be able to say they did it."

"But if you do not go to Somos Santos, who will know that you are ducking anyone? Perhaps in time this incident will die down and be forgotten."

"I wish it were so," said Dawson. "But I didn't go looking for those three. They came here looking for me. There'll be others now that they know where I am. The more I let them push, the harder they *will* push. The more I let them take, the more they will take from me." Without mentioning the telescope or the fact that the three men had been spying on them, he added, "I can't let them have the next move, Carmelita. I've got to get ahead of them and turn this thing around . . . for both of our sakes. Do you understand what I mean?"

She nodded in silence, avoiding his eyes on hers. Then she took a step back from him in resolve, put an arm around his waist, and said, "Come. I must feed you and help you keep up your strength."

Chapter 9

Eddie Grafe and Joe Poole didn't slow down long enough to rest their horses until they'd reached the bottom of the hill line and traveled across a three-mile stretch of high, rolling ground dotted with mesquite, scrub juniper, and piñon. When they finally stopped at the crest of a creek bank, Joe Poole jumped down from his saddle, raised his horse's right front hoof and examined it. "Just my luck, he's stone-bruised sure as hell!" he said in disgust.

"We ain't got time for no stone-bruised cayuse, Joe, damn it to hell!" Eddie Grafe exclaimed, looking back across the undulating trail at a distant rise of dust. "That gunman's onto us! We're going to have to go fast!"

Joe Poole dropped the horse's hoof from his hands and winced, studying the rise of dust. Then he said, "Well, we ain't no match for facing a cold-blooded gunman like Crayton Dawson straight up."

"We sure as hell can't outrun him riding double," said Grafe, nodding at Poole's injured horse.

"If we start dragging along, he'll kill us both the way he did poor Higgs."

"You're right," said Grafe, looking all around. "We better find a good spot to put an ambush on him."

"There ain't no better spot than right here," said Poole "I say we get ready, drop him as soon as he clears that rise."

"Then we better hit hard. He'll get real suspicious once he sees we're not making any more dust in front of him," Grafe said.

"I ain't going down without a fight," Poole vowed.

"Me neither," said Grafe. He dropped from his saddle and pulled his rifle from its boot.

Beside him Poole did the same, saying "We should've done this in the first place, instead of letting him run us down out of the hills."

"It's too late to worry about what we *should've* done," said Grafe, checking his Spencer rifle before levering a round up into the chamber. "We won't get a second try at saving our own lives here. Soon as he tops the rise, turn him into chopped mutton!"

Jerking a double-barreled shotgun from his saddle boot, Poole said, "don't worry, he won't know what hit him." He broke open the shotgun, quickly checked to make sure it was loaded, then snapped it shut. They waited tensely, watching the dust until the sound of pounding hoofs came into hearing range. Then the two separated, putting the thin trail between them, letting their horses' reins fall to the ground.

In moments, the hoofbeats had grown closer, coming up on them from the other side of the rise. "Get ready!" said Grafe.

"I am ready," Poole hissed in reply, his hands tightening on the shotgun. As the ground beneath his feet vibrated to the rhythm of the coming hooves, he cocked both hammers on the shotgun and raised it to his shoulder.

Poole whispered as the horse and rider sprang into sight, "This is for Jewel, you son of a bitch!" He fired both barrels, unable to stop himself when he saw at the last second the terrified face of the very man he had just sworn to avenge.

"Oh, no!" Jewel Higgs screamed a split second before the shots from Poole's double-barrel and Grafe's rifle hit him at the same time. The blasts launched him upward from his saddle and flung him backward and to the ground like a bundle of rags.

"My god, Poole! What have you done?" Grafe shrieked, running to the bloody body lying sprawled in the dirt.

"Me?" shouted Poole, running alongside him. "What about you? We both shot him!"

"I didn't mean to!" cried Grafe, throwing himself onto his knees beside Higgs, whose entire body quivered and tried to rise up, his face, chest, and belly mangled by buckshot and lead, and covered with dark blood. "No, Jewel! You lay still now," said Grafe. "You're hurt really bad. We'll save you!"

"Get . . . get the—" Higgs tried to talk, his voice a choking, halting rasp.

"What's that?" asked Poole, staring down and shouting close to Higgs's face. "Speak to me, Jewel! What did you say?" he asked the bloody face staring up at him, the eyes glazing and slipping fast.

Jewel Higgs struggled hard to speak. "Get . . . get, the . . ."

"Yeah, Jewel!" said Grafe, "Tell me, what is it you want? You just tell us!"

"Get . . . get—" Higgs was fading fast. Grafe and Poole saw it. "Get the . . . hell, away, from me . . ." he managed to say, his voice faltering and ending in a deep sigh as his face went slack and he gave in to death.

"Lord, Eddie, we've killed the poor bastard," said Joe Poole, turning loose of Higgs and standing up, dusting his knees. "How the hell are we going to explain this to Lematte?"

"Explain what to Lematte?" asked Eddie Grafe. "How we got ambushed up in the hills? How somebody shot poor Higgs dead with a rifle?"

"No, I mean about us killing him!" said Poole, not getting what Grafe was trying to tell him. "It wasn't Dawson who killed him, it was us. His own pals!"

"I don't know about you," said Grafe, "but the last time I saw Higgs we were all three up in the hills above the place we tracked Dawson to. If Lematte wants to know, Higgs got himself shot clear out of his saddle. I ain't saying it was Dawson who shot him, and I ain't saying it wasn't. We just tell it like it happened, except we drop the part about him riding in and you blowing him to hell with that shotgun."

"Why do you keep acting like I'm the only one who shot him, Eddie?" Poole protested. "We both had a hand in it."

Ignoring Poole's question, Grafe said, "Does that sound about right to you? We just stick to our story on this. Don't try to get clever and make up a bunch of details. It's them added details that trip a man up every time." His hand dropped close to his holstered pistol. "Are we agreed on what I'm saying?"

"I ain't adding no details; I've never tried to be clever in my life," said Poole.

"Are we agreed on what I'm saying?" Grafe repeated in a stronger tone.

Joe Poole swallowed a dry knot in his throat and stared down at the body of Jewel Higgs in the blood-splattered dirt. "Yeah, I understand you, Eddie," he said quietly. "I believe that's the best thing we can do."

"Come on then, give me a hand," said Grafe, bending back down beside Jewel Higgs's body. "Let's drag him off a ways and get him underground." He grimaced with remorse. "This is the awfulest mess I ever seen."

Poole bent down with him and together they picked the bloody body up between them and carried it off the trail. "It's a shame them boots are going to have to go to waste," Poole said quietly, nodding at Higgs's limp feet.

"If you're thinking what I think you're thinking, you best put the notion out of your mind, Poole," Grafe warned him.

"I'm just saying it's a shame is all," said Poole, struggling along with his end of the body.

They found a sunken spot alongside the creek bed, dropped Higgs's body in it, and covered it with rocks. When they had finished their task they mounted their horses in silence and rode the rest of the way into Somos Santos as evening shadows began to overtake the land.

In the back room of the Silver Seven Saloon, Sheriff Martin Lematte looked three new girls over with a gleam in his eyes, a gray wisp of cigar smoke curling upward and drifting above his head. "You gals are in luck, arriving today. I just saw the owner of the Double D Ranch and a few of his hands ride into town. They're over at the hotel settling in right now.

You'll all three get to make some fast money starting off."

"Good," one of the young women murmured, all
three of them looking at one another and nodding.

"But first," said Lematte, "I want each of you to
tell me a little about yourself." He blew a thin stream
of smoke studiously between his lips, then said,
pointing the wet end of the cigar, "You there. What's
your name and where did you come from, sweetheart?" He asked this of a young black girl who
stood in the middle of the three, who were standing
abreast, facing him for inspection.

Stepping forward the young woman stood erect,
leveling her shoulders, jutting her breasts beneath the
low bodice of her red dress. "My name is Miami . . .
Miami Jones, after the town where I grew up."

"Miami, eh?" said Lematte, motioning her closer.
"I'm not paying your travel fare all the way from
Florida. Where were you when you took up my offer
to come here?"

"Houston," she said. "I tore one of your flyers off
of a post outside an opium parlor."

"Yeah, Houston," said Lematte, "that's more like
it." He gave a gesture toward the tight buttons of
her dress. "Open up wide for me, Miami. Let's see
what those brown puppies look like without their
muzzles on."

She looked surprised. She'd only been in the business a couple of years, but so far no one she'd ever
worked for had asked her to undress for them, not
for free anyway. Seeing her hesitation, Lematte said,
"I've just got to see what my good customers will be
paying for."

Miami Jones passed a guarded glance at the other

two women as if for guidance. When none came, she replied, "Sure, why not?" Reaching her hands up, she began to unbutton her dress, noting the flushed look on Lematte's face as she spread it open and raised her exposed breasts for him to see.

"Oh, yes . . ." Lematte whispered, reaching a hand out and caressing the firm warm skin as she stood stonelike, staring into his eyes. "I think you're going to do well for yourself here."

"Are you going to be one of *those* kind of owners?" Miami asked boldly.

"What kind is that?" Lematte asked.

"The kind who's always dipping into the cookie jar for samples," said Miami.

Lematte chuckled. "Believe me, sweetheart," he said, "the kind of money you're going to be making here, you'll be grateful enough to give me whatever I want from you." He cupped her breast for a second, then lowered his hand.

"I see," she said. "So that's how it's going to be." She closed her dress and began to button it.

Lematte smiled. "If you object, just say the word. I can put you on a mule and point you back toward Houston." He puffed on his cigar, staring at her.

"No, I don't object," said Miami. "I'm just trying to understand what's required of me."

"And now you know." Lematte grinned, giving her a gentle nudge backward. He turned to the next young woman, saying, "Your turn. Come up here, Red. Let's see what you've got."

"How did you know my name?" said the young woman in surprise, stepping forward with her shaky hands already up on her dress buttons.

Looking at the flaming red curls spilling down

onto her shoulders, Lematte smiled and said, "Just a lucky guess, sweetheart."

"Well, anyway," she said, "I'm Angel Andrews— everybody calls me Red Angel. I came from over near El Paso, and this will be my first professional job! So, I'm going to be a little nervous at first, doing it for money and all."

"You'll do fine. I'll train you myself," said Lematte. He reached out a hand and stopped her from unbuttoning her dress and exposing her breasts. "For now let's leave something to the imagination," he said.

"Oh, okay." She shrugged, dropping her hands clumsily to her sides. "Sorry."

"Not at all, dear," said Lematte. Then, cupping her chin in his palm, he studied her full, red lips and said, "I can already see where your talent lies. We're going to be *real* close friends, you and I." He ran his thumb back and forth across her lips. "Yes, indeed, we are. I think I can soon bring out the best in you, *Red Angel*."

"Oh, I hope so, Mister Lematte!" she said, wide-eyed. "Thanks for all your help, and for paying my way here. You won't be sorry, I promise you."

"I bet I won't, dear," said Lematte.

As Angel Andrews stepped back beside Miami, Lematte watched the third young woman step forward without being asked. This one appeared a bit more experienced than the other two. "What have we here?" asked Lematte, wearing a different sort of grin as she stopped and put a hand on her hip, and tossed back her long auburn hair.

"I'm Suzzette," she said, "and I never thought last names were important in this business. I came here from Eagle Pass. It cost me six dollars for stage fare, food, and lodging." She looked him up and down, then said crisply, "The flyer said you would reimburse stage fare and expenses upon arrival. I'd like that money now, if you please."

"Whoa now!" Lematte chuckled. "Pleased to meet you too, Miss Suzzette. "How about telling us a little about yourself first. Maybe show us some wares." Lematte stepped forward, raising a hand toward the tie-string on the bosom of her dress. But Suzzette stepped away skillfully.

"Uh-uh, now," she said, wagging her finger with a friendly but no-nonsense smile. "Nobody pays a toll *after* they've crossed the bridge, Mister Lematte." She gave the other two women a glance, then added, "I came here to sell favors, not give them away."

"But I enjoy having my girls feel as if we're all just one big happy family, Suzzette," said Lematte. "Are you going to be one of those hard-headed types, too tough for anyone to get along with?"

"I'm a whore, Lematte," said Suzzette, "and it looks like I'm going to be one the rest of my life. I'm good at it, and I get paid good for doing it. If that's not enough, tell *me* where to find that mule and point me back toward Eagle Pass."

"Not so fast, honey." Lematte chuckled, as if she might turn and leave without another word on the matter. "I like a woman who knows her business and how to run it. Have you ever ran your own string of women?"

"No," said Suzzette, "but I always figured I could when and if the opportunity ever presented itself."

"Well," said Lematte, "the opportunity just has presented itself." He pointed at her with his cigar. "I don't usually do this—hire somebody to take charge of something without knowing them first. But I need a lead woman, sort of a working madam, to take charge of these newer girls and show them how to squeeze every dollar they can out of these customers." He shrugged, saying, "Of course, for the time being you'd still be servicing *some* men, but only the special customers. Most time you'd be keeping everything running smoothly. Can you be that person for me?"

"For how much of the take?" Suzzette asked firmly.

"We'll work that out later," said Lematte. "The main thing is, can you handle the job?"

"I can *handle* the job," said Suzzette. "The main thing is, for how much of the take?"

Lematte laughed under his breath, liking her boldness, the way she handled herself. "Yep, we're going to get along fine, Suzzette. We're both going to make lots of money, I can see that already." He took a long draw on the cigar and proudly blew a stream of blue-gray smoke.

As Suzzette and the other two women picked up their bags from the floor, Karl Nolly opened the door to the room and said, without stepping all the way inside, "Begging your pardon, Sheriff Lematte. Eddie Grafe and Joe Poole are riding into town."

"Oh, really," said Lematte. "Didn't Jewel Higgs ride out with them?"

"Yes, he did," said Karl Nolly, "but he ain't riding with them now."

"I see," said Lematte. He turned to the women. "Suzzette, take Miami and Red upstairs. You'll find your way around. Now, if you ladies will excuse me." He turned and followed Karl Nolly out the door.

When the three women were alone, Miami and Red Angel turned to Suzzette for direction. Miami said in a friendly manner, "Well, congratulations to you. It looks like you just cut a nice, soft spot for yourself." She stood close beside Red Angel, awaiting word from Suzzette.

"Thank you," said Suzzette, hefting her carpetbag up from the floor, "but if there's *any* nice soft spot to be cut in this lousy business, I haven't found it yet." She nodded toward the door leading to the stairwell. "Come on, let's go upstairs, see how bad the bedbugs are here."

Chapter 10

The rest of the deputies joined Sheriff Martin Lematte and Karl Nolly in the middle of the street, and watched Eddie Grafe and Joe Poole coax their tired horses the last twenty yards along toward the Silver Seven Saloon. "What the hell has happened to them?" Lematte asked idly under his breath. "Where's Jewel?"

"I don't know," said Nolly, standing beside him, "but I've got a feeling the news ain't good."

Poole's horse limped along on its bruised hoof. Both riders wore sweat-streaked layers of trail dust on their faces and swayed wearily in their saddles. When the gathered gunmen made room for them to stop their horses at the hitch rail, Joe Poole's horse faltered and almost fell as Poole stepped down to the ground. Seeing the sour look on Lematte's face, Poole shook his lowered head, saying, "Something terrible happened, Sheriff. You ain't going to believe it."

"I'm certainly going to try," Sheriff Lematte said sarcastically. "What's happened to Jewel Higgs?" He looked back along the dirt street as if Higgs might appear.

Stepping down beside Joe Poole, Eddie Grafe said, "That damned gunman killed him, that's what happened to him." He looked around at the others, checking their expressions, trying to gauge whether or not anyone would believe his story. "Shot him from a long way off . . . wasn't a thing we could do about it."

Lematte looked stunned. "I told you three to go check on him, just see where he was holed up! Just keep an eye on him! I didn't want you to start any trouble!"

"We didn't!" Joe Poole cut in, seeing that Eddie Grafe needed help with the story. "It's like Eddie said! We had just finished breakfast and looked down over the edge of a cliff and there was the gunman and this Mexican woman, both of them as naked as a couple of jaybirds—"

"The sheriff didn't ask for every *detail*," Eddie Grafe said, cutting in, hoping that Poole would get the hint about details and shut his mouth.

"Oh," said Poole, catching himself. "Sorry, Sheriff. The fact is, we didn't cause the trouble. If you want my take on it, this gunman figured we were deputies from Somos Santos and just lit into us, rifle blazing. Poor Jewel caught the brunt of his anger." He looked around at Grafe, then at the stonelike faces staring at him.

A deep silence fell upon the men as Lematte and Karl Nolly stood staring at Poole. Henry Snead had been eating an apple, but he'd stopped chewing and stood with a large lump of it in his jaw. Finally Lematte said, "Go back to the part about them being naked as jaybirds."

Jesus . . . ! Eddie Grafe felt like clubbing Poole into the ground. Before Poole could speak, Grafe said, "All right, we did see a thing or two that we shouldn't. Not to speak badly about the dead, it was

Jewel doing all the looking. As soon as we saw what he was doing we stopped him, of course. Although by then it was too late. The gunman had spotted us. But the whole point is, this gunman is going to have to be reckoned with. Poor Jewel is dead . . . and that's what this is really about." He looked back and forth nodding his head nervously. "Ain't that right, boys?"

The men continued to stare at him in silence. Lematte gave him a dubious look, but decided if there was more to the story he wasn't going to get it out of them right then. "All right, both of you get your horses over to the livery barn. Then get back to the saloon. We're not through talking about this."

"Sure thing, Sheriff," said Grafe, turning wearily and leading his horse away from the rail, Joe Poole doing the same. On their way across the dirt street, Grafe growled at Poole under his breath, "You just couldn't keep your big, stupid mouth shut, could you?"

"What did I do?" Poole asked, his horse limping along behind him.

"We agreed not to go adding any details, remember?" Grafe whispered harshly.

"I had to tell him something, didn't I?" Poole replied.

Watching the two men walk away, Lematte said to the other deputies, "All right, everybody get back to the job. Keep this town *safe*." He grinned slyly. As the deputies began breaking up and walking away, he said to Nolly in a more serious tone, "This thing with Dawson has to be dealt with before it gets out of hand. I'm thinking somebody has to go talk to Dawson, make peace with him if we can."

"It sounds like he's awfully riled up," said Nolly. "I don't know if it'll work, trying to make peace with him."

"I think it might, if I give him Henry Snead," said Lematte.

"Give him Snead?" Nolly sounded surprised.

"Why not?" said Lematte. "Snead *is* the one who brought all this on."

"But *you're* the one who told Snead to do it," Nolly said in disbelief.

"Dawson doesn't know that," said Lematte, as if not seeing his responsibility in the matter. "If it settles things, I think we ought to do it. I've got some big plans in the works. I can't let stuff like this get in the way."

"Maybe we should give it a few days before we do anything else," Nolly suggested. "Let things cool down a little, see what move Dawson makes next."

"Yes, we'll give it a few days," said Lematte, "but only a *few days*." He puffed on his thick cigar and looked away toward the distant hill line. "I don't want nothing messing up what we've got going here."

A block away, at the second-floor window of the hotel, Councilman Roy Tinsdale turned loose of the curtain he'd held to one side and turned back to the men gathered around an oaken fold-up poker table that had been set up for a meeting in the middle of the room. "They're still talking in the middle of the street," said Councilman Tinsdale, "but I don't think Lematte has any idea we're meeting here."

"Very well," said Councilman Deavers, sitting down across from Gains Bouchard. "Let me get straight to the point." He looked solemnly around at the faces of the men. "Gentlemen, I'm sure you've all heard about what Sheriff Lematte did to our head councilman. Poor Councilman Freedman is still convalescing at his sister Pauline's over in Uvalde. It could be weeks before he's back on his feet after such a terrible whipping."

Heads nodded in sympathy.

Looking around again, Deavers continued. "I'm afraid we've got a bad situation on our hands that is going to have to be dealt with in the strongest of manner. On behalf of the town, I'm asking for the support of the Double D Ranch to help us get rid of this monster Lematte before more innocent people suffer."

Across the table Gains Bouchard poured himself a tall glass of rye whiskey, weighing his words before speaking. Beside Bouchard sat his foreman, Sandy Edelman. Behind Bouchard and Edelman stood three Double D cowhands, Stanley Grubs, Jimmie Turner, and Mike Cassidy. Finally Bouchard lifted his bushy eyebrows, glancing first at Councilman Tinsdale, then at Councilman Deavers. "Councilmen," he said, "I had a notion this was what it would come to with a man like Lematte becoming sheriff of this town. But the fact is, you townfolk *voted* him into office. I believe the first step you ought to make to get rid of him is to *vote* him out."

"I couldn't agree more, Mister Bouchard," said Deavers. "But the problem is, by next election time, Lematte will have this town dragged down so far with his gambling and his whores, the only folks left here will be his kind of cutthroat trash. Decent folk will be so outnumbered they won't have a chance at *voting* him out. By then he will have won. Our only chance is to remove him right now, by any means necessary, before he gets a deeper foothold. Believe me, if there was any other way we would come up with it. But there isn't. That's why we asked you here today, Mister Bouchard. We need your help badly."

"I see," said Bouchard, contemplatively. He sipped his whiskey. "This is nothing new for Martin Lematte, you know, trying to take over a town and turn it into his own enterprise. He almost got away with the same thing in Hide City."

"Yes," said Deavers, "we heard that same thing from Councilman Freedman . . . although he didn't know much of the particulars of the story."

"Neither do I," said Bouchard, "except that he had things going pretty good for himself until he fell for one of his own whores and she drove him out of his mind." Bouchard stopped and sipped his whiskey. "But I reckon that's all water under the bridge. The only thing is, once a man gets that close to what he's worked for and loses it, he'll hang on harder the next time around."

"Indeed he will," said Deavers.

Bouchard looked back and forth at the faces of the two councilmen, then said, "Lematte will kill any man who tries to get in his way this time, you can count on it." He gave them a flat, wise grin. "Of course, you've already thought of that. I reckon that's why you don't want to risk calling for a special election. After what Lematte did to Freedman for just approaching him, imagine what he'd do to you two for trying to unseat him."

"I'll admit that has crossed our minds," said Tinsdale. "But you wouldn't have that to worry about. You've got as many men working for you as he has."

"I have good, hard-working drovers," said Bouchard. "Lematte has gunmen, thieves, and murderers. My men will fight if I ask them to . . . they'll die for the Double D if I ask them to. But I won't ask them to. I won't put them against men like Lematte's. I have no right to ask that of them. If you want this man out of office, you best get busy doing it legally."

"And meanwhile," said Tinsdale, "when he hears of it and begins tearing this town apart, killing us! What then, Bouchard?"

Gains Bouchard stood up and said, "Councilmen, you brought me here to ask me to break the law . . . but I won't do it. I reckon I'm not as crude and uncivilized as you thought I am." He looked at Tinsdale and said, "If Lematte got out of hand, went on a killing rampage the way you seem to think he will, it goes without saying that I'd try to stop him. It would be my civic duty. But that's all I can say on the matter for now. If all you want is somebody to do some killing for you, go hire yourselves a gunman." He gestured toward the door. "Right now, I plan on taking these men to the saloon and buying them whiskey. I don't think that would be out of line, do you, Councilmen?"

"No," said Deavers, grudgingly, standing up with Gains Bouchard. "Nobody will consider that out of line. But I hope you'll think this thing over and change your mind. You're our only hope."

"Sorry, gentlemen," said Bouchard. "I've given you my answer on it. I ain't likely to change my mind." Then he turned and left, his men following close behind him.

"Now what do we do?" asked Tinsdale, staring at the closed door.

"Perhaps he's right," said Deavers. "Maybe we need to hire ourselves a gunman."

"Sure," said Tinsdale sarcastically. "and just where do we go to do that?"

Carmelita stared out the window toward the steady sound of pistol fire coming from the wide creek bed a half mile behind the *hacienda*. She counted six quick shots. Then came a short pause, followed by four more explosions; these shots fired farther apart, with greater deliberation, she supposed. In the following silence she saw a mental picture of him standing there alone, evaluating himself, scrutinizing his skill in the dark contest of killing. She saw him standing relaxed now—relaxed but still poised, his big Colt pistol smoking in the morning air.

She knew that moments after the last of the four shots rang out Cray Dawson and his horse Stony would soon appear in sight, coming back toward the house at an easy gait. This had become Dawson's new routine. In the four days that had passed since the incident with the deputies from Somos Santos, Cray Dawson had spoken very little on the matter. But every morning Carmelita would watch him sit on a short bench outside near the *chimnea,* and count out ten cartridges and inspect each one closely while he drank his coffee.

Each morning the routine had been the same, yet each morning Cray Dawson had been slightly different. An edginess had developed around him, and with it an economy of movement and expression. His eyes had taken on a wariness, and with it a cold resolve that seemed to strengthen itself more and more with each fall of the gun hammer, with each explosion of metal and fire.

"*Sante Madre,*" she whispered to herself, making the sign of the cross on her breasts as a revelation

swept her consciousness with a slight chill. Watching
him step down from his saddle and hitch the horse's
reins near the back porch, she realized that the more
time he spent conditioning and hardening and pre-
paring himself for battle, the more desirous she became of him. Dawson had come to her wounded, not
only in his flesh but in his heart and in his spirit. He
had suffered hurt that she was certain he would
never reveal to her. She had taken him in because
she too had known pain, and her nature was of a
kind that healed best by healing others.

"Carmelita, I'm back," Dawson called out, stepping inside and closing the back door behind himself.

"*Si*, you are back," Carmelita said quietly to herself. She walked toward the sound of his voice, but
then stopped mid-step as he said his next words.

"It's time I go to Somos Santos and get supplies."

"Oh, I see," she said, standing in the doorway between the two rooms. "It would not be better for you
to wait another day, or even two?"

"No," said Dawson, gently but firmly, as if he had
struggled with that same question himself. "It's time
I go." He looked away for a moment, then said, "It
will be late when I get back tonight . . . but I'll ride
straight back unless the weather turns bad. Don't
worry about me. I'll be all right."

"*Si*, of course," she said, as if dismissing it. "I have
made a list of things we need. I will get it for you."

She went to a small desk in the front part of the
house. When she returned with her list, the rear door
had been left open and Dawson stood beside his
horse, adjusting the cinch on the saddle. She took the
folded paper to him and watched him take it in his
gloved hand and put it inside his riding duster with-

out reading it. "If you think of any other things we need . . ." Her words trailed. Supplies were the farthest thing from his mind, she reminded herself.

Dawson led the horse to the side yard. Carmelita walked with him in silence, sensing that he did not want to hear words of any kind. He lifted his hat from his head and drew her against him. They kissed, tenderly. Then he continued to hold onto her for a moment as if taking in the essence of her. He whispered into her ear, "I'll be back."

"I know," she whispered reassuringly.

She stepped back and watched him swing up onto the horse's back. With a glance and a final touch of his hat brim, he was gone, leaving a low rise of dust in his wake. She stood for a moment longer, scanning both the hill lines and the rocky flatlands stretching out in every direction. Then she walked back inside the *hacienda* where the world felt smaller and closer to her.

Three hundred yards along the trail Cray Dawson stopped at a rise and looked back at the empty yard. He thought of the many times in the past when he sat his horse at this very spot and looked back to see if his beloved Rosa still stood in the side yard, watching him ride away. It dawned on him that for the past few days, since his run-in with the deputies, he had not thought of Rosa Shaw. He had not seen Rosa's face, not when Carmelita came to him in the darkness, not when he held her naked and warm against his bare chest, not when they made love.

A dark wave of loss and guilt started to sweep over him, but he managed to head it off and brush it aside. He had to admit to himself, it felt good not being haunted by the memory of a woman he could

never have—a woman whose love he'd had no right
to in the first place. Carmelita was all the woman
any man could ever hope for. The fact that she resembled her sister Rosa so closely could be both a
blessing and a curse, Dawson reminded himself. But
so be it, he thought. For now Carmelita was everything life could have to offer . . . Rosa Shaw was
everything death could take away. "Let's go, Stony,"
he said, turning both his horse and his thoughts
toward the trail to Somos Santos.

Chapter 11

It was early afternoon when Cray Dawson rode into town. He stayed close to the boardwalk without drawing any attention to himself and stopped his horse out front of the mercantile store. Being from Somos Santos he knew it wouldn't be long before someone recognized either him or Stony. Keeping his head ducked, he hitched Stony's reins and stepped up quickly onto the boardwalk and inside the store. But he hadn't made it across the floor to the counter when the store owner, Mort Able, called out to him, saying, "Well, well, Crayton Dawson. It's about time we heard something from you!"

There were no other customers in the store, so Dawson tipped his hat and said, "Howdy, Mort." He pulled the folded supply list from his pocket. "I'd be much obliged if you could fill this for me while I take care of some important business."

"Why certainly, Crayton," said the store owner. "Anything I can help you with?"

"No, but thanks for the offer all the same," said Dawson. He thought about something then said, "Mort, you've been here on the main street about as long as I can remember. Tell me something—how long would you say it takes for news to make its way from one end of the street to the other?"

Mort hesitated for a second. "Do you means *news* like you riding into town?"

Dawson nodded.

Mort Able rubbed his chin in contemplation. "Oh . . . I'd say five to ten minutes, giving that you didn't ride in whooping and yelling."

"That's about what I had figured," said Dawson. He nodded toward the rear of the store. "Do you mind if I use your back door?"

"Well, no . . ." Mort Able gave him a curious look, asking quietly, "You ain't in any trouble are you?"

"No, Mort, I'm not in any trouble," said Dawson, already headed toward the back door.

"Well, that's good news, Crayton," Able said. "I heard what happened to you here awhile back. It was a damned shame, that bullying punk doing what he did to you."

Dawson stopped before reaching the back door. "I don't suppose you might know where I would find him this time of day, do you?"

"Henry Snead? Ha!" said Mort Able. "He's the same place he's been all day . . . over at the Silver Seven. I was there less than an hour ago, getting me a beer. Henry was bragging to Gains Bouchard and a couple of his Double D cowboys about how he beat you up."

"He was telling that story to Bouchard and his men?" Dawson asked.

"He sure was . . . and I could tell they didn't like hearing it one bit," said Able.

Dawson smiled. "That's good to know, Mort." He looked around and saw a keg filled with hickory ax handles. "Mind if I borrow one of these?"

"No, sir," said the store owner, a sly grin coming

to his face. "You just help yourself . . . and if you break it, just consider it on the house."

"Thanks," said Dawson, picking up one of the handles and heading out the back door.

As soon as the rear door closed, Mort Able snatched his clerk's apron from around his waist and hurried to the front door, grabbing his bowler hat from a peg on the wall. Quickly he flipped a sign around in his glass door, turning it from OPEN to CLOSED with a flick of his wrist. Then he hurried out, slamming the door behind him, and heading for the boardwalk directly across the street from the Silver Seven Saloon.

Inside the saloon, Henry Snead stood with his back against the bar, a froth-capped mug of beer in his right hand, his tight shirtsleeves rolled up high enough to show his thick muscles. Gathered around him a few local drinkers had been listening closely to his version of the fight between himself and Cray Dawson. At the far end of the bar stood Gains Bouchard and his drovers, staring at Snead with expressions that showed little appreciation for his story. Beside Bouchard, Sandy Edelman clamped a hand firmly on Stanley Grubs's right forearm to keep him from jerking his pistol from his holster and going toward Snead.

"Let it lay, Stanley," Edelman said in a private tone. "You heard what the boss told the councilmen. We ain't starting no trouble."

"Cray Dawson has always been on the square with me," said Grubs, relenting, but glaring at Snead with contempt. "I don't like listening to this fool lie about whipping him."

Nor do I, Stanley," Gains Bouchard cut in, speaking barely above a whisper. "But it's a plain simple fact that this turd sent Dawson out of here on his belly. Until Dawson changes the outcome, that *is* how things stand, whether we all like it or not."

"Damn it!" Grubs growled. He spat a stream of tobacco into a brass spittoon and ran a hand across his mouth. Beside him, Jimmie Turner and Mike Cassidy nodded in agreement with him and sipped their whiskey, glowering at Henry Snead as he continued his fight story.

Finally Mike Cassidy said, "You boys listen to this horse shit if it suits you . . . I'm going upstairs and grab the first whore who shows her face."

"Hell, yes," said Jimmie Turner, setting his empty whiskey glass on the bar. "That move has my name written all over it." The two shoved away from the bar and climbed the stairs. No sooner than they had disappeared behind two separate doors, an old man stuck his head inside the saloon and called out, "Crayton Dawson is in town! I just now got the word! He's coming this way!"

Henry Snead stopped his story, saying to the gathered drinkers, "You gentlemen will have to excuse me. I better get out to the street. It appears I might have to whip this man all over again." He grinned with a feigned sigh. "Some people never learn." He unbuckled his gun belt and laid it up on the bar. Turning in a slow circle with his arms raised, he said, "I want everybody here to witness the fact that I am *unarmed*."

Having heard the old man shout from the doorway, Martin Lematte stepped in from the back room and looked back and forth, saying, "Did I hear that Crayton Dawson is in town?"

"So the man said," Henry Snead called out to him. "But don't worry, this will only take a minute."

At the end of the bar, Gains Bouchard gave his men a nod. They turned as one, walked out the rear door of the saloon and hurried along the alley back out to the street. They arrived in time to see Henry Snead step down off the boardwalk and face Cray Dawson from less than ten feet away. The saloon emptied, men shuffling along the boardwalk for a good view. Others gathered around in a half circle in the dirt street. Lematte's deputies appeared from every direction. They gave Lematte a glance, looking for some direction from him as he stepped out onto the boardwalk.

Lematte spotted Gains Bouchard and his drovers spreading out behind the crowd. Realizing where Bouchard's loyalties would lie, Lematte shook his head slightly, signaling his deputies to stay out of it. At a window above the saloon, Mike Cassidy stood looking down without his shirt on. Behind him, Miami Jones peeped over his shoulder, then said, "Come on, cowboy, what's it going to be, me or a street fight?"

Cassidy reached around, grabbed his gun belt, and threw it around his waist. "Keep it warm for me, Ma'am. I best get on down there."

Following him out the door of the room, Miami met Suzzette coming along the hallway. "What's all the commotion outside?" Suzzette asked, stepping into Miami's room, toward the open window.

"I don't know," said Miami. "A fight of some sort." She reached out to close the curtains, but Suzzette looked down and caught a glimpse of Cray Dawson.

"Wait!" Suzzette gasped, grabbing Miami's arm.

"Not you too!" Miami laughed. But she stopped laughing when she saw the look on Suzzette's face. "Oh, I see . . . you know this man, don't you?"

"Yes," said Suzzette, her voice hushed and without breath in it.

"Uh-oh," said Miami, looking closely at her. "I mean you *really* know this man."

On the street, Henry Snead hooked both thumbs in his belt, liking all the attention that he felt focused on him. "Well, well now," he said, grinning, standing firm as Cray Dawson took a step forward, closing the distance between them. "I see you brought along an equalizer." He nodded at the ax handle in Dawson's fist. "I hope you don't think I'm going to give you the advantage of—"

His words stopped in his mouth. He heard the ax handle slice through the air, but before he could see it or make any attempt to get out of its way, his jaw exploded. The impact of the blow sent his head flying sideways, but then the ax handle sliced the air again, this time catching the other side of his jaw and sending his head swinging in the opposite direction. A wincing moan rose from the crowd. Snead tried to shake his batted head and come forward, his fists raised as if to protect his face and do battle. "Come on!" he bellowed, managing to steady himself on wobbly feet. "I ain't hurt!"

But now the ax handle paid no attention to Henry's face. The exploding he'd felt in his jaw had moved down to his knee. He crumbled straight down and rocked back and forth, addled, unable to fight, unable to fall.

Cray Dawson took his time now, stepping a bit to one side and looking around at the deputies as he spoke. "Anybody who knows me, knows that Somos Santos is my home," Dawson called out to the crowd, focusing on Lematte and his deputies. "I want to be able to come here without any trouble from anybody." The ax handle streaked through the air and struck Snead across the small of his back. Snead snapped upright, then started to fall slowly forward.

"You all know that I live with a woman right out there off the Old Spanish Trail," said Dawson, giving a nod out across the rocky land. With a quick step forward, he swung the handle again, this time stooping slightly to make certain it hit Henry Snead just below his ribs, sending a gush of air from his bloody mouth. "I won't tolerate anybody coming around uninvited." Snead's gold tooth hit the dirt at Dawson's feet.

"We're putting a stop to this," said one of the deputies. But before he made a move, a pistol barrel nudged against the side of his cheekbone. Mike Cassidy stood bare-chested beside him.

"You're not going to do anything but *behave* yourself," Cassidy warned him, cocking the pistol.

In the dirt Snead buckled forward, his arms wrapped around his stomach, his cheek on the ground, his behind in the air. Dawson raised his boot and shoved the helpless man over onto his side. Snead groaned pitifully. "Does everybody here understand what I'm saying?" said Dawson. He looked back and forth at the faces of the deputies, the cowboys, and the townsmen. A silence set in. The only sound on the street was that of Snead groaning. Cray Dawson pitched the ax handle atop Henry Snead with disregard and walked to where Martin Lematte stood with his cigar in his mouth.

"Sheriff Lematte," said Dawson, "I want to report a robbery."

"A robbery?" Lematte looked surprised, and worried.

"That's right," said Dawson. "The last time I was in Somos Santos I had four hundred and eighty dollars in my shirt pocket. After I left the Silver Seven it was missing." His gaze narrowed and riveted on Lematte. "I'm counting on you and your deputies clearing this thing up for me. I'm getting my money back before I leave town this evening."

Lematte looked stunned. "Dawson, I hope you don't think I had anything to do with Snead doing what he did to you here the other day!"

"He's wearing a deputy's badge," Dawson said firmly. "He's one of your boys."

Karl Nolly cut in, saying, "That's right, Snead is a deputy, Dawson! That means you just beat the hell out of a deputized lawman!"

"Nolly! Shut up!" Lematte demanded. He looked past Dawson at the crowd growing closer around them. "Everybody break it up now!" he shouted. "Go on home! There's nothing else to see here!"

"About that money, Lematte," Dawson said flatly.

"I've been hoping you'd show up, Dawson," said Lematte. "I want to talk to you about that money."

"I'm here," said Dawson. "Start talking."

"Excuse me just a second," said Lematte. As the townsmen drifted away, leaving only the deputies and Gains Bouchard and his drovers, Lematte turned from Dawson and called out to two men who were dragging Snead out of the street. "As soon as that bum is able to ride," said Lematte, "stick him on a horse and run him out of here."

Turning back to Dawson, Lematte said, "I hope you never thought that I had anything to do with what happened to you in the Silver Seven."

"The thought never entered my mind," Dawson said with a trace of sarcasm.

"Good," said Lematte. "I'd like for you and me to be friends, Dawson."

"What about that money?" said Dawson.

Lematte stared at him for a moment, seeing that he wasn't going to let up on the subject. "All right, Dawson," he said. "It just happens that someone found a handful of dollars in the street the night after you left here. I counted it and it came to exactly four hundred and eighty dollars. If you say it's yours, feel free to pick it up at my office." He nodded toward the sheriff's office down the street, where a large wooden star hung above the door.

"I will," said Dawson.

"But I meant what I told you," said Lematte. "I do want us to be friends. There's a lot we could do for this town, working side by side, Dawson."

"I doubt it," said Dawson. He glanced around at the faces of Bouchard and his drovers, giving Bouchard a look that said everything was under control.

Gains Bouchard jerked his head toward the saloon, saying to his men, "Come on, boys, I'm going to set us all up a drink." He said to Dawson as he and his men moved toward the Silver Seven Saloon, "Crayton, you've got one coming too, soon as you can join us."

"Obliged, Mister Bouchard," said Dawson.

"Don't turn me down without even thinking about it," Lematte said to Dawson.

"I already have turned you down," Dawson replied.

"But surely there's something I can do to change your mind, Dawson," Lematte coaxed.

"I'll be by to pick up my money," said Dawson. He started to turn away. But he stopped abruptly at the sight of Suzzette standing on the boardwalk out front of the saloon. Their eyes met and Suzzette offered a slight smile.

Lematte saw the way they looked at one another and said quickly, "Dawson, that's Suzzette . . . one of my new girls. I bet you and she would hit it right off. She's a Texas gal. Quite a looker if I might say so."

"Suzzette . . ." Dawson murmured almost to himself, still surprised at seeing her in Somos Santos.

"That's right, Suzzette," said Lematte, misreading the look on Dawson's face. "Go on over and say howdy to her." He grinned and called out to Suzzette, "Sweetheart, I've got somebody here I want you to meet. Why don't you take him upstairs and pour him a *private* drink."

Cray Dawson just looked at Lematte, speechless.

Lematte slapped him on the back, saying, "Well, go on, Dawson. What are you waiting for? This one is on the house. Call it an offer of friendship from me to you." He leaned closer to Dawson and said, "And don't worry about your money; it'll be waiting for you at my office. Come get it when you please."

Cray Dawson walked to the boardwalk slowly, not taking his eyes off of Suzzette.

Beside Lematte, Karl Nolly said, "Sheriff, I don't like this a bit. These two act like they know one another."

"Maybe that's good," Lematte replied in a lowered voice. "This whore might have come along at just the right time. Snoop around some. If you find out there's anything between them, let me know first."

"What are you thinking, Sheriff?" asked Nolly.

"You saw what was going here," said Lematte, "the way Bouchard and the Double D boys were ready to back Dawson's play? We can't afford to have all of them against us, not if we're going to run this town the way we want to." He dropped the cigar to the ground and crushed it under his boot heel. "They've all just about worn out their welcome with me."

"Cleveland Ellis and Moon Braden said they're both itching to take Dawson on," said Nolly. "Think we ought to sic them on him, see if they might get lucky?"

"Sic them on him," said Lematte. "Just make sure he doesn't see that it's us standing behind them."

Chapter 12

———

Inside the Silver Seven Saloon, Gains Bouchard and his cowhands stood with their drinks in hand and watched Suzzette Sherley lead Cray Dawson up the stairs and through the door to her room at the end of the hall. Sandy Edelman raised his drink toward Dawson in acknowledgment, but Dawson never gave him a glance. "Well"—Edelman grinned—"I reckon he's got his head on right. I wouldn't be paying no mind to nothing else either if that little gal had me by the reins, leading me to the barn." He and the others laughed and threw back their drinks.

"Give him a few minutes," said Gains Bouchard. "He'll be down here picking pillow feathers out of his hair."

Upstairs, Cray Dawson closed the door to Suzzette's room and turned, facing her. "Oh, Cray!" she cried out, throwing herself against him in an embrace.

Dawson returned her greeting, but after a moment had to tactfully hold her back at arm's length. "Suzzette, it's good to see you," he said. "I never expected I'd see you in Somos Santos." Glancing around the room, he said, "But I see you didn't quit the business after all."

"No," Suzzette sniffled, touching a dainty kerchief

to her eye. "My circumstances took a bad turn right after you left Eagle Pass. I *couldn't* quit . . . at least not right then. But now I've got to quit. I'm getting desperate."

"I don't like seeing you work for Martin Lematte," said Dawson, letting her last few words slip past him. "I think he's a dirty dealer." Then he stopped and backtracked over what she had said. "Desperate? How do you mean?" he asked.

She hesitated, studying his eyes, as if wondering whether or not to tell him. But then she let out a sigh, saying, "Cray, I'm going to have a baby."

Dawson looked stunned. "A baby?" A short tense silence set in. Then Dawson said, "But how do you know? It hasn't been long enough to—"

"Cray, it's not your child," Suzzette said, interrupting him. "I was afraid I might be pregnant when you and I were together. But I wasn't certain yet. Now I am." Her hand touched her stomach idly.

"My goodness, Suzzette," Dawson said quietly. "You can't go on doing this." He gestured around the room.

"I know," she answered quietly. "But right now there's nothing else I can do. I'm setting aside all the money I can get my hands on. I can't have this baby in the street."

Looking into her eyes, Dawson had to ask himself if this was the reason she'd wanted to stay with him. Had she only been turning to him for help? Had he stayed with her much longer would she have told him this was his child? He brushed the questions aside. It made no difference what she might have done, or why she did it. This was the only way she had known to deal with her situation. He couldn't blame her. She had been as honest as she knew how to be. The fact was, she had seen him through a tough time. Now that she needed his help, he had to make the offer.

"You won't have your baby in the streets, Suzzette, I promise you," he said, wanting to hold her, to comfort her, but knowing it might not be a good idea.

"Cray," she said softly, "I didn't come here to cause you any trouble. I heard what you said out there a while ago . . . that you have a woman living with you. I don't want to interfere."

"Suzzette, you're not interfering," he said. "I am living with someone. But that has nothing to do with this. I'll help you find a place to live. I'll help you through this. But you've got to leave here right now. You can't be doing this in your condition."

"I'm not getting on the bed with anybody," said Suzzette. "Lematte pays me to oversee the other girls. The deal is, unless it's a special customer or one that I choose to be with, I don't have to service anybody. So far I've been lucky. I've kept myself busy and stayed out of Lematte's way. But I know that, sooner or later, he'll require more of me."

"Then we've got to get you out of here," said Dawson, "the sooner the better. I'll see about getting you in at a boarding house."

Suzzette reached out and placed a hand on his cheek, saying quietly, "Cray, no boarding house is going to take me in. If they did, I'd soon be the only guest there." She offered a sad smile. "Don't forget what I am. I'm a whore. The world isn't going to change what it thinks of me just because I'm carrying a baby. To them it's nothing but a bastard child."

"Don't talk that way about yourself and your baby," said Dawson.

But she continued, saying, "Most folks would wonder why I didn't pay some blackleg doctor to gouge this baby out of me."

"Stop it, Suzzette!" Dawson said. "I won't listen to you talk that way."

"Cray, I'm just being honest about it," Suzzette said. "The fact is I started to get rid of it when I first found out. But I couldn't. Something just told me not to . . . that this baby was meant to get here. So it looks like I'm going to have it. The rest I'll have to figure out as I go along."

"That's right," said Dawson. "And I'll help you figure things out, until you get back on your feet."

"Thanks, Crayton," Suzzette said, stepping forward, putting her arms around him again, this time resting her head against his shoulder. "It's good to know I've got a friend here."

This time Dawson didn't resist. He held her and stroked his hand down her hair. "Don't mention it, Suzzette," he said. "I'm here for you, just like you were for me . . . for as long as it takes."

They stood in silence for a moment, then Suzzette said, "Cray, this woman you're living with . . . is she someone you met after you left me in Eagle Pass?"

"No," said Dawson, "I knew her before. But I never mentioned her because there was nothing between us then. It's only, when I came here she and I decided to—"

"Shhh," Suzzette said, cutting him off. "I'm not asking for any explanations. I just wanted to know if she came along after me."

"I knew her before," Dawson said quietly. "This is not something I had planned. It just happened."

"Has she replaced the woman you told me about, the one who died?" Suzzette asked.

Dawson had to think about it before answering. It was a question he had asked himself lately, but not one that he had yet answered for himself. "I don't know, Suzzette. She's a good woman . . . so are you. But it's still not the same." He held her against him, thinking it over.

"No one can replace Rosa," she whispered.

Dawson stiffened. "How did you know that name? I never told you her name."

"Yes, you did, Crayton," Suzzette said. "You told me her name a dozen times . . . while you slept and I held your face to my breasts and took care of you. You called her name throughout the night." She sighed. "So, you see, I knew I was up against a lot, trying to win you over."

"I'm sorry, Suzzette," he whispered, drawing her even closer against him. "I don't know what makes life play itself out the way it does. I just wish I had more to say in how things happen."

Another silence passed, then Suzzette whispered, "Are you going to have any more trouble with Henry Snead or any of Lematte's men?"

"I hope not," said Dawson. "What happened with Snead is something I couldn't afford to let pass. Lematte's men came snooping around where I'm staying. I had to put a stop to it before it got out of hand. I hope that will be the end of things."

"I hope so too," said Suzzette. She moved back enough to look up into his eyes. "If I hear anything from Lematte or his deputies, I'll tell you right away."

"Thanks," said Dawson. "But I'm hoping you won't be here much longer." He considered something for a moment, then asked, "Will you be all right here for a couple of days?"

She smiled. "I'll be all right here for a while. Don't worry about me. I'm good at looking out for myself."

"I know," said Dawson, "But I'm going to find you a place, somewhere for you to rest and take it easy until after the baby's born. Then maybe you can go get some other kind of work. Maybe even go back east if you have to, where nobody knows how you made your living."

"Somewhere where I'll be *respectable*?" Suzzette asked with a tired smile.

"Somewhere where you and your child can live in peace is all I meant," Dawson said.

"I know what you meant, Crayton," said Suzzette, "and I appreciate it."

"I'll be back for you, Suzzette," he said. "I promise."

"I believe you," she replied. "I'll be waiting."

At the bar Gains Bouchard and his men looked up from their whiskey in surprise, seeing Cray Dawson come down the stairs only a few minutes after he'd followed Suzzette up, hand-in-hand, into her room. "Looks like Cray Dawson must be a man with lots on his mind if he can't settle in with that little dove for the rest of the evening," Sandy Edelman commented quietly to Gains Bouchard.

Shooting a guarded glance along the bar at Stanley Grubs, Jimmie Turner, and Mike Cassidy, Bouchard replied privately to his foreman, "Keep your comments to yourself, Sandy. You know how these boys can get started teasing a man and not know when to let up."

Arriving at the bar, Dawson saw the questioning looks on the drovers' faces, but he offered them no explanation. Before any of the drovers could make a remark, Bouchard shoved a whiskey bottle along the bar in front of him and said, "Here, fill you a glass from a Double D bottle."

"Obliged," said Dawson. He motioned for the bartender to set him up a shot glass. Then he filled it from the bottle and took a drink. "I appreciate you boys riding herd on Lematte's deputies out there."

"Don't mention it," said Bouchard, a grin forming beneath his thick mustache. "I'd give a twenty-dollar gold piece to see the whole thing over again." He looked Dawson up and down with close appraisal. "Although, I have to say, you do look plumb tuckered out." He nodded at the whiskey glass in Dawson's hand. "Better drink up, get some energy back."

Smiling, Sandy Edelman cut in, "Yeah, in case any more of the sheriff's deputies decide to take you on."

Dawson sipped his whiskey. "I'm hoping that'll be all I hear out of that bunch. I don't want any trouble with them."

Bouchard winced. "For a man who doesn't want trouble, you sure manage to keep a bunch of it on your trail."

"This thing with Snead couldn't be helped," said Dawson. "The longer I put it off, the more of these thugs I would have had to deal with."

Bouchard looked at Edelman, then back at Dawson. Lowering his voice he said, "It might interest you to know that the town councilmen are looking for somebody to stand up against Lematte and run him and his men out of town."

Dawson nodded. "That figures. They vote this man in, now they can't wait until the next election to vote him out. They want to go against *their own* laws."

"I know what you mean," said Bouchard. "I get

the same bad taste in my mouth from it. They asked me to do something, but I turned them down. After them seeing what happened out there today between you and Deputy Snead, I wouldn't be at all surprised if our *honorable* councilmen come sneaking around, asking you for help."

"Well, they can ask all they want," said Dawson. "But if they're not going to abide by their own law, I'm not going to strap on a gun for them."

"That's good to hear," said Bouchard, raising his glass toward Dawson in a short salute, "coming from a man with a big gun reputation. Usually a man gets known as a gunman, he begins to think of himself as above the law."

"Not me," Dawson said. He finished his drink and looked along the bar at the other drovers, who stood watching him. "I thank all of you for being out there today."

The drovers nodded as one. "Don't mention it," said Edelman.

Dawson set his glass on the bar, then said privately to Gains Bouchard, "The woman I went upstairs with?"

"Yeah, what about her?" Bouchard asked.

"Do me a favor . . . pass the word around for everybody to leave her alone?"

"Leave her alone?" Bouchard mused. "Dawson, you are asking one hell of a lot. Everybody here has been interested in her ever since the two of you climbed the stairs together."

"Will you do this for me?" Dawson asked.

Bouchard grinned, then asked, "What's wrong, Crayton, have you gone and fell head over heels for that young fancy woman?"

"No," said Dawson, "it's not like that at all. But I have my reasons. Will you help out?"

"All right," said Bouchard, "I'll try to keep my boys away from her. But I have to do it my own way."

"Thanks," said Dawson. "Looks like I owe you twice for today."

Bouchard grinned again. "You don't owe me nothing, Crayton Dawson; you never did."

Dawson left the saloon with a touch of his hat brim, taking a quick glance up at the door to Suzzette's room. Once he'd left the saloon, Gains Bouchard stood leaning on an elbow, looking across the saloon in contemplation as he worked on a lump of chewing tobacco in his jaw. Down the bar, Mike Cassidy tossed back the rest of his drink and said, "Boys, it's time I get up them stairs and take up where Dawson left off. If you smell smoke that'll just be wallpaper burning."

Cassidy stepped back from the bar and started toward the stairs. But as he passed Gains Bouchard, he felt a big hand snatch him by the back of his shirt and pull him back. "Where do you think you're going?"

"Hell, you heard me, Boss!" said Cassidy. "I'm going upstairs and dust my shirttail!"

"No you ain't," said Bouchard flatly. "Go back over there and have another drink."

"Whoa, hold on now, Boss," said Cassidy, getting an edge to him. "I'll ride to hell and back for you and never bat an eye over it . . . but you don't tell me who I can and can't bed myself down with."

Without raising his voice, Gains Bouchard said matter-of-factly, still leaning on his elbow, "Dawson just told me he's in love with that woman. Why don't you pick yourself somebody else?"

Cassidy let out a breath of disappointment. "Well, damn it, Boss. I was all set to fall in love with her myself."

"Do us all a favor, Cassidy," said Bouchard. "Dawson's been one of us for a long time."

"Ah—hell, I know it," said Cassidy grudgingly. He looked all around the bar until he spotted Miami Jones standing near a gaming table with a hand on her hip. She gave him a seductive smile. "Well now, one door shuts, another always opens." Giving the other drovers a look, he said, "I reckon I'll just have to *fall in love* in a different direction."

Chapter 13

———

Cray Dawson managed to leave the Silver Seven Saloon unseen and slip into an alley. He walked along the backs of buildings to the end of the block and turned toward a tall, white clapboard boarding house sitting back off the main street in the shaded canopy of two live oaks. At the rear of the large house, he opened a gate in the white picket fence and went to the back door. A young white housemaid let him in and led him to a cool, darkened parlor and introduced him to the proprietor, Miss Lillian Hankins.

"You're from here, aren't you, Mister Dawson?" Miss Hankins asked once the introductions were made. She eyed him up and down, Dawson standing with his hat in his hand. Her eyes went to the Colt on his hip. "I believe I heard somewhere that you are renowned for your ability with a handgun?"

"That is true, Miss Hankins," said Dawson. "But I am not a gunman, or a rounder of any sort . . . I'm a drover by trade."

"Oh, I see," she said, the look on her face suggesting that being a drover made him no better in her estimation. "No offense, Mister Dawson, but the fact is, I have a hard, fast rule against letting rooms and board to drovers."

"Well, you see, ma'am," said Dawson, "the room wouldn't be for me. No, I'm looking for temporary room and board for a young woman I know." He already realized how difficult this was going to be. "I wanted to find out what it would cost to put her up here for say . . . eight to ten months?"

"Eight to ten months, eh?" Miss Hankins eyed him skeptically. "Do I look like I'm just a newcomer to this business, Mister Dawson?" she asked.

"Ma'am?" said Dawson.

"This young woman is in trouble I take it. And if I was to guess, I'd say that you're the one responsible." She tossed a hand. "My goodness, young man, do you realize how many times a year somebody stands right there where you're standing, asking me the same thing, if I have room for some poor young woman carrying their child?"

"Ma'am, it's not like that," said Dawson. "The fact is, this woman is, well . . ." He let his words trail for a moment. "The fact is she's a saloon gal . . . a working girl as they say."

"Oh, one of those poor *soiled doves* out to change and make a new life for herself," said Hankins with a sharp twist to her voice. "I should have guessed." She stared at him coldly and murmured under her breath, "A gunman and his swollen harlot." She shook her head. "What's coming next to my door?"

"I apologize for taking your time, Ma'am," said Dawson, controlling his anger, as he saw that this was getting him nowhere. He excused himself and walked to the rear door. No sooner than he was gone, Miss Hankins called the young housemaid in and said, "Beverly, do you know this man?"

"Oh, no, Ma'am!" said the startled maid. "He's

from around here in Somos Santos! I recognize him . . . but no Ma'am, I don't know him, not at all."

"I hope you're not lying to me, Beverly!" said Miss Hankins, giving her a dark stare. "Do you know which saloon gal he's been fooling with? Have you seen the two of them together any time?"

"No, Ma'am! I never go near the saloon! I don't know any of those women! I'm a good girl, Miss Hankins! I swear to you I am!"

"You better stay that way, Beverly, unless you want to go back to that Nebraska orphanage and work there until the whole world thinks you're simple-minded."

"Yes, Ma'am," said Beverly with a crushed expression on her face. "Is there anything else, Ma'am?"

"Yes," said Miss Hankins, "I want you to go tell the sheriff I'd like to see him. I want him to know that one of his whores is big in the belly." She chuckled under her breath in contemplation, then said quickly before the young maid could leave the room, "No, wait, this will keep for now. Go on about your work. I'll tell the good sheriff tonight."

"Yes, Ma'am, will that be all?" Beverly asked, her voice a bit shaky.

Miss Hankins stood up and plucked at the seat of her long gingham dress. "Yes, that will be all for now," she said absently. Craning her neck, she looked out the window and saw Cray Dawson walking along the side of the street toward the mercantile store. "How dare he, thinking I would allow the likes of a saloon gal staying here among decent folks . . ."

Outside on the street, Dawson kept his head ducked slightly to avoid bringing attention to himself. At a hitch pole out front of the mercantile store,

he spun the horse's reins, stepped onto the board-
walk and walked inside. Behind the counter Mort
Able grinned and rubbed his long hands together.
"My oh my, Crayton! That was the most excitement
I've had in years!"

Dawson stopped and snapped his fingers, remembering the ax handle he'd borrowed. "Mort, I'm
sorry. I didn't bring your handle back like I said I
would."

"That's all right, Crayton, I picked it up myself
after you wore it out on that deputy." He grinned
broadly. "I'm going to hang onto it, bloodstain and
all; call it a *keepsake*."

"I'm glad you're happy with it, Mort." Dawson
offered a slight smile. "Now I have to ask you, how's
my credit here for a few weeks?"

"As good as it is for a few months, far as I'm
concerned, Crayton," Mort Able said, gesturing with
a hand toward a feed sack filled with the items he'd
gathered that were on the list Dawson had left
with him.

"Good, said Dawson. "I need to get more supplies
than I had planned on when I came here."

"That's no problem at all," said the store owner.
"Just tell me what else you need and I'll help you
gather it up."

"Just double everything for me, Mort," Dawson
said. "I can see this is going to be too much for my
horse. Have you got a buckboard I can borrow?"

"No, but I've got a mule out back that's been itching to get out and stretch his legs some. You're welcome to borrow him as long as you want."

"I'm much obliged, Mort," said Dawson. Looking
around at the shelves of goods he said, "I better get

some strong lye soap and a new scrub brush." He thought at something for a second then asked, "You don't happen to have some curtains already made, do you?"

"Curtains?" Mort Able gave him a strange look.

"Yes, curtains, Mort . . . something bright . . . something a woman might like."

"My wife Martha made some curtains for her mother last year, right before the old woman died," he said. "I bet they're still around here somewhere. You gather up what else you need. I'll go in the back and look for them."

Dawson filled another feed sack with supplies and set it on the floor while Mort disappeared into the back room. When the store owner came back he carried a rolled-up bundle of red-and-white cloth in his arms. "Here we are"—he beamed—"three sets of checkered curtains, already made up and ready to use." He laid the bundle on the counter. "They might need some adjusting here and there . . . if they don't fit at all, just bring them back to me and I'll mark the price off your bill."

"I won't forget this, Mort," Dawson said. He gathered the curtains and shoved them down into a third feed sack.

With a nod toward the front window, Mort Able said, "It looks like we've got rain coming. You best get yourself a canvas and wrap everything before you tie it onto the mule."

Dawson gathered the three bags and carried them out the rear door to a stall in the alley behind the mercantile. When he had the bags covered and tied to the pack frame on the back of a gangly red mule, he led the animal out front and unhitched Stony from the rail. The horse sniffed at the mule and shook out its mane as if in protest as Dawson stepped up into his saddle. Leading the mule behind him, Cray Dawson left Somos Santos as the first drops of rain began to spill from the gray afternoon sky.

By the time he'd gone two miles, the weather had turned fierce. Thunder pounded. Wind-lashed rain blew in hard, causing him and the animals alike to hunker sidelong against it. Having unrolled his rain slicker from behind his saddle and put it on, he held it closed tight at the throat. He pressed on, wondering how Carmelita would take the news about Suzzette.

Traveling slowly on the mud-slick trail, it was close to midnight when he rode into the yard of the *hacienda*. The storm continued to rage. Inside the barn, Dawson struck a match to the wick of an oil lamp and hung the lamp on a post over his head, giving himself a circle of light in the darkness. He stripped off his rain slicker and hung it over a stall rail. He took the supplies off the mule and the saddle and bridle off of Stony and led both animals into adjoining stalls. He took up a scoop of grain from a grain bin and poured it into each animal's feed trough. While the animals crunched on their feed, he dried each of them down with handfuls of clean straw. He had just finished his tasks when he heard the door creak open and looked around to see Carmelita step inside.

"I saw the light from the window," she said. "I was afraid the storm would keep you away all night." She lowered a blanket she carried above her head and shook water from it. Her thin cotton gown had gotten soaked and it clung to her breasts. She took note of the red mule standing in the stall.

"He belongs to the store owner," said Dawson, seeing her curiosity.

"I see." Carmelita nodded.

"I pushed on through the storm," said Dawson, finishing with Stony and giving a shove on his rump. "I didn't want to worry you." He walked out of Stony's stall and closed the wooden stall door.

Carmelita came closer and said with hesitancy, "Was there— Was there trouble?"

"None to mention," said Dawson. "I made it clear that I wanted us to be left alone. There was some unpleasantness with the man who hit me in the stomach. But I believe it's all settled now." He slipped his arms around her. "I hope so anyway."

"*Si*, I hope so too," she replied. "I'm glad you came back tonight. I have been frightened for you." She pressed herself against him in an embrace. Then she stepped back, looking down at the bags of supplies sitting in the straw on the floor of the barn.

"I was not expecting you to bring back so many supplies," she said.

"I wasn't expecting to," said Dawson. "That's why I borrowed the store owner's mule." He watched her step away from him and bend down slightly, spreading the top of the bag holding the curtains. "Something's come up . . . something I need to talk to you about."

"Oh?" she said. Rasing the bundle of checkered curtains she asked, "What is this, a tablecloth?"

"No," said Dawson, reaching out, taking the curtains from her hand gently. "They're curtains . . . for the windows on my old place."

"You are going to be leaving here?" Carmelita asked, looking surprised.

"No," said Dawson. "That is, I sure hope not." He dropped the bundle of curtains back into the feed sack. "I'm going to carry these things inside. Then we need to talk."

Carmelita watched him shoulder the feed sacks as she threw the blanket back around her, covering her head. Then she took the lantern down from the post and followed him through the storm to the house as lightning twisted and curled in the black sky.

In front of a crackling fire in the stone hearth, Dawson told her everything over a cup of hot coffee. He told her how Suzzette had helped nurse him through his stomach wound, and how she had wanted to travel with him but he told her no. When he had finished telling her about the predicament Suzzette was in, Carmelita only nodded. She stood up slowly from the divan where they sat and moved closer to the fire. Finally she said softly without turning and facing him, "Do you love this woman?"

"No, Carmelita," Dawson said, being honest. "I don't love her. I never told her I love her. We were together for awhile, I won't deny that. But there was never anything between us. Not like there is between you and me."

"You and me . . ." she said, letting her words trail.

"I mean, I never felt toward her like I feel toward you, Carmelita," he said.

"And you are not the father of her child?" Carmelita asked quietly, studying the flames.

"No," said Dawson, "She said I'm not the father . . . I believe her."

"But still you will put her into your family's house?" she asked.

"Yes," said Dawson, "that's what I mean to do, just until after the baby is born. She can't stay where she's at. I wouldn't feel right letting her . . . not when my place is just sitting there empty."

"And once you get her settled in," Carmelita asked, "then what will you do? Will you leave her there and forget about her?"

"No, of course not," said Dawson. "I will have to go by and check on her. You're welcome to come along with me if you like. That is, if it makes any difference to you."

"*Si*, we sleep in the same bed," said Carmelita. "Of course it makes a *difference* to me."

Dawson heard the change of tone in her voice, a bitterness. Perhaps it was not directed at him but rather at the circumstance itself, directed at the forces unseen that brought about such incidents in people's lives. "Carmelita, I'm sorry," he whispered, stepping over behind her, reaching out to put his arms around her. "I never meant for anything like this to happen."

She stepped out of his reach, avoiding his arms. "You must get some rest," she said, Dawson noting a hurt in her voice that she hadn't managed to hide. "Tomorrow when the storm has passed, we will go to your place and hang curtains."

But when morning came the storm had not passed. With gray dawn came a renewed round of heavy thunder and sharp, splitting lightning. From the front window Carmelita and Dawson watched the large bough of a cottonwood tree slip away from the trunk in an arch of blinding white light and topple to the ground. Dawson saw Carmelita stiffen in fear, but she did not reach for his hand for comfort. Instead, after a short, startled gasp, she turned silently, walked to the hearth, and picked up the coffeepot from the night before.

"Can I do anything?" Dawson asked quietly. Lightning licked downward, casting an eery glow on the dark morning.

Carmelita didn't answer. If she did her words were lost in the deep rumble of thunder.

They spent the day in silence and fell asleep that night to the sound of rain still pounding the roof. The following day the storm had broken up and left, yet the rain held fast, falling heavy and straight down. "Maybe I ought to try to go on," said Dawson, knowing that the quicker he got this done, the sooner the tension might settle between them.

"When you go, I will go with you," Carmelita said with determination.

"We'll wait until the rain passes," Dawson said, not wanting to press a raw nerve. Outside, rain fell from the roofline like a silver, shimmering veil.

Chapter 14

————

Inside the saloon, Sheriff Martin Lematte sipped his morning coffee and cursed the rain under his breath. His head pounded from a rye hangover as he brooded over the news he'd received the night before from Miss Hankins after she'd sent her housemaid to summon him to the boarding house. "Dawson, you son of a bitch," he hissed into his steaming coffee cup. Behind the bar, a nervous bartender kept his distance and polished shot glasses with a clean white cloth. He gave Karl Nolly a cautioning look when Nolly walked through the doors and slung water from his hat brim.

Nolly returned the bartender's nod and walked forward warily, the way a man might approach a growling dog. "Rough night, huh, Sheriff?" he said, keeping a few feet of bar between him and Lematte.

Ignoring Nolly's question, Lematte looked at him through blood-shot eyes and said with acid in his tone, "Nolly, the conniving little bitch is carrying that gunman's kid in her belly."

"Who? What gunman? Whose belly?" said Nolly, looking bewildered. "What are you talking about, Sheriff?"

Lematte slowed down and took a sip of his coffee.

Speaking more clearly he said, "Yesterday evening I talked to Miss Hankins at her boarding house. She told me Dawson was there looking for a place for a saloon girl to live until her baby is born." He gave a sidelong nod toward the stairs.

"Her baby?" Nolly looked stunned. "Damn! Looks like I was right . . . they *did* know each other before."

"Yeah, you were right about them," Lematte said flatly. "But now what? I can't stand for this. This is like having a spy right in our midst. I feel like she's lied to me, the deceitful little whore! To think I put her in charge of these other whores. All the while she was playing along with me, just waiting to join up with her *gunman*!"

"Sheriff," said Nolly, not liking where this thing could be going, "I don't think she was deceiving you . . . you offered her the job, right? She didn't come asking you."

"That makes no difference," said Lematte. He shoved the coffee away, and called out to the bartender. "This stuff tastes like horse piss! Raymond! Bring me a bottle of rye!"

"If you don't mind me saying so, Sheriff," said Nolly, "you're letting this gunman get to you. I'm thinking if we let things go, he'll just back away and leave us alone."

"That's not the way you were talking yesterday, Nolly," said Lematte, watching the bartender pull the cork from a new bottle of rye. Impatiently, Lematte snatched the bottle from his trembling hand, poured a sloshing drink into a shot glass and glared coldly into Raymond's eyes until the bartender backed away.

"I know it's not what I said before," said Nolly.

"But now, I look at what it's doing to you, I think we need to cool off, sober up, and get a better grip on this thing."

"Shut the hell up, Nolly!" Lematte snapped. "I need muscle, not *mouth*! We've got a good thing going. I can't have it end up like it did in Hide City!"

"Sheriff," Nolly asked, "what exactly went wrong at Hide City? All I hear is how things went to hell there. But you never mention *how*!"

Lematte tossed back a drink, emptying the shot glass. Then he settled, filled the glass, and said, "Everything just got out of hand. One thing led to another and before I could get things under control, it was too late."

Nolly just looked at him for a moment. "Ain't that what's going on here, with this Dawson? With this whore? With these councilmen, the Double D boys—"

"Yes, hell yes, that's what's going on here, you idiot!" Lematte bellowed, cutting him off. "That's what I'm talking about! I've got to keep it from happening here! We've got to stop these people and their deceit, and their greed, and their envy from screwing things up for us!"

Nolly looked troubled, watching Lematte toss back another drink, then another. "All right then, just relax a little. I sent Cleveland Ellis and Moon Braden after Dawson right before the storm hit . . . let them take care of him if they can. They're probably waiting to ambush him somewhere right now."

"That's good," said Lematte, "but not good enough." He shot a glance up the stairs toward the door to Suzzette's room. "I was counting on that gal! I would've made her into something if she would have played straight with me."

Nolly tried to talk him down, saying, "Sheriff, you can't count on a whore. You know that. Just be glad you found all this out now instead of later on."

Lematte swiped a hand across his forehead and let out a tight breath. "You're right, Nolly. I've let her get under my skin. I have to admit I was going to get a little *close* with her, more than I would with one of our *doves*." He shrugged and poured another shot of whiskey. "But what the hell." He gave a crooked whiskey grin. "There's plenty more where she came from, ain't that right?"

"Damn *right* it's right!" Karl Nolly said.

"There's pretty whores all over the world." Lematte drank his whiskey, then let his eyes follow the stairs upward, along the hall toward the door to Miami Jones's room. "I know where there's one just waiting for me any time I want her." He looked as if he was ready to turn and climb the stairs.

"You're right, Sheriff," said Nolly, "but it's awfully early. Let that woman rest. She worked hard last night. Here, let me pour you another drink." He hurriedly raised the bottle and filled the shot glass.

But Lematte pushed the drink away. "A whore doesn't need to rest . . . they spend all their time in bed!" He laughed under his breath.

"Come on, Sheriff," said Nolly trying to turn his attention in another direction. "Let's go across the street and get us some breakfast. What do you say?"

"I just *had* breakfast," said Lematte. "Coffee and whiskey. What I want now is a woman. What's the use in having a string of whores on hand if you can't cut one out and ride her now and then?" He turned and staggered slightly, heading for the stairs.

"Damn it . . ." Nolly cursed under his breath.

Lematte snatched the bottle off the bar and carried

it with him. He made his way up the stairs as the
bartender sidled up, across the bar from Karl Nolly.
"What are we supposed to do when he gets in this
shape?" Raymond asked.

"Just let him get it out of his system," Nolly replied quietly, watching Lematte walk along the hall
toward Miami Jones's door. "I just hope he's not
going to make a habit of this kind of stuff. This is
what happens every time."

"What do you mean?" the bartender asked.

Nolly looked at him, realizing he shouldn't have
said anything about Lematte. "Never mind, Raymond," he said, "Just keep your mouth shut and
pour me some coffee."

At the door to Miami Jones's room, Lematte
knocked loudly until the woman opened the door a
crack and pushed her hair back from her face. "What
do you want, Sheriff?" she asked, her voice gruff and
blurry. She looked past Lematte, down at Nolly and
the bartender, who stood looking up at her from
the bar.

"What do I *want*?" said Lematte. "I want *you*,
woman! What do you think I'd want, stupid whore!"
He tried shoving the door the rest of the way open,
but Miami had her foot against the bottom of it,
keeping it secured. "Damn it! Let me in!" Lematte
shouted. "I'm the one you work for!"

Giving a quick glance down at Karl Nolly, seeing
him give her a nod, Miami said, "All right, Sheriff.
But give me minute. I have company—"

"Company?" Lematte cut her off, again trying to
open the door completely, but only gaining a few
inches. "What sonsabitch is up here this time of
morning?"

"It's not a man, Sheriff," Miami said, holding him back, "it's my friend, Red Angel."

"Your *friend*?" Lematte sneered. "Well, I just bet she's your *friend*!" He pressed harder against the door. "Let me in!" he demanded, "we'll all three be *friends*!"

As they spoke back and forth, Lematte could see that she was naked except for a thin cotton robe hanging open down the front. The sight of her dark, bare skin caused him to struggle harder.

"She's too new for that, Sheriff," said Miami. "Please! Let me send her out . . . it will just be you and me!" The door opened a few more inches. Angel Andrews tried to hurry through it and past Lematte, letting out a shriek in fear. She held a towel wrapped around her.

"Come here, *Red Angel*!" Lematte shouted, dropping the bottle of rye. The bottle broke at his feet. He grabbed the frightened young woman by her curly red hair. I've been wanting to see your patch of *fur* anyway!"

"Let her go, Sheriff!" Miami demanded, striking at Lematte with her fists, letting the door fly all the way open.

"*Jesus . . . !*" the bartender whispered, seeing Angel Andrews naked, the towel she'd held around herself coming undone. Her pale, freckled skin and flaming red hair stood out starkly in the gray morning.

"Damn it!" Nolly cursed, hurrying toward the stairs, seeing things turn uglier by the second.

"Whoa! Lookie here!" Lematte shouted drunkenly. Holding Angel by her hair from behind with one hand, he reached his free hand down and shoved it between her trembling legs. He grabbed her by her crotch, raised her up off the floor as she screamed and flailed wildly.

"Turn her loose, Sheriff!" Nolly shouted, running up the stairs, seeing Lematte stagger forward, raising the girl higher up off the floor in front of him, taking her dangerously closer to the handrail.

"Let's watch a *Red Angel* fly!" Lematte shouted.

Nolly's eyes caught Miami coming up behind Lematte, her cotton robe off of one shoulder. "Stop!" he shouted at her, racing as fast as he could along the hall. He saw her right hand raised above her head, grasping the neck of the broken whiskey bottle. His hand went to his gun, but not in time to keep Miami from plunging the long shard of broken glass deep into Lematte's shoulder.

Nolly ran into her, shoving her aside, knocking her to the floor as Lematte turned wide-eyed, dropping Red Angel to the floor and kicking her out of his way. Woodenly he raised his left hand over his right shoulder and felt the warm blood and the thick neck of the bottle there.

Having heard the commotion from inside her room, Suzzette had awakened and come running at the sound of Angel's screams. She froze for a second at the sight of Miami Jones coming up from the floor, slinging her arm free of the cotton robe and hurling herself at Lematte. Then Suzzette screamed herself, seeing Lematte's Colt come up from his holster and fire repeatedly.

"No!" Suzzette screamed. On the floor near Lematte's feet, Angel Andrews also screamed, covering her head with her arms.

The first shot stiffened Miami Jones, stopping her mid step. Each of the four following shots jolted her backward, closer to the handrail. The sixth shot sent her through the handrail in a spray of broken wood and splinters.

Outside on the boardwalk, Mad Albert Ash had already heard the commotion as he hitched his horse and started inside the Silver Seven. Stepping through the bat-wing doors he'd heard the gunfire. Without flinching he instinctively threw his hand on his gun and saw the woman crash down through a gaming table and lie there spread-eagled, covered with blood, six bullet holes in her naked breasts. Her white cotton robe lay wadded up under her arm.

"What a town!" said Ash, taking in the scene, then grinning at the terrified bartender, "Whores falling out of the sky!"

Upstairs, Lematte turned toward Suzzette, seeing her run to Angel Andrews. He pointed his double-action Colt Thunderer at her and pulled the trigger three times before realizing he'd emptied the gun into Miami Jones. "You caused this, you conniving bitch you!" he shouted, drawing the gun back, stepping over to the two women who huddled sobbing on the floor.

Angel screamed and tried to grab his hand as soon as his pistol barrel swiped across Suzzette's face and sent her sprawling sidelong on the floor. But Lematte kicked Angel away, screaming loudly, "Do you want some too?"

"Stop it, Sheriff!" Nolly tried to grab Lematte from behind, but Lematte slung him away, raging out of control. "Don't you pass out on me, damn you!" he screamed at Suzzette. She lay dazed, a streak of blood rising from the large welt along her cheek.

"Plea—Please," she managed to murmur through a swelling red haze.

"Please *hell*!" said Lematte, shaking her violently.

"You lousy lying whore!" He swiped the pistol barrel back across her other cheek. She rolled sideways with the impact. He kicked her twice, hard, in the ribs, even though she was unconscious. "There now! That's what I've got for you!" He kicked her again. "For you and your gunslinger's bastard kid!" He reached down to grab her by her throat, but a powerful hand clamped around his wrist and jerked him upright. He turned his face and stared into the cold, blank eyes of Mad Albert Ash.

Mad Albert gave him a flat, mirthless grin, up close, almost nose to nose. "You're jumping awfully ugly on the hired help, ain't you, Sheriff?"

Lematte settled down instantly, letting out a breath, wiping his bloody gun barrel on his trouser leg and holstering it while Mad Albert still held his wrist, keeping a tight grasp, the same flat crazy grin. "Howdy, Ash," Lematte said in a much calmer voice. "I've been wondering what was taking you so long to get here."

"*Things*," said Ash, finally letting go of Lematte's wrist slowly by raising one finger at a time until he held him with just his thumb and finger circling his wrist. Then he jiggled Lematte's wrist back and forth before turning it loose altogether.

"Things, huh?" Lematte said, rubbing his wrist as if it had just been released from steel cuffs. "Well, I'm glad you finally got here."

"Want me to get that for you?" Ash asked quietly. Nolly stood back watching. Angel crawled over to Suzzette and raised her head into her lap.

"Get what?" Lematte asked.

"You have a bottle growing out of your shoulder," said Ash, reaching up and clasping the bottle neck.

"Oh, yeah," said Lematte. "Be careful though."

"I will," said Ash. But instead of pulling the bottle neck straight up, he snapped it sideways, breaking off a long shard, leaving it embedded deep in Lematte's flesh.

Lematte winced and gasped in pain as blood ran down his chest and back under his clothing. "God almighty, Albert! You broke it off in me!"

"Did I?" Ash shrugged. "Hell, I'm no doctor," he said. "Want me to cut it out for you?"

"No! Please!" Lematte said quickly. "I'll go have it taken care of!"

Wearing the same strange, crazy grin, Mad Albert nodded at the naked body of Miami Jones lying below, staring shamelessly up at them. "I knew Miami Jones." He sighed. "There was a time I'd have rode all night and half the next morning just to hear her whisper in my ear."

Lematte looked down at the dead body, then back at Ash. "I never got to hear that."

"And now you never will," said Ash. He looped an arm over Lematte's shoulder and said close to his ear, "Is this man back here a friend of yours?"

"Yes," said Lematte, glancing over his bloody shoulder at Karl Nolly. "He's been my right-hand man for a while."

"Then you might want to tell him to quit thinking about reaching for his gun . . . else I'm going to jerk around there and blow his head off."

"Karl!" Lematte called out over his shoulder. "Stop thinking about grabbing your gun. This is Albert Ash, the gunman I told you about. He's on our side."

Karl Nolly didn't say a word.

Ash stared into Lematte's eyes expectantly until

they both heard Nolly walk toward the steps and start down them. "How could you tell he was thinking about grabbing his gun?" Lematte asked in a hushed tone.

"Knowing things like that is what you're paying me for," Ash whispered near his ear, as if it were a secret strictly between them. "Now let's go get that shoulder looked at, then get us some breakfast."

Chapter 15

―――――――

Before leaving the Silver Seven Saloon, Lematte sent Nolly to gather the deputies and see to it they removed Miami Jones's body and straightened up the place before morning customers began coming in. Nolly returned to the saloon in a few minutes followed by Delbert Collins, Rowland Lenz, Joe Poole, Eddie Grafe, and Hogo Metacino. The deputies looked at the body, the broken gaming table, and up at the broken handrail.

"Men," said Lematte, seeing the curiosity in their eyes as they looked Ash up and down, "I want you all to meet Mister Albert Ash. You've all heard of Mister Ash . . . I'm proud to say he will be working with us now, upholding the law here in Somos Santos."

The deputies nodded and looked Ash up and down again, this time with a sense of guarded respect. Hogo Metacino said in a straightforward manner, "Do we all call him *Mister* Ash?"

Before Lematte could answer, Ash cut in, saying, "No. Just call me *Deputy* Ash . . . now that I'm the head deputy."

"Head Deputy?" said Delbert Collins.

"Is that right, Sheriff?" asked Hogo Metacino.

Lematte gave Albert Ash an inquisitive look. This was the first he'd heard of the gunman being the head deputy. But seeing the unyielding look on Ash's face he went along with what he'd said. "Uh, yes, that's right. From now on this man speaks for me on the streets of this town." Lematte looked back and forth, saying, "Now get this place cleaned up and get that dead whore out of here. Let's get back to business as usual." He looked up at the doors along the hall for a second, then said to Nolly, "Take over, Karl . . . get things in order."

"Yes, sir, *Sheriff*," said Nolly, with a trace of sarcasm in his voice. He stared after Lematte and Ash as the two turned and left the saloon.

"What is this all about, Nolly?" Hogo Metacino asked, stepping over beside him and looking at the bat-wing doors still swinging back and forth from Lematte's departure. "We knew he had a gunman coming, but we never thought it was somebody who was going to replace you!"

Nolly flared, turning to him. "Get busy Hogo! Nobody is replacing me! Lematte is just edgy . . . worried about Dawson, the town council, the Double D boys. You think it's easy running a town?"

"All right, Nolly," said Hogo, backing off. "I meant nothing by it. It's just that we're used to you being the *segundo* in charge here. We weren't expecting this."

"I'm still the second in charge here!" Nolly said, raising his voice as he looked from one deputy to the next. "Don't none of you forget it!"

"All right," said Hogo Metacino, agreeing with him. "But just to get this straight, you tell us, if the situation comes down to it, who do we listen to, *you* or Mad Albert Ash?"

"Don't worry about it," said Nolly, "I'm still Lematte's right-hand man. Now get busy."

With no further discussion on the matter, Hogo shrugged at the others and walked toward the naked body of Miami Jones lying spread-eagled on the broken gaming table. "Somebody give me a hand here, get rid of this dead whore before she starts to stiffen up on us."

Upstairs, Angel Andrews sat on the side of Suzzette's bed, comforting her, gently pressing a cold, wet towel to the cut on her swollen cheek. Suzzette lay curled up in a ball, her arms wrapped around her waist. She moaned deeply as Angel tried to take a look at her battered ribs and stomach. "No, please, don't touch me," Suzzette sobbed. "It hurts too bad."

"Oh God, Suzzette!" Angel sobbed, "I don't know what to do! I heard what they said, that you're pregnant. How can that poor baby live through something like this?"

"Don't talk," Suzzette moaned. "Go out the back way, get the doctor."

"But Lematte went to the doctor to get the glass out of his shoulder!" said Angel. "Won't he try to stop me?"

"Wait until you see him leave the doctor's office," said Suzzette. "I'll lay here and rest awhile."

"Are you sure you'll be all right?" Angel asked, already standing up ready to go.

"Just hurry, Angel, bring him back as soon as he can get here," said Suzzette.

Angel Andrews had also taken a beating, but she ignored her pain and hurriedly grabbed a coat from a coatrack and threw it around herself. "I'll hurry, Suzzette!"

She managed to slip out the door and along the

hallway without being seen. It was only a few feet from Suzzette's room to an upper rear door at the end of the hall. Angel eased the door open and rushed down a long set of steep wooden stairs to an alley that ran from the main street to the backs of its long row of clapboard buildings. Looking back over her shoulder, she ran along the rutted alley until suddenly she stopped abruptly as two powerful hands caught her by her shoulders. Startled, she stared into two bloodshot eyes and smelled the bittersweet scent of burnt opium.

"Hey, little gal," said Jimmie Turner, one of Bouchard's Double D cowhands. "Where you off to this hour of morning?"

"Please, turn me loose!" Angel pleaded with him. "Something terrible has happened to Miami and Suzzette!"

"Aw, now," said Turner, his voice slurred, his eyes red and shiny from a night of smoking opium. "How terrible can it be?" He held her firmly as she struggled against him.

"Turn me loose," she shouted. "Miami is shot dead and Suzzette has been pistol-whipped! I'm gone for the doctor."

Even in his opium stupor he began to realize the gravity of Angel's words. "Dead? Pistol-whipped?" He tried shaking his head to clear it a bit. "—I heard some shots awhile ago," he said, still holding Angel by her shoulders. "Who did it?"

Seeing his condition, Angel pleaded, "Please, let me go! I need to get help!"

"Who did it? Turner demanded, his temper flaring, fueled by the opium.

"The sheriff did it!" Angel said. "He went crazy,

killed Miami and tried to kill Suzzette! Please let me go!"

"The sheriff, huh?" said Turner, turning her loose, staggering a step forward. "What kind of sheriff would do something like that!"

But Angel Andrews didn't answer. She had already hurried along the alley away from him, in the direction of the doctor's office.

On their way back from the doctor's office where Lematte had the shard of glass removed from his shoulder, Mad Albert took note of the glaring eyes of the townsfolk. "How bad has it gotten between you and the town leaders?" Ash asked, the two having already talked some while the doctor gathered and sterilized his surgical tools.

"I had to bullwhip a councilman," said Lematte, "if that tells you anything." He wore a sling around his shoulder supporting his right forearm, but the doctor had to run the sling across his chest to his left shoulder to keep it off of the wound.

"Mad Albert chuckled darkly. "I always seem to miss the fun times." They walked on toward a restaurant across from the sheriff's office.

Lematte gave a wicked grin. "You might have missed the *get-acquainted* part of the show, but I'm counting on you being here for the main attraction."

They stopped out front of the restaurant for a moment before stepping inside. Lematte gestured with his free hand, taking in the whole town from end to end. "When I get this town whipped into shape, I expect to have at least three more saloons running night and day. Gambling, whores, liquor, dope, entertainment! You name it, Somos Santos will have it!"

"Sort of a Sodom and Gomorrah right here in *Tejas*, eh?" said Mad Ash.

"Yeah," said Lematte. "Something like that."

"At any rate," he continued, "I've already had some resistance from the town council, and I expect more at any time." He pointed toward a drover hotel a half block away, where a line of Double D horses stood at the hitch rail. "I've also got trouble coming from this bunch of cowhands and a friend of theirs."

"Cowhands, *opposed* to gambling, whoring, and drinking?" Mad Albert shook his head. "What is happening to this great nation of ours?"

"It's not that they're opposed to drinking, gambling, and whatnot," said Lematte. "I think it's a matter of just because I'm a lawman I'm not supposed to make any money."

"Shame on them," said Ash, looking back and forth along the street.

"Yeah," said Lematte, looking perplexed. "I've never understood that way of thinking. I always say the best way to control human vice is to *own* it." He shrugged. "You know how cowhands get these stupid notions about what's right and wrong."

"What's the story on you and those three whores?" Mad Albert asked.

"That was mostly personal," said Lematte. "I brought all three of them here, paid their fares, their expenses. Then the one I had to pistol-whip betrayed me. I put her in charge, gave her some respect. Damned if she's not carrying a baby by the man who's been causing most of the trouble here."

"Trouble?" Ash asked, "What kind of trouble?"

"He's a local cowhand who went off and got himself a reputation as a gunman," said Lematte. "I wanted to get him on my side . . . but it hasn't worked out. Everything just seems to go wrong between us. I don't know why."

"A reputation, huh?" said Ash, already getting an idea who Lematte was talking about, but not wanting to be the one to bring it up. "What's his name?"

"His name is Crayton Dawson," said Lematte. He watched Ash's eyes for a response. "I suppose you've heard of him?

"Yes, I have," said Ash, his expression unchanging. "He took a bullet in the gut that was meant for me."

"He did?" Lematte was taken aback. "Then— Then you two are friends?"

"Not that I know of," said Ash.

Lematte stammered, "But you said—"

"I know what I said." Ash stared away, along the other side of the street, seeing two more of Lematte's deputies walking along the boardwalk. "He *might* have saved my life . . . but I can't say he did for certain." He seemed to consider it. "And if he *did*, I didn't ask him to." He chuckled under his breath. "And if he *did*, it weren't all that big of a deal. I always figure if a man doesn't die in one place, he'll just die in another."

Lematte tried to look into his eyes and gauge his sincerity, but Ash looked away, avoiding his stare. "Then it's not going to be a problem for you to kill him, when the time comes?" Lematte asked.

"Is it going to be a problem you *paying* me for doing it, when the time comes?" Ash asked in reply.

"None at all," said Lematte, feeling better.

"Then we're both walking on the same side of the line," said Ash, turning back to face him with a level gaze. "Dawson is a gunman himself . . . he better realize by now that this ain't the kind of business to be in owing favors."

"We're going to get along fine, Ash," said Lematte, allowing himself a grin.

"I knew we would, once you got to know me," said Ash.

Lematte nodded toward the Silver Seven Saloon, where two councilmen hurried along the boardwalk away from the bat-wing doors. "Look at those two," he said sidelong to Ash. "They can't wait to start spreading it all over town about more *'trouble at the Silver Seven.'* Before it's over I bet I have to bullwhip both of them."

"Relax, Sheriff," said Ash, "I'm on the job now." They both turned and walked into the restaurant as the two councilmen hurried on to the drover's hotel.

Inside the hotel, Councilman Deavers hurried to a window and looked out nervously toward the spot where Lematte and Mad Albert Ash had been standing. "Do you think they saw us?" he said to Councilman Tinsdale.

"I'm certain they saw us," Tinsdale replied, "but I don't think it matters to Lematte right now. He thinks we can't do anything to stop him."

"You're right," said Deavers, letting go of a tense breath, turning from the window in time to see Gains Bouchard and his men walking down the stairs to the lobby.

"Morning, Councilmen," said Bouchard, seeming to be in a hurry. "What was all the shooting about?"

"Mister Bouchard! We're certainly glad to see you," said Deavers. "All hell has broken loose at the

Silver Seven! One girl is dead and another beaten senseless! It was all Lematte's doings!"

Bouchard slowed to a halt at the bottom of the stairs. "He didn't kill Dawson's gal, Suzzette, did he?"

"Suzzette is Dawson's gal?" Deavers asked, looking astounded.

"No," Tinsdale cut in, "he killed that dark gal, Miami. But Suzzette took a beating, trying to stop him is my guess."

"Then Lematte has more trouble coming than he'll be able to handle is *my guess*," said Bouchard. "But right now, gentlemen, you'll have to excuse us. I've got a man missing. He took off last night, drunk and on his own. He didn't show up come daybreak . . . so something is wrong."

"Mister Bouchard, you're going to have to help us!" Deavers pleaded. "We have no other way to turn!"

From the middle of the street came the sound of a pistol shot, followed by Jimmie Turner's blurry voice yelling in rage toward the restaurant. "Lematte! You dirty whore-whipping son of a bitch! I seen you go in there! Come out here and face a *man* for a change!"

"That's Turner!" said Sandy Edelman.

Gains Bouchard stepped quickly out the door of the hotel and into the muddy street, Edelman, Stanley Grubs, and Mike Cassidy right behind him. In the lobby of the hotel Tinsdale and Deavers stood peeping out through the curtains.

"There he is," Bouchard said in a lowered voice, nodding toward Turner. Jimmie Turner stood in the middle of the muddy street facing the restaurant as Sheriff Lematte and Mad Albert Ash stepped out

onto the boardwalk. Lematte calmly stuck a fresh
cigar into his mouth and took out a match to light
it.

"You don't have time for a smoke!" Turner raged,
shoving his smoking pistol into his holster. "I'm
sending you to *hell* where you belong!"

"Take it easy, cowboy," said Lematte, striking the
match with his thumbnail. "Who do you think you
are, coming here firing your gun at this time of morning? Decent folks are still having breakfast." He offered a short, tight laugh. "*We* were having
breakfast!"

"Come on down in the street, Lematte! I'm going
to shoot you to pieces!" Turner said to Mad Albert
Ash, not knowing who he was speaking to, "You
step away, Mister. I ain't here to kill you!"

"*Gracias*," said Ash with a thin flat smile. "But my
breakfast is getting cold. You best hurry this up. I
hate cold eggs."

Lematte puffed the cigar to life while Ash took a
step sideways, putting some space between them.
Ash's attention went from Turner, to Gains Bouchard
and the other three men spreading out as they
walked across the street.

Blowing a stream of smoke, Lematte said to
Turner, "You've already earned a couple of days in
jail for disturbing the peace if I want to push it." He
also lifted a glance toward the drovers crossing the
street. From the doors of the Silver Saloon he saw
his deputies stepping down into the muddy street
and spreading out as well. "But you and the Double
D boys have been good customers and model citizens
up to now. So I'm going to overlook this. You turn
yourself around right now, go sleep it off somewhere."

"Step down here, Lematte!" said Turner. "Else I'll have to kill you where you stand!" He staggered forward a step. Gains Bouchard and the drovers quickened their pace.

"Be ready for anything, men," Bouchard whispered, seeing the deputies coming from the other direction.

"You're covered, Boss," said Sandy Edelman.

"Turner!" Bouchard called out. "Go get your horse and let's get going, right now!" As Turner turned, half facing him, Bouchard called out to Lematte, "Sheriff, you see the shape he's in. Pay him no mind. I'll get him out of town."

"You do that, Bouchard," said Lematte, "and don't forget that I did this favor for you the next time you hear somebody bellyaching about me behind my back." He cut a glance to the hotel window where the two councilmen stood peeping out like frightened children. Then he looked back at Bouchard.

"People tell me lots of things, Lematte," said Bouchard. "That doesn't mean I act on it." He came to a halt a few feet from Jimmie Turner. The other drovers spread in a half circle on his right. On Bouchard's left he saw the deputies form a matching half circle.

Lematte nodded. "I understand. Take your man and straighten him out." He grinned. "No harm done."

"Come on, Turner," said Gains Bouchard, "I ain't telling you again!"

"Boss, damn it!" said Jimmie Turner. "You don't know what he's done to those women!"

"Yes, I do know," Bouchard said firmly. "Now come on, let the law deal with Lematte when the time comes."

"But damn it to hell, Boss! He is the law!" Turner shrieked. "What kind of men are we, letting him treat these poor women that way?"

With a wide, sarcastic grin Hogo Metacino cut in, his hand resting on his pistol butt, "Yeah, Bouchard, what kind of men are you anyway?"

"Shut up, Hogo!" Lematte shouted. He turned to Bouchard and said quickly, "Take him and go! You see what kind of pot we've got boiling here."

"Come on, Turner," Mike Cassidy called out, staring hard and cold at Hogo Metacino. "Let these *deputies* crawl back under their rocks."

"That's enough, Cassidy!" said Bouchard, half turning toward him. "Lematte is right, we've got a bad situ—"

Bouchard's words stopped short at the sound of a pistol shot exploding. A stunned silence froze everybody in place. Everyone except Jimmie Turner. He staggered backward a step and spun, facing Gains Bouchard. A gout of blood streamed from the center of his chest. Blood spilled from his lips as he said, "Now look what they've gone and done to me . . ." Then he fell forward, splashing facedown in a puddle of mud.

"On the boardwalk Mad Albert Ash stood with his pistol smoking and a strange grin on his face. "I guess that settles that," he said. "Now can we get back to our breakfast?"

"You murdering bastard!" Gains Bouchard shouted, spitting out his wad of chewing tobacco as his hand streaked to his holster and started back up, cocking his Colt on the upswing. The street seemed to spring back to life all at once. Seeing the deputies respond to Bouchard's move by reaching for their guns, Sandy Edelman and the Double D men made their own move to protect the old rancher. Within a split second eleven pistols blazed back and forth with less than fifteen feet between the two warring groups.

Mad Albert Ash's shot slammed into Gains Bouchard's chest, sending him backward into the mud as a terrified horse yanked its reins loose from the hitch rail and found itself rearing high amid the fracas. But Bouchard wasn't done for. He came up onto one knee, his left hand gripping the flow of blood from his chest. With the rearing horse between him and Ash, Bouchard saw the deputies firing on his men. He saw Sandy Edelman go down in a spray of blood, two bullets hitting him at once. Instinctively Bouchard swung his Colt toward them and emptied all six shots into the gunmen.

Lematte took a long dive along the boardwalk and found cover behind a stack of shipping crates out front of the harness shop.

Mike Cassidy took a bullet in his upper left shoulder but kept firing, one shot hitting Rowland Lenz squarely in the forehead and turning him in a backward flip. Another shot sent Hogo Metacino sprawling into the mud, although the bullet only grazed the side of his head. His gun slipped from his hand and sank in the mud. He crawled frantically, reaching for it, only to have it squirt from his grasp as a bullet whistled above his head.

"Look out, Stanley!" Mike Cassidy shouted, seeing Delbert Collins taking an aim at him. But Stanley Grubs didn't act quick enough. Collins's bullet sliced through his heart and left him lying dead in the mud.

"Kill him, Delbert!" shouted Hogo Metacino from

the mud, still trying to get a grip on his slippery pistol.

Delbert Collins and Mike Cassidy fired at the same time at one another. Cassidy's bullet sent Collins writhing in pain with both hands clutching his crotch. Collins's shot sliced through the center of Cassidy's right ear, leaving the lower half of it hanging limply. Cassidy clasped a hand to the bloody ear and turned toward Mad Albert Ash, seeing the frightened horse run out from between Ash and Gains Bouchard.

"Get down, Boss!" Cassidy shouted, seeing that Bouchard had gone down again, but that he was struggling back up to his knee, raising his Colt toward Mad Albert with all his effort.

"Whooie!" said Ash, grinning wildly. "What a shootout this *is*!"

Bouchard pulled the trigger on his Colt before realizing he'd used all his shots. As he fumbled for bullets from his mud-covered gun belt, Ash calmly looked at Mike Cassidy and put a bullet in his chest. As Cassidy hit the ground, Ash walked slowly toward Gains Bouchard, taking his time, still grinning. He stopped two feet from Bouchard and held his gun pointed down at his face. Bouchard stared up the long gun barrel. Knowing that it was all over for him, he let the bullets spill from his muddy hand.

"Now tell the truth, old man," said Mad Albert Ash. "Was all this worth one lousy cowhand?"

"Damn you, sir!" said Gains Bouchard, remaining defiant to the end.

"And you as well," said Ash. He pulled the trigger and Bouchard's head snapped back violently, a blast of blood and brain matter raising a splatter of mud in the street.

Lematte came down from his hiding spot and cocked his head sideways quizzically, looking down at Bouchard's dead, blank expression. "I'm going to miss his business," he said with regret.

Chapter 16

From an outhouse behind the Silver Seven Saloon, Karl Nolly had come splashing through the mud with his holster belt over his shoulder at the first sound of gunfire. But he slowed to a halt a few feet back from where the bodies of both deputies and cowhands alike lay spilling blood. "Good God!" he said, one hand holding his Colt, his other hand holding his unfastened trousers gathered at his waist. He watched Hogo Metacino struggle to his feet like some creature rising from the bowels of the earth.

"Lower that pistol and attend to yourself, Deputy," said Mad Albert Ash, standing over Gains Bouchard's body as he reloaded his Colt. "You're too late to be any help here."

Nolly stared at him, seething, but he lowered the pistol and began fastening his trousers. "How the hell did all this happen?" he asked of anyone there.

"If you had been here," Ash said flatly, "we wouldn't have to tell you. Ain't that right, Sheriff?" he asked Lematte.

"Yes, that's right," Lematte agreed. He had stepped down from the boardwalk and stood beside Ash. "Since you missed the party, you can stay for the cleanup." He pointed down at Bouchard's body, saying, "Drag him away from here. It looks bad, bodies laying around."

In the middle of the street, Mike Cassidy was still alive and struggling through the mud toward the other side of the street. Ash hurriedly finished reloading and cocked his Colt, taking aim. But Lematte stopped him, saying, "Let him go, Ash. He's done for anyway."

"Mercy is low on my list of virtues," said Ash. Yet he lowered the gun and looked around at the other men rising up from the mud.

Lying dead on the Double D side were Jimmie Turner, Sandy Edelman, Gains Bouchard, and Stanley Grubs. Of Lematte's deputies only Rowland Lenz lay dead, his blank eyes staring skyward, a bullet hole in the center of his forehead. As the rest of the wounded deputies arose, Delbert Collins stayed balled up in the mud, his hands gripping his bloody crotch as he sobbed and moaned loudly. Lematte winced looking at him, then said, "Somebody get him on his feet! Get him to the doctor's."

"No, please!" Collins sobbed. "I can't stand up!"

In spite of Collins's pleading, Hogo Metacino pulled him up, saying, "We're all wounded, Delbert, stop your bellyaching!"

Across the street, out front of the hotel, Mike Cassidy had managed to pull himself up the side of his horse and roll himself up into the saddle. While Lematte and his men were busy taking stock of themselves, Cassidy managed to ease the horse around into an alley and along the back of the town.

Inside the hotel, Tinsdale and Deavers had seen Cassidy slip away. "I hope to God he makes it,"

Deavers said. "Maybe he'll bring the rest of the Double D boys back with him to avenge Bouchard."

"Good Lord, man!" Tinsdale remarked. "A vengeance war is exactly what we *don't* need here right now—not on top of everything else!"

"After what we've both just witnessed in the street," said Deavers, "I think the only way we'll get rid of Lematte and his band of murderers is to kill them where they stand."

"Take hold of yourself, Deavers," said Tinsdale. "We're civilized men! We can't stoop to murder. That makes us no better than Lematte."

"You're right, Tinsdale," said Deavers, giving it some quick consideration. "We can't stoop to *his* level. We have to act fast. We have to get the Double D cowhands on our side while their blood is boiling over what these men did to Gains Bouchard. I'm sure we can count on them now."

Tinsdale nodded. "And don't forget Cray Dawson. I understand he and Bouchard were real close."

"Then that has to be our next move," said Deavers. "We have to appeal to the Double D and Cray Dawson; see if they'll take up our fight. That's the only civilized way to do this sort of thing."

Dawson and Carmelita had arrived early at the old Dawson place and spent most of the day hanging curtains, sweeping the floors, and checking the place thoroughly for rattlesnakes. The rain had quit at dawn, leaving the land sodden and strewn with wide puddles of muddy water that would take days to seep down into the sated land. Only the trail was dry, the sun having spent the day baking it back to its hardened state.

They had spoken very little since the night Dawson had told her about Suzzette. But now that they had gotten out and gone about cleaning up the old, weatherbeaten house, Dawson could see Carmelita's attitude softening a bit. By the time they had finished with the house, mounted up, and taken the Old Spanish Trail back toward the Shaw *hacienda*, Dawson could see she felt better about things.

"Tell me this, Cray," she said as they rode along easily through a cut of high-reaching rock walls. "If you were not with me, would you be staying with this woman?"

Cray looked her up and down, seeing she was getting over any bad feelings she'd had, but still working things over in her mind. "No," he said. "She is a good woman, I think, in spite of her profession. But we had already talked it over . . . I had no interest in staying with her. I don't think she really had any interest in being with me. She had a friend who took up with a gunman. She told me she thought it would be a good life."

"A good life with a gunman," Carmelita said, pondering it to herself. "I watched how my sister and Lawrence Shaw lived. I do not think she had a good life."

"I know," said Dawson, not wanting to think about Rosa Shaw right then; certainly not wanting to talk about her. "I tried to tell Suzzette that life with a gunman was no way to live. She didn't want to hear it."

Casting him a sidelong glance, Carmelita said as if in some sense of personal reflection, "So, you left this woman for her own good?"

"I left her because I didn't have the feeling a man

ought to have for a woman before he takes up living with her," Dawson said bluntly. "I could see no good ever come from me lying 'bout it."

"I see . . ." Carmelita rode beside him quietly for a second, then asked, "And do you have this kind of feeling for me, Cray Dawson?"

"Yes, I do, Carmelita," said Dawson. They rode on in silence for another moment, then he asked her, "What about you? Do you feel as strongly toward me?"

"*Si*," she said, "I feel very . . . *strongly* for you."

Dawson smiled to himself, noting how they both had carefully avoided saying they loved one another. He started to stay something more on the subject, but the sound of a hoof against a rock along the trail ahead caught his attention. He halted his horse and gave a hand gesture, cautioning Carmelita to stay behind him.

"What is it?" she whispered, drawing the red mule over between Dawson and the rock wall.

"Someone on horseback, I think," said Dawson, staring forward where the trail bent out of sight. They waited quietly as the sound of slow hoofs against rock grew closer. When the horse finally turned into sight, Carmelita gave a short gasp, seeing the rider lying limp in the saddle, bowed forward on the horse's neck. His right arm hung down the horse's side, dripping blood.

"It's Mike Cassidy! Wait here," Dawson said to Carmelita. He heeled Stony forward, still looking around warily until they reached Cassidy's horse.

"Easy, fellow," Dawson said, calming the jumpy dun. Reaching down he picked up the dangling reins, then stepped down from his saddle.

"Daw—Dawson, is that you?" Cassidy said in a weak, broken voice.

"Yes, Mike, it's me," Dawson replied, reaching up and pulling him down from the saddle into his arms. He laid him gently onto the ground and motioned for Carmelita to ride forward. "What's happened to you, Pard?" he asked the wounded drover, opening Cassidy's shirt and seeing the gaping wounds in his chest and shoulder. The lower half of Cassidy's ear was dangling and caked with thick, dried blood.

"Lematte . . . and his men," Cassidy rasped. "They killed everybody but me. Bouchard . . . Grubs, Turner, and Sandy, all of them dead in the street."

"Take it easy, Mike," Dawson said, taking a canteen from Carmelita as she stepped down from the mule, uncapped it, and handed it to him. "We're going to get you to the ranch, get you taken care of." He poured a trickle of water on Cassidy's dry lips.

Cassidy gripped Dawson's forearm. "I won't make it to the ranch, Crayton."

"Sure you will," said Dawson. "You're going to be all right, Mike, hang on." He gave Carmelita a doubtful look, then asked Cassidy, "What was all this about, Mike? What started it?"

"Lematte killed one of the saloon women," said Cassidy.

"Why?" Dawson asked, stunned.

"Because he's a rotten . . . bastard," Cassidy gasped. Gripping Dawson's arm he added, "And he beat up Suzzette, real bad."

"He beat up Suzzette? How bad?" Dawson asked, concerned about her condition.

"I never saw her . . ." Cassidy said weakly. "Jimmie Turner went wild . . . called Lematte out on it."

"Mike, listen to me," said Dawson, seeing him fading. "I'm going to take you on out to the ranch. We've got to get you some help. Can you try to stay in your saddle, if I lay you in it?"

"I'll try . . . but I ain't going to make it, Crayton," Cassidy whispered. "Get Lematte for me," he pleaded, "for Bouchard, for all of us . . ." He slumped onto the ground, his eyes going empty, his jaw slack.

Dawson checked his pulse. "He's dead," he said to Carmelita. Prying Cassidy's clenched hand from his shirt sleeve, Dawson stood up and said, "I'll take him on out to the Double D. You can take the mule and go on home. I'll be along later, as soon as I can."

"*Si*," said Carmelita. "I will be waiting for you. But please do not go to town looking for vengeance."

"I won't go looking for vengeance," said Dawson. "But I can't promise you that I won't get involved in this thing. Bouchard and his men would have done the same for me."

"I understand," said Carmelita, deciding this wasn't the time to talk about it. She watched him stoop down and close Cassidy's eyes. Then she walked to the mule, mounted, and rode away.

Dawson laid Cassidy's body over the dun's saddle and led the horse by its reins along the Old Spanish Trail until he rode up to the closed gates of the Double D Ranch. Sonny Wells had spotted him coming from a long ways off, with the body lying over the dun's back. He had opened the gates and stood watching in dark anticipation as Dawson halted Stony, looked down at him and said, "It's Mike Cassidy, Sonny. But I'm afraid I've got more bad news."

Sonny Wells took the reins to the dun and led it

along as Cray Dawson relayed the news about Gains Bouchard and the others being dead. Shaney the cook and his helper, Frenchy, stood up from the tailgate of his chuck wagon in the side yard and watched Dawson and Sonny walk along the path to the house.

"Boys, this ain't looking good," Shaney said to the drovers who began to walk over from the corral and the bunkhouse yard to see what was going on.

Arriving at the chuck wagon, Dawson touched his hat brim and said howdy to the old cook.

"What happened to him?" Shaney asked, recognizing Cassidy. He wiped his hands on his grease-spotted apron as he stepped around and took a closer look, shaking his head grimly.

Dawson said, "Let everybody draw around first, Shaney. I only want to have to tell this once."

As the rest of the drovers came in and circled close to the dun, taking off their hats and looking at Cassidy's body, Dawson called out to them, saying, "Pards, Mike Cassidy is not the only one dead. Gains Bouchard, Sandy Edelmen, Stanley Grubs, and young Jimmie Turner are all dead."

A low murmur went up from the drovers. Then they settled down respectfully and listened to Dawson relay to them what Cassidy had told him. When he'd finished telling them, Broken Nose Simms said, "Jimmie Turner could never stand seeing a woman mistreated, even if she was a whore."

"Gains Bouchard showed the world that he'd stand with his men and die with them if need be," said a seasoned drover named Alvin Decker.

"Everybody keep their heads," Dawson cautioned them, seeing the anger flare.

But Alvin Decker would have none of it. "Boys,"

he said, "I've heard enough talk. I say we go take Somos Santos apart and put it back together, without Sheriff Lematte and his murdering rats in it!"

A cry of support arose from the drovers until Shaney raised a hand and called out for silence. When they quieted down, he said, "I'm just as upset about this as the rest of yas. But before we go shooting up the town, we've got some other important things that has to be done first."

"Yeah? Like what?" said Broken Nose Simms testily.

Shaney said firmly, "Like getting everybody's body back here and giving them all a proper burial! That's *what*!"

"You know he's right, men," said Dawson, stepping down from his saddle. "Bouchard loved this place. He wouldn't want to be buried anywhere else. And none of the others would want to be laid in boot hill, if they had any say in the matter."

The drovers stood watching silently as Dawson helped Sonny Wells lower Cassidy's body onto a wool blanket that Frenchy had run and grabbed from inside the chuck wagon. Finally Barney Woods called out what had been on all their minds, "Are you going to ride with us to take on these murdering bastards, Dawson?"

Sonny Wells stepped forward before Dawson could answer, saying, "Crayton Dawson is one of us! Don't none of you ever forget that! He'll do what he knows is best . . . the way Bouchard would do if he was here!"

Barney Woods stepped back, giving Dawson a repentant look, saying, "Sorry Dawson, you know how I am. I get riled and don't always think real clear. I meant nothing by it."

"I know that, Barney." Dawson gave him a nod, then said to everybody, "Listen up, men. I don't know what will happen to the Double D now that Gains Bouchard is dead. He was a prudent man, so I'm thinking his attorney in Houston has a will, and some sort of plan for this place in the event of Bouchard's death. We'll notify his attorney, but for right now, until we hear otherwise, somebody is going to have to take charge here." He looked around at Shaney, and called out, "I think Shaney's the man Bouchard would pick, since his foreman died with him." He looked all around. "Does anybody say otherwise?"

Heads shook back and forth slowly. But Shaney called out before Dawson could continue, "Men, I'm a cook. I don't claim to know how to run an outfit. I can feed, doctor, punch boils, and cut snakebites. But I can't keep this place together full time and I ain't ashamed to admit it. I'll run things until we hear from Gains's attorney, but when I write to his attorney I'm going to ask to be relieved."

"You're quitting us?" Frenchy asked.

"No, idiot, I ain't quitting!" Shaney barked at his helper. "I'll still cook . . . but I won't run this spread." He looked straight at Cray Dawson and said, "All of you know that I thought the world of Sandy Edelman, both as a man and as a foreman. But you all know as well as I do that had Cray Dawson been here when Bouchard appointed a foreman, it would have been him running this crew instead of Sandy."

"Wait a minute, Shaney," said Dawson, seeing where this was going.

Ignoring him, Shaney said, "So I say we all ask that Cray Dawson be appointed to run this spread until such time as a heir or a new owner shows up to take over. Who agrees with me?"

Dawson looked around at a unanimous show of hands. "All right, we'll see," he said. But first things first. I'm taking a buckboard to Somos Santos to pick up Bouchard and the others. I'm going to bring Suzzette back with me if she'll come. I want two men to go along with me."

"Only two?" Shaney asked.

"That's right, only two," said Dawson. "I don't want to turn it into a fight. I just want to get our dead and get them back here. If I take more men, it looks like I'm coming for a showdown."

"I say I ought to be one of the men you take with you," said Barney Woods, stepping forward, "and I say Alvin Decker ought to be the other."

"You're not going with me, Barney," said Dawson. He gave Alvin Decker a look, stopping him from coming forward. "Neither are you Alvin. You'll both lose your tempers. That's what we *don't* want to happen." He looked around; then, spotting the Furry brothers, he said, "Eldon, Max. Can I count on you two keeping cool heads in town?"

The Furry brothers looked at one another blankly, then back at Dawson. "We'll try, Crayton," said Eldon, the older of the two.

"All right then," said Dawson. "That's all I ask. We'll leave right now and ride through the night. The quicker we get the bodies out of there the better." He looked at the others, then said, "I want the rest of you to ride with us until we get a quarter of a mile from town. I know the land is still wet, but the sun has already dried the trail. Raise as much dust as you can, so they'll get the idea we've got men coming if we need them. But everybody will stay out of Somos Santos unless you hear shooting." He looked straight at Barney Woods. "Is that clear, Barney?"

"Yeah," said Barney Woods, sincerely. "I'll stay in line, Dawson. You've got my word on it."

"Mine too," said Decker.

"That goes for everybody here," Dawson said, looking from one drover to the next as if asking each one for their word. "We've got burying to do . . . let's do it with respect."

PART 3

PART 3

Chapter 17

———

Cleveland Ellis and Moon Braden sat atop a ridge and watched the Dawson house for a full hour before deciding to ride down and take a closer look. Afternoon shadows stretched long across the land as they rode cautiously into the yard and stepped down from their saddles with their pistols coming up from their holsters, cocked and ready. "Hello, the house," Ellis called out, motioning for Moon Braden to put some distance between them as they approached the front porch. Stepping up quietly and crossing the porch, he slowly shoved the door open a few inches, then looked inside. He turned back to Braden, taking a breath of relief.

"Just like we thought, Moon," he said. "There's nobody here. But it looks like there has been."

"Are you sure this is the old Dawson homestead?" Braden asked, looking down at the fresh prints that Stony and the red mule had left behind.

"Yes, I'm sure," said Cleveland Ellis. "One of the hands from the Double D showed it to me once when we was pushing some steers past here."

"Then these must be his tracks," said Braden. "It looks like there was two riders here." He pointed at the ground near the hitch rail and added, "They weren't just passing by either. They hitched their mounts."

"All right," said Ellis, still holding his pistol, but uncocking it. "Let's go inside, see what we can learn about mister *hotshot* gunman."

After a close look at the newly hung curtains, scrubbed floors, and cleaned hearth, Moon Braden said, "Looks like Dawson is about to move back in and set up housekeeping here."

"Not if you and I have anything to say about it." Ellis grinned. "Come on, give me a hand." He picked up an oil lamp, shook it to see if it was full, then unscrewed the cap.

"What are you doing?" Braden asked.

"What the hell does it look like I'm doing?" Ellis replied, chuckling under his breath.

"We don't have to do this!" said Braden. He'll be coming back before long. All we got to do is wait, and be ready to ambush him!"

"That's right," said Ellis, shaking the lamp fuel all over the table, the floor, and up and down the new curtains. "But he'll see this a long ways off and come riding in fast, before he has time to realize what might be waiting for him along the trail."

"That ain't sound enough reasoning to suit me," said Braden, shaking his head.

"Sound reasoning, hell," said Ellis. "Some things you have to do just for the fun of it. Don't forget this gunman peckerwood cost us our jobs at the Double D."

"I thought we was getting ready to quit that job anyway," said Braden.

"You just ain't with me on nothing today, are you, Moon?" said Ellis, cocking a menacing eye at him.

"All right, damn it," said Braden. "I'll go along with you. But let's get done and get out of here. Don't forget how he got his reputation."

"You're starting to worry worse than an old woman, Moon," said Ellis. "Now grab a lamp and shake it out."

When the two had finished emptying fuel oil all over the inside of the house, they walked out onto the porch and Cleveland Ellis took a wooden match from his pocket. "Go get the horses, Moon. I'll do the honors here."

He watched his partner hurry down to the hitch rail and pull the horses back a few feet. As soon as Braden was mounted, holding Ellis's horse by its reins, Cleveland Ellis struck the match, pitched it inside the open door, and hurried away from the house as the fuel ignited quickly, sending a roaring ball of fire out through the front door. "Whooie!" Ellis laughed aloud, seeing the flames licking high inside the house as he jumped atop his horse. "Now that is what I call a *fire!*"

"Let's get going, Cleveland!" Moon Braden said nervously, looking all around as if Dawson might appear at any second.

"I'm just waiting on you, Moon." Ellis laughed, turning his horse and batting his heels against its sides.

They rode their horses quickly along the Old Spanish Trail, following the hoof prints left by Stony and the red mule, until they looked back and saw the black smoke billowing high above the rocky cliff line. Slowing their horses to a walk, Ellis said, "I figure we can stay on these prints awhile longer. We can always get up into the rocks as soon as we hear somebody coming."

"That's a risky way of dealing with a man like Dawson," Braden said, sounding concerned.

Cleveland Ellis had began feeling big about himself after setting the fire. He jutted his chin and said, "Instead of me worrying about dealing with Dawson, maybe Dawson better start worrying about dealing with *me*."

Moon Braden just gave him a doubtful look and rode on. When they reached the spot in the trail where Dawson and Carmelita had met up with the ill-fated Mike Cassidy, Ellis halted his horse and looked down at the dark blood on the dirt. Then he saw where the hoof prints had split up, two going in the direction of the Double D Spread, and one still headed along the trail. "Now what have we here?" he asked, stepping down from his horse's back and stooping down for a closer look.

"Now there's three of them," said Moon Braden in a shaky voice. "I don't like this one bit." He looked around again.

"You're starting to get on my nerves something awful, Moon," Ellis warned him. "Stop acting like you're about to soil yourself."

Braden took a deep breath and calmed himself, but still kept a wary eye on the trail ahead. "All right, what now? There's three of them . . . which do we follow? Which set belongs to Dawson?"

"Dawson ain't riding no mule," said Ellis, "that's for damn sure."

"How can you tell those are mule hoof prints?" Moon Braden asked.

"I'm from Ohio, Moon. Don't ever ask me how I can tell a mule from a horse! It's insulting," he snapped.

"All right, sorry!" said Braden. Again he looked around nervously. "So what are we going to do?"

"We're not going to ride into the Double D Spread after him, that's for damned sure," said Ellis, nodding in the direction of the two sets of horse prints.

"But you just said Dawson ain't riding no mule!" said Braden, getting more and more nervous sitting there. "There's no point following *it*!"

"I know what I said, damn it!" Ellis shouted, getting nervous and edgy himself. He looked back and forth for a moment as if giving things some careful consideration. Finally he said, "All right, here's the plan . . . we're going back to town. I'll tell Lematte we couldn't find him."

"Back to *town*?" Braden gave him a disbelieving look. Poking his thumb back over his shoulder, he said, "You mean we just burnt down a good house for nothing?"

"It's Dawson's house, so don't say we burnt it for nothing!" Ellis snapped.

"It sure feels like it was for nothing to me." Braden shrugged.

Cleveland Ellis gritted his teeth to keep from snatching his gun from his holster and killing Moon Braden on the spot. Taking a deep breath and getting himself under control, he said, "All right . . . I'm going to follow the mule because it might be that woman that Dawson was talking about, the one who lives at the Shaw *hacienda*. If it is, he'll soon be coming back to her."

"Well, I expect he will," Braden said sarcastically, "now that we've burnt his house to the ground . . . for *no good reason*!"

"Keep it up about that house, Moon," said Ellis,

pointing a gloved finger at him. "See if I don't kill you."

"Are we going or not?" said Braden, ignoring his threat.

Grumbling under his breath, Cleveland Ellis jumped into his saddle and angrily jerked his horse around in the direction of the single set of hoof prints. "Yes! We're going back to town, but first we're going to the Shaw *hacienda*. I want to see that woman for myself.

Carmelita spotted the black smoke in the distance above the jagged hillside as she looked out along the trail. She'd known it was too early to see Cray Dawson riding in, yet she nervously watched for him all the same. When she first saw the smoke she did not instantly think that it might be the Dawson house burning. But upon consideration she couldn't think of anything else in that direction that would raise this kind of smoke, especially after the heavy storms had left much of the land still standing in water. The smoke made her even more anxious and restless. She walked back and forth near the window. Nearly an hour passed.

She stopped pacing and stared out the window, seeing that the black smoke had dissipated slightly. She'd told Dawson she'd wait here for him, but now she wasn't sure she could. She looked at the stone hearth, at the bullet hole still in its facing, and reminded herself of the terrible thing that had happened to her sister in this house.* She walked out front and paced back and forth on the porch. Another

* See Book I: *Gunman's Song*

half hour passed. She stopped and looked at the smoke, noting that it had slackened and drifted far across the rocky hill land. Dawson would understand, she told herself, suddenly stricken by an overpowering need to get away from there.

She walked inside, grabbing her riding coat and the big Colt Dawson had placed in a drawer for her in case of emergencies. Then she hurried out and around to the barn, driven by dark intuition, an inner voice urging her to flee. There, she quickly saddled the red mule and rode away, the mule running stiffly as she batted her boot heels against its sides. Instinctively, she rode away from the rear of the *hacienda*, ducking slightly to avoid the low, thick branch of a live oak standing close to the barn. She took a seldom-used elk path that led upward and parallel to the main trail.

Once in the shelter of rock and juniper and scrub piñon she slowed the mule to a steady pace and calmed herself down. But before she had gone a full mile she spotted a drift of dust rising from the trail below. She stopped the mule, dropped from the saddle, and led the animal close to the edge of the cliffs. Looking down from a well-hidden position, seeing the two riders, she crossed herself and whispered the name of the Holy Mother under her breath. Seeing the glint of the deputy badges on their chests she whispered to herself, "Sheriff Lematte's *asesinos*."

She had no doubt what these men had been up to, and she had no doubt where they were headed now. She watched them ride along at a quick, steady pace toward the *hacienda*, looking back over their shoulders. "*Animals cochinos!*" she said to herself in her native tongue. Raising the big Colt with both hands, she squinted one eye shut and aimed down at them, her hands swaying under the weight of the gun. But she did not cock the hammer on the Colt; instead she lowered it and shook her head, her pulse pounding. She was no killer. She stood up, dusting herself off, and hurried to the mule. She shoved the Colt down in her belt and rode away quickly, going another full mile before cutting down onto the main trail.

Once down on the stretch of flatlands Carmelita hurried the mule along until she saw a lone rider racing toward her in the fading evening light. For a moment she could only stare, her breath seeming stuck in her chest. But as the horseman came closer and she recognized both Dawson and his horse, Stony, she sighed and allowed herself to slump in the saddle. She let the mule stop in the trail and waited for Dawson to slide the horse to a halt beside her.

"Carmelita! Are you all right?" Dawson said, out of breath. Before she could even answer, he embraced her, lifting her from the mule and onto his lap.

"*Si*, I am all right," she said with relief. She saw the worried look melt in his eyes, then she felt him press her against him. She returned his embrace, saying, "You saw the two men?"

"Yes," he said, "That is, I saw what they did. They burned my house. I knew their next stop would be the *hacienda*." He hesitated, conjuring up his own dark memories of what had once happened at the *hacienda*. "I—I rode ahead of the others." He nodded back toward the trail, where dust from the Double D riders and the buckboard was just beginning to loom on the purple horizon.

"These men were deputies," she said. "I saw the badges on their chests."

"I figured as much," said Dawson. He let her down from his lap, then stepped down beside her. They looked toward the Double D men riding ever closer.

"Why are so many men riding with you?" she asked.

"They asked me to ride in and bring back the bodies of Bouchard and his men for proper burial," Dawson said. "I want Lematte to know that I'm not alone."

"Before it's over there will be much bloodshed, no matter how we try to avoid it, *si*?" she asked.

Dawson's voice lowered as he replied, "Yes, Carmelita . . . I'm afraid so."

Chapter 18

When Cleveland Ellis and Moon Braden arrived at the *hacienda*, again they stopped their horses a long ways back and watched the place for any sign of life before venturing forward into the yard. "Seems like everywhere we go lately there's nobody at home," said Ellis.

"Is that why we just burn their houses down and ride on?" Moon Braden asked sharply, the two of them stepping down from their saddles.

"Keep it up," Ellis warned him. Then, nodding toward the *hacienda*, he said, "If nobody's home now, they must be on their way. Let's get these horses out of sight and wait inside. They'll least expect something to happen as they come through their front door."

"Yeah," said Moon. "Maybe we can rustle up something to eat in there, too. I'm starving."

"Me too," said Ellis. "I didn't see a thing to eat at that last house."

"If we hadn't been so quick to stick a match to it," we *might* have found something," Braden said, leading his horse around the side of the *hacienda* toward the barn. Cleveland Ellis just looked at him.

Inside the barn, instead of putting the two horses

in a stall, they hitched them to a pole near the rear doors and opened the doors halfway in case they had to make a hasty exit. Then they entered the rear door of the *hacienda* and rummaged the pantry for food. Ellis found a canvas bread bag containing a half loaf of sugar-sprinkled sweet bread, and they began breaking off chunks of it and wolfing them down. "God almighty, I love Mexican *pan dulce!*" he said with his mouth stuffed. "I'll say one thing about this little filly, she sure can cook!"

"Um-hmm!" Grunting in reply, Moon Braden looked around, found a bottle of wine, pulled the cork and tossed it away. Raising the bottle, Moon swigged long and deep until Ellis forced his hand down and took the bottle from him.

"Damn it! Show some manners," said Ellis, standing beside him. He took a long drink himself and started to hand the bottle back to Moon.

But Moon had found another bottle. "Keep it," he said, shaking the bottle slightly, pointing it toward a shelf lined with more dark wine bottles. "There's enough here to start our own little *fiesta!*"

Ellis nodded, grinning. But then the seriousness of their being there set in and he said, "You've got to keep an eye on the trail, while I go through this place, see what I can find."

Finishing a drink of wine, Braden wiped a hand across his mouth and said, stifling a belch, "I agree we've got to keep an eye on the trail . . . but I didn't know we're trying to *find* anything, except Cray Dawson.

"Don't you think it would be helpful to look around, find out what we can about the man we're looking for?" Ellis asked.

"Sure," said Braden, shrugging. "But I believe you just want to sniff around at the woman's stuff."

Ellis's expression grew hard. "What the hell is that supposed to mean?"

"It means just what I *said*," Braden repeated. "You're wanting to snoop around and go through the woman's stuff."

"So what if I am?" said Ellis. "That's what a normal man does, ain't it?"

Instead of answering his partner, Braden tore off a mouthful of sweet bread with his teeth and threw back another long drink of wine.

Ellis looked him up and down. "Now, if you don't have any more comments on the matter, I'll go look around some. Whatever you do, don't light a lamp. Anybody riding the trail will see a match strike halfway to the hills."

"Don't worry," said Braden, eating vigorously. "I know better then to strike a match." He added sarcastically, "I don't want to give you any ideas." He let out a short laugh at his own humor.

"Smart son of a bitch," Ellis cursed under his breath, walking away. He prowled his way to the bedroom, leaving opened drawers and disheveled whatnots and belongings in his wake.

Moon Braden took a large chunk of the *pan dulce*, the opened bottle of wine in his hand and a fresh bottle under his arm, and walked to the front window where he could keep a clear lookout on the winding trail. "Don't take all night *looking*," Braden called out toward the bedroom. Chuckling again at his humor, Braden took another long drink, feeling the strong Mexican wine beginning to glow inside him.

But Moon Braden's words didn't cause Ellis to get in any hurry. Nearly an hour passed before Ellis came back from the bedroom, carrying his boots in his hand and his gun belt over his shoulder. "Moon, you can go on back there if you want to," he said, barely above a whisper. "I'll keep watch for awhile."

Moon had dozed off leaning against the window frame, but Ellis's voice snapped him out of it. "Huh? Go where?" he asked, having heard Ellis through a veil of sleep.

"You fell asleep keeping watch, didn't you?" Ellis asked accusingly.

"I wasn't asleep," said Braden. He wiped his blurry eyes and looked Ellis up and down curiously in the pale moonlight coming through the window. "What do you mean '*I can go back there awhile*?' " he asked, staring at Ellis's empty boots and shouldered gun belt.

Ellis set his boots down and began stepping into and pulling them on. "Never mind," he said with a snap.

Braden looked him up and down again, this time with a disbelieving grin, saying, "What on earth was you doing back there all this time, *Pard*?"

"I was just looking," said Ellis, adjusting his boots and swinging his gun belt around his waist. "You can go look if you want to . . . that's all I was saying."

"Just looking?" Braden asked. He sniffed the air, catching a scent of women's lilac cologne. "Are you wearing perfume?"

"You go to hell, Braden!" Ellis snapped. "I might have spilled some on me . . . it's too damn dark in here!"

"Yeah, it's dark, but *still* . . ." said Braden, his words trailing.

Trying to change the subject, Ellis pulled out a handful of cigars and wagged them back and forth in front of Braden. "Look what I found! I suppose you won't turn one of these babies down, will you?"

"We can't light them in here, remember?" said Braden. "We don't want any light to be seen."

"I know," said Ellis, "but give me a match. I'll go light them out back, then bring them back in here. There's no reason we can't be comfortable while we wait."

"Nothing doing," said Braden, turning back to the window. "I ain't trusting you alone with a match. I still wonder what you was doing in that woman's bedroom all this time."

Outside, leading the riders around the last wide turn in the trail, Cray Dawson saw the flash of fire in the front window of the *hacienda* and heard the single muffled gunshot. He halted the group and said to the Furry brothers, riding with Carmelita in the buckboard beside him, "Did you see that? It came from inside the house."

"We all saw it," said Max Furry. "What does it mean?"

"I have no idea," said Dawson. But we're not taking any chances. We're going to dismount, circle the place and close in all at once."

Cleveland Ellis came back from the bedroom for the second time, this time bare-chested and hatless with a pair of women's pantaloons draped around his neck. He finished his second bottle of wine in a long gulp and saved enough of it to spit a stream down on Moon Braden's body. "What do you think of this trinket, Pard?" He jiggled a large beaded women's necklace on his chest. Then he said, mockingly, "What's that? I don't hear you giving me any back-talk, *Mister* Braden! Looks like you've finally learnt to keep your mouth shut." He gave the blank, dead face a short kick, causing Braden's head to rock back and forth on the hard tile floor.

Staggering, he walked back to the pantry and opened another bottle of wine, pulling the tall cork with his teeth and spitting it away. "Care for some more *pan dulce,* Mister Ellis," he said aloud in a mock feminine voice. Then, tearing himself a large handful of the sweet bread, he lowered his voice to a manly tone and said, "Well, thank you . . . I don't mind if I do." He staggered back to the front room chewing a mouthful of sweet bread as he struck a match and lit one of the cigars.

Out front, seeing the match flare through the window caused Cray Dawson to turn to Carmelita and say, "I'd feel better if you'd stay back here until we get inside. They could have met up with some others. We don't know how many might be in there."

"I understand," said Carmelita. "I will stay back here until it is safe to come in."

Creeping up silently beside Dawson, Frenchy said, "I checked the barn; there's only two horses there."

"Good enough," said Dawson. "Let's get it down." He raised a hand in the pale moonlight and waved the others forward, the circle of armed men moving as one, silent and fast.

Dawson leaped onto the porch and without a second of hesitancy kicked the front door open and charged inside, his Colt cocked and aimed. Behind him the Double D men spilled into the room and formed another circle, their pistols and rifles pointed at the shadowy figure and the glowing cigar in the center of the room. "Don't move!" Dawson shouted.

"Don't shoot!" came Cleveland Ellis's startled reply.

A tense moment passed as Dawson moved sidelong to a lamp on a table. He picked it up and held it out to Max Furry, who lit it and lowered the globe into place, casting a bright circle of light.

"What the hell?" said Shaney. The rest of the men stared with stunned expressions at Cleveland Ellis, with the pantaloons around his neck, the large woman's necklace sparkling on his hairy chest, and his eyes wide and red-rimmed from too much wine. "It's Cleveland Ellis!" Shaney's eyes went to the body on the floor at Ellis's feet.

"And there's Braden! Shot from behind!" Frenchy added, nodding at Braden's body, with a gaping hole in his chest where Ellis's bullet had exited.

"Drop the gun!" said Dawson, as surprised as the rest but not allowing himself to be distracted from the task at hand. The scent of women's lilac cologne wafted heavily in the air. Empty wine bottles lay strewn across the floor, one of them broken, from when Braden fell dead on the floor.

Ellis let his pistol drop onto Moon Braden's bloodstained belly. "You would never have gotten the drop on me if I hadn't got drunk, Dawson," Cleveland Ellis sneered, sticking the cigar into his mouth. Looking at the Double D boys, he said, "I wish I could have managed to kill a bunch of you poltroons before I went down."

"String him up!" shouted Barney Woods.

"Wait!" Dawson said firmly to Woods. Turning back to Ellis he asked, "Did Lematte send you two after me?" He eyed the badge on Ellis's chest as he stepped around, picked up the dropped pistol, and shoved it down into his belt.

"Yeah." Ellis shrugged. "He sent us. I ain't going to lie about it. Lematte sent us to kill you. We burned your house down." He nodded down at Moon Braden's body, then lied shamelessly, saying, "Burning the house was all his idea . . . I tried to stop him, begged him not to. Burning that house is what started the trouble between us. I told him we shouldn't have done it. He wouldn't listen."

"String him up!" Barney Woods said again.

"Hold on," said Dawson, stopping Woods from reaching out and grabbing Ellis. Woods stepped back, but he turned to Alvin Decker and said, "Get a rope. Soon as Dawson's through talking to him, we're stringing him up!" As he spoke he gave Ellis a cold stare. Ellis swallowed a knot in his throat, sobering quickly.

Carmelita stepped into the room from the porch. Upon seeing the pantaloons and necklace around Cleveland Ellis's neck, she said angrily, "What are you doing with these things?"

"Yeah, Ellis," said Barney Woods, "what *are* you doing wearing women's jewelry and under-garments?"

Ellis looked sick, but he said defiantly, "I don't have to explain myself to you, Woods!"

Carmelita stepped forward and tried to snatch the pantaloons from him, but Ellis jumped a step to the side. His eyes darted back and forth wildly. "Carmel-ita, get back from him!" Dawson shouted, seeing that Ellis was about to make a move. But before Carmelita could even respond, Ellis gave her a hard shove toward Dawson, then turned and bolted straight through the Double D men between him and the rear of the *hacienda*.

"Grab him!" shouted Woods. A shot went off from Eldon Furry's rifle, but Ellis had shoved the barrel up away from him as he streaked past. "He's making a break!" Woods barked.

Cleveland Ellis raced along a hallway and out the rear door, the Double D boys right behind him. But he managed to pull ahead of them and make it inside the barn. He gave the barn door a shove and dropped the long wooden bolt into place just as the men ran into it. "*Adios!* You sons-a-bitches!" he shrieked, hearing them pounding and shouldering the doors.

He knew it would only be seconds before some of the men ran around to the rear of the barn, so he rushed to the horses he and Braden had left standing near the rear door. Hearing boots pounding the wet ground around the side of the barn, he grabbed one of the horses' reins, flung himself up into the saddle and nailed his spurs into the horse's sides. As the horse bolted away he ducked low in his saddle, slap-ping the ends of the reins wildly, putting the horse into a full run. Reaching down with his right hand he jerked his rifle from his saddle boot and straight-ened up enough to turn and fire a shot back at his pursuers.

As the shot sounded, Dawson and the rest of the men heard a loud *thunk* in the darkness and felt a slight tremor in the ground beneath their feet. "What was that?" Alvin Decker asked, dumbfounded.

"Shhh, quiet!" Dawson said, listening closely to the night. A silent second passed, the only noise being the sound of Cleveland Ellis's horse's hoofs slowing to a halt thirty yards away.

"Is he turning, coming back?" asked Frenchy, in a whisper.

"I don't think so," Dawson said. He motioned everybody forward with his pistol barrel. They moved quietly and cautiously until they saw a dark lump lying on the moonlit ground beneath the low, outreaching limb of the live oak tree.

"Lord have mercy," Shaney said in a hushed tone. "He hooked that low branch!"

"Boy, I'll say he did," Frenchy whispered in reply. He had carried the lit lamp with him from the house. He held it out at arm's length and winced at what the glow revealed.

"He's broke his damned neck," said Woods in disbelief.

"Boy, I'll say he has," said Frenchy.

Cleveland Ellis lay flat on his back, spread-eagled on the ground, his neck at an odd angle to his body. A trickle of blood ran down from one corner of his mouth. His eyes stared upward with a startled expression.

"He never knew what hit him," said Alvin Decker. A few feet away Ellis's horse came walking back slowly, looking down, then poking its muzzle against its downed rider.

"Saved us stretching his neck for him, far as I'm concerned," said Woods.

"What do you want to do with these two, Crayton?" Shaney asked quietly.

"We didn't kill them," said Dawson. "Let's get them on the buckboard. I'll haul them to Lematte. They're his men. Let him figure what he wants to do with them."

Chapter 19

———

At daylight, on their way to the restaurant for breakfast, Sheriff Lematte asked Karl Nolly, "Where's Ash?"

"He was just getting up when I left the hotel," said Nolly. Then, in a critical tone, he said, "I reckon a *big gunman* needs more rest than us common folk."

"Yep, I suppose that's it all right," said Lematte. He smiled to himself, liking the way Mad Albert Ash got under Karl Nolly's skin. It kept Nolly on his toes, Lematte thought.

"Shouldn't we be hearing something from Cleveland Ellis and Moon Braden?" Nolly asked.

"Most any time now, I expect," said Lematte, seeing a buckboard and a single horseman top the horizon, headed toward town. He squinted slightly, studying both the rig and the rider for a moment. "Who's this coming here?"

"It could be most anybody at this time of morning," said Nolly. "Why? What's your concern?"

"My concern is all that dust rising aways back *behind* them. As wet as the land is, it takes a lot of riders to raise this much dust.

"I see what you mean," said Nolly, craning his neck slightly for a better look.

The two stepped up onto the boardwalk out front of the restaurant and stared out at the lone wagon in the early morning light. "To just be a rig and one rider they sure are leaving a lot hanging behind them," said Lematte.

"Think I better get the deputies together?" Nolly asked, without taking his eyes off the buckboard.

"Yes, I think you better," said Lematte, "as much craziness as there's been going on lately."

As Karl Nolly left and headed back toward the hotel, Hogo Metacino came walking over leisurely from the other side of the street staring out in the same direction, toward the buckboard, as he adjusted his silver-studded leather gauntlets on his wrists. "Who's this coming here, Boss?" he asked Lematte.

"I don't know, Hogo," said Lematte, "but we're going to find out." He nodded at three horses standing at a hitch rail. "Take one of these hay-burners and ride out close enough to see who this is raising all the dust."

"Whose horses are these?" Metacino asked, looking the animals up and down.

"I don't give a damn," said Lematte. "We're borrowing one in our capacity as peace officers."

"Sure thing then." Metacino grinned. He unhitched one of the horses, stepped up into the saddle, and heeled the animal out toward the approaching wagon. Lematte watched him ride out fast, three hundred yards, then turn short of reaching the wagon and race back. As he watched Metacino return, Nolly came back from the hotel with a perplexed look on his face.

"Where's Ash?" Lematte asked without facing him. He stared at Metacino as he spoke to Nolly.

"He's shaving!" said Nolly. "Told me he'd be along when he's done."

"Did you tell him *why* I sent for him?" Lematte asked.

"I told him there was a wagon and a rider coming to town raising a lot of dust. He said to tell you that if he don't get his shave first thing in the morning he'll be cross and irritable all day long."

Lematte gave Nolly a strange look.

Nolly shrugged. "I'm saying what he told me to tell you. If you ask me, he's not—"

"I didn't ask you, Nolly," said Lematte cutting him off, seeing Metacino ride in hard and slide the horse to a halt in front of the boardwalk.

"Boss, it's that gunman, Crayton Dawson, and a couple of other men," Metacino said. "Looks like they've got the whole Double D crew riding a quarter of a mile behind them." Metacino dropped down from the saddle and spun the horse's reins around the hitch rail.

"Damn it," said Lematte, "I figured it might be Dawson.

"Why do you suppose he has the Double D boys riding so far behind him?" Nolly asked.

Lematte pulled a fresh cigar from his lapel pocket. He bit the end off of it, blew it away, and adjusted the cigar in his mouth as he searched for a match. "It's his way of showing he's not coming here looking for trouble," he said.

"Good," said Nolly. "If he's wanting to talk, maybe we can all get something settled between us without any bloodshed."

"Ha!" said Lematte, "If you think he's wanting to do that, you're easily fooled. He's got something up his sleeve. Keep your eyes open."

"I always keep my eyes open," said Nolly, looking at him curiously. "But I don't think he's got anything up his sleeve, Sheriff. If you want my opinion on the matter."

Lematte ignored his comment and said to him and Metacino, "Both of you round up the men. I'll see what Dawson has to say. Tell everybody to be prepared for anything he does. He's full of surprises."

As the two men turned and hurried away to gather the rest of the deputies, Metacino said to Nolly, "Is Lematte going *loco* because of this gunman?"

"It's sure starting to look that way," said Nolly. "He can't seem to put things to rest between them. I don't think Dawson wants anything but to be left alone. Lematte can't seem to get a grip on how to *do* that!"

In the window of his hotel room overlooking the street, Mad Albert Ash stood back far enough to keep from being noticed as he looked out on the street below. Seeing the wagon roll into town with the two canvas covered bodies in its bed and Dawson riding alongside it, he smiled to himself and murmured quietly, "*Dalton,* You beat all these eyes have ever seen." He wiped the remaining streaks of shaving soap from his cheeks and tossed the towel aside. "I'll just let you and the good sheriff jaw things over while I get dressed." His smile widened. "Nothing like a dramatic entrance I always say . . ."

On the boardwalk, Sheriff Lematte spread his coat open, making sure Dawson could clearly see his badge. A few townsmen began to gather cautiously, eyeing the covered bodies as soon as Dawson brought Stony to a halt out front of the restaurant. Beside him, Max Furry stopped the wagon. Lematte stood tall and silent and looked out at Dawson, then down at the wagon. He saw a shotgun in the hands of each of the Furry brothers. Dawson's right hand rested on the big Colt on his hip.

"We're not here looking for trouble with you, Sheriff," Dawson said, seeing him eye the two shotguns. "We're here to pick up the bodies of Gains Bouchard and his men . . . and drop these boys off to you." As he spoke, Eldon Furry reached a gloved hand back and flipped a corner of the canvas, uncovering the blue-white faces of Cleveland Ellis and Moon Braden.

Seeing his deputies coming across the street from different directions, Lematte grew bold. "You killed them both!" he said, holding his hand poised near his gun butt as if it took all his effort to keep from grabbing his pistol. "I heard that you gave them some trouble, cost them their jobs at the Double D!"

The Furry brothers waited in silence, their thumbs across the shotgun hammers.

Dawson said calmly, "Yes, I had some words with them awhile back out at the Double D, but nothing came of it. I didn't kill them." He stared coldly in Lematte's eyes. "I would have killed them though, had I came home and found them waiting to ambush me, the way they had planned."

"Then what happened to them?" Lematte asked impatiently. Dawson turned slightly and nodded down, first at Cleveland Ellis then at Moon Braden. "This one blew his pardner's brains out, then he hung chin on a tree limb trying to get away from me and the Double D boys." He nodded toward the distant sheen of settling dust. "They're out there waiting for us to bring back the bodies for burial."

Lematte bit the inside of his lip, not seeing any sign of Mad Albert Ash, and not wanting to push a fight with Dawson and the Double D boys right then. Finally, as the deputies came gathering around in the street, half circling Dawson and the buckboard, staring down at the bodies, he said, "All right, Dawson. You'll find Gains Bouchard and his *gunmen's* bodies in the shed behind the livery barn." He turned to his deputies and said, "Get Ellis and Braden out of there. Take them to the barbershop; get them looked after."

"This is the third man of ours he's killed!" said Hogo Metacino, "and we ain't going to do nothing about it?"

"He says he didn't kill these two!" Lematte snapped at the deputy. "Now unless you'd like to take over my job, get these bodies out of there!"

"You heard him, men," said Karl Nolly, stepping forward, throwing off the large sheet of canvas.

The deputies stepped in, Hogo Metacino grumbling under his breath, and lifted the bodies from the wagon bed.

Dawson gave Lematte a questioning look, saying, "What's he talking about, the third man of yours I've killed?"

"Dawson," said Lematte, "I could arrest you right now for the murder of Jewel Higgs. But since I'm so busy and it would take all my time to prove you did it, I'm not going forward with any charges against you right now." He looked out toward where the Double D cowhands were waiting for Dawson. "I believe in holding down trouble whenever I can. If you stay out of my town, away from my deputies, and keep your nose out of Somos Santos's business, I'm going to overlook Higgs's murder."

"If you're talking about one of the three men I caught spying on me awhile back, Lematte," said Dawson, "he was alive and well when I let him go." Dawson looked around among the deputies and said boldly, "If your deputies say I killed him, they're lying through their teeth."

Lematte said quickly, "The two deputies with him said *somebody* shot him with a rifle. You were the only person out there."

"If I were you I'd be asking those deputies if they had anything against the man," said Dawson. "Maybe they're the ones who killed him. Next time I catch anybody sneaking around where they don't belong, there won't be any doubt who shot them. It'll be me."

"Those men were out there in their official capacity, Dawson, keeping an eye out for any undesirables headed toward town," said Lematte.

"They had no business out there doing what they were doing, and you know it, Lematte," said Dawson. "Send them again. Badge or no badge, I'm going to send them back to you facedown."

"Careful, Dawson," said Lematte. "You just made a threat on officers of the law."

"That I did," said Dawson. "I just gave all of you a warning; now let's see if you're smart enough to listen to it." He heeled Stony forward slowly. Max Furry jiggled the reins to the team of wagon horses, sending them forward as well.

Feeling his face redden in embarrassment, Lematte stood watching in silence, seeing Dawson and the wagon turn in a wide loop and head toward the street alongside the livery barn. Stepping up beside Lematte, seeing the anger and humiliation on his face, Karl Nolly said, "Let it go, Sheriff. He'll take the dead and leave."

Lematte snapped his head around, facing Nolly with rage in his eyes. "Did I ask you for any of your half-assed opinions, Nolly?"

"No, Sheriff," Nolly said, backing off. "You sure didn't."

"Then kindly keep your stupid mouth shut!" Lematte hissed at him. "I know how to handle this gunslinger!" He looked all around wildly, then asked, "Where the hell is Ash?"

"Still shaving," Nolly said bluntly.

With the bodies of Gains Bouchard and the others in the buckboard, Max Furry reined the wagon back out onto the street, following Dawson until he stopped Stony out front of the Silver Seven Saloon. Across the street, Lematte still stood watching, Nolly standing back behind him, and most of the deputies gathered in front of the boardwalk. "What's he doing now?" Lematte asked no one in particular.

"Maybe he wants a couple of drinks before he leaves town," said Nolly, working at keeping the bitterness out of his voice.

"He's going to that whore!" said Lematte. "Can you believe this? Brazen as all get-out!" He looked toward the hotel again. "What the hell is keeping Ash?"

"Maybe he needed to trim his toenails too," said Nolly.

But as they looked, Mad Albert Ash stepped out of the door of the hotel and stood for a moment, smiling, taking in a long, deep breath of morning air.

"It's about damn time," said Lematte.

"What is it you want Mad Albert to do, Sheriff?" Nolly asked, taking a chance on getting yelled at again.

"Lematte didn't answer again, as if having to think it over first. Finally he said, "I want to see Dawson show me some respect."

"Good luck," said Nolly.

"What's that suppose to mean?" Lematte asked.

"It means, Dawson has no respect for you, Sheriff. He's got no respect for *you*, me, or *any* of us. So what? To hell with him. Let's put him out of our mind and go on with business."

"You're starting to show me a side of you I don't like, Nolly," said Lematte. "You're acting just a little too weak to suit me."

"Sheriff, I'm just trying to go on with business, not let this man get under my skin. This ain't worth all the—"

Nolly tried to continue, but Lematte cut in, saying, "Come on, let's see if meeting Albert Ash face-to-face will take some starch out of Dawson's attitude."

Leaving the Furry boys in the wagon with their shotguns ready, Dawson went inside the Silver Seven Saloon and walked straight across the floor to the stairs. "Hey, you can't go up there!" the bartender called out, seeing him start walking up the stairs. But Dawson only gave him a sidelong look without slowing his pace. The bartender shrugged, saying to himself, "So, what the hell?" Then he went back to polishing shot glasses with a clean white bar towel.

Dawson didn't have to knock. Suzzette had seen him through the window as he rode into town. Her ribs and stomach were bruised and sore. Her face was swollen and blue, with a bandage over the cut left by the pistol barrel. But she had hurried as fast as she could and gotten herself and Angel Andrews dressed. She met Dawson at the door, ducking her face slightly, although unable to conceal her injuries from him.

"What the—" Dawson was taken aback by the sight of her. Dawson looked at her, then past her to where Angel Andrews sat on the side of the bed, dressed and wearing a thin traveling duster. At her feet sat their luggage. "Who did this?" Dawson demanded. But he really didn't have to ask.

"Let's just go, Cray," Suzzette said, her voice sounding shaky. "All I want is to get out of this town and forget I was ever here."

Dawson asked, "What about your baby, Suzzette? Is everything all right?"

She had a guarded expression as she replied, "Yes, I'm all right . . . or I will be, as soon as I get away from here."

Dawson looked at Angel Andrews, seeing her bruises, seeing that she seemed to be addled and unaware of what was going on around her. "What about her? Is she all right?"

"She's coming too," said Suzzette. "Is that all right? I can't leave her here. Next time he might kill her."

Dawson felt himself hesitate, but only for a second. Then he said, "Sure, she's coming too." He stepped over and picked up the luggage. Turning, he said to Suzzette, "I wasn't able to find you a place. You're going to stay with us, Carmelita and me that is."

"Have you talked this over with her?" Suzzette asked.

"Yes, we talked about it on the way here," said

Dawson. "It's all right with Carmelita, you staying with us. She even helped me fix up my old family house for you, but some of Lematte's men burnt it down."

"Is that who the two bodies were?" Suzette asked. "I saw you ride in with two bodies in the wagon. Is that the two men who burned it? Did you kill them?"

"Yes, that's them," said Dawson, "but it's a long story how they died." He looked Angel Andrews up and down, then said to Suzzette, "Can you help her along? We need to get out of here before Lematte or his men do something else crazy."

Chapter 20

Coming through the doors of the Silver Seven Saloon, Dawson stopped and found himself standing almost nose to nose with Mad Albert Ash. "Well, well, look who's here," Ash said, wearing an almost friendly grin. "How come every time I see you you're on some kind of tight spot, *Dalton*?"

Dawson saw Lematte and the rest of the men in the street behind Ash. In the buckboard the Furry brothers had stood up back to back, their shotguns pointed and ready. With both hands full of luggage, Dawson kept calm and said to Ash in a flat manner, "Who said I'm on a tight spot?" He set the luggage down and straightened up, showing no fear.

On the street Lematte whispered sidelong to Karl Nolly, "See how arrogant he is? That's what I can't stand about him!"

"What the hell is he supposed to do?" Nolly whispered in response. "Between him and those shotguns, he's got no reason to crawl."

Realizing that Dawson wasn't going to back an inch, Ash chuckled and turned toward Lematte, saying, "It looks like *Dalton* here is leaving, taking all your whores with him! Whatever shall we do now for entertainment?"

"Those two whores aren't going anywhere!" said Lematte, stepping forward boldly. They still owe me for transportation and expenses, bringing them here!"

"It's a free country, Lematte. They can come and go as they please," said Dawson. "Figure up what they still owe you. If it's a reasonable amount I'll pay you back. You're holding my marker on it."

"Your marker is no good with me, Dawson," said Lematte.

"Then you best consider the debt paid, Lematte," Dawson replied. "You've already killed one of them. I'm not leaving these two here to be beaten and misused by a tub-of-guts *coward* like you."

"Coward?" Lematte bristled, his hand coming close to reaching for his Colt. But he saw that Dawson's temper had started to flare, and he eased down, not liking the look Dawson suddenly had in his eyes. Mad Albert Ash and the rest of the men in the street saw that look as well. The men took a short step away from Lematte. But Mad Albert didn't let it affect him.

"Whoa, *Dalton*!" he said, still being playful, but taking Dawson more seriously. "You've been a good friend to me, saving my life and all. But damn, son! Calling a man a *coward*? A tub of *guts*? I can't let you stand here and offend my *employer* that way! How does that make *me* look?"

"I have no concern how it makes you look, Ash," said Dawson, straight and bluntly. "Step out of my way; they're leaving with me."

Something flickered in Ash's eyes. His hand almost snapped to his gun butt. But then he caught himself, stopped, and said to Lematte, "What say you, Sheriff? Should I kill him? Yea or nay?"

Dawson's cold stare moved from Ash to the Furry brothers and their shotguns, then to Lematte. Without Dawson saying a word, Lematte got the message loud and clear from the cold determination in Dawson's eyes. No matter how quickly Ash killed Dawson, Lematte could see himself lying dead before Dawson hit the ground. "Let them go," Lematte said meekly, sounding defeated.

"What was that, Sheriff, I didn't hear you. Speak up!" Ash said sidelong, teasing Lematte as he also stared steadily into Dawson's eyes.

"I said, let them go," Lematte repeated, feeling more humiliated, the eyes of all his men upon him.

Another short silence passed before, "*Whooie!*" said Ash, speaking so suddenly that Lematte and his men were taken aback by him. "Now that's what I call a tense moment of self-revelation!"

Letting out a short breath, Ash grinned and half turned toward Lematte, leaving Dawson and the women room to get past him without appearing to have stepped aside or backed down. He watched Dawson and the women walk across the boardwalk and step down into the street. Lematte's men moved slowly aside, unsure of what they should do. Seeing the look of uncertainty on the faces of all the men, Ash called out as if in amazement, "*Dalton,* I declare, you seem to have won the day!"

Dawson didn't answer him as he helped the women up onto the wooden seat of the buckboard. Suzzette took the reins to the team of horses. The Furry brothers still stood rigid in the wagon bed, the canvas-covered bodies at their feet. Dawson took Stony's reins and stepped up into the saddle. He tightened his hat down onto his head and said to

Lematte, "Don't send your men out spying on me, Lematte." He paused for a second as if to let it sink in. Then he said, "I'll be coming to Somos Santos on occasion for supplies and such. Advise your men to leave me be, or I'll hold you responsible." Then he gave Suzzette a nod and she slapped the reins to the team of wagon horses and rode the rig forward on the dirt street. Dawson rode beside it, keeping Stony cantering quarterwise for a few yards before turning his back on Lematte.

"There goes my whores," said Lematte flatly. Mad Albert chuckled under his breath, looking at the sour expression on Lematte's face.

"Why didn't you stop him, Ash?" Nolly asked, stepping up beside Lematte. "You're the gunman here!"

"Indeed I am the *gunman* here," Ash replied, still grinning, staring at Nolly with his hand resting on his pistol butt. "I make it a point to always follow my employer's orders."

"He's right, Nolly," said Lematte, sounding deflated. "I should have told him to stop Dawson . . . I didn't."

"There now, you see?" Ash said to Karl Nolly. "The sheriff should have asked, but he didn't." He turned and looked out at the wagon as it rolled onward, growing smaller and smaller. "And so Mister Dawson departs from us driving a wagon loaded with dead men and whores. How poetic." Ash seemed to ponder things for a moment, then added, "But don't worry, Sheriff, I'll still kill him for you when the time comes. Next time be more sure of yourself." Ash turned and grinned to himself as he walked away along the boardwalk.

"And that time will come," Lematte said quietly, "I'll see to it." He waved the waiting deputies away. "All of you back to your jobs!" The men walked away slowly, some of them shaking their heads.

Beside Lematte, Nolly said, "Sheriff, this is a good place to stop everything."

"Oh, yeah," Lematte growled. "What about the money it cost bringing those whores here?"

"There's plenty more whores where they come from," said Nolly. "We've got a good thing going here; let's not let it fall apart on us."

"You mean the way I let it fall apart in Hide City?" said Lematte, taking offense.

"Sheriff, I don't know anything about Hide City except what I've heard from you and from folks who were there. Alls I know is sometimes a man can be so careful about not making the same mistake *twice*, that he makes it over and over."

Lematte stared at him with a disgusted look. "That makes less sense than anything I've ever heard in my life." He turned and walked away, leaving Nolly alone on the boardwalk.

When Dawson and the buckboard arrived back at the spot where the Double D cowhands awaited them, Max Furry stood up and wiped an exaggerating hand across his forehead and grinned, letting the men know what a tense situation it had been. Dawson stepped down from his saddle and into Carmelita's arms. "Are you all right?" she asked him, the two embracing for a moment while Suzzette and Angel Andrews looked on.

"Yes, I'm all right," Dawson whispered to her. Turning to the wagon, he introduced Carmelita to

the women as the Double D men gathered respectfully, hats in hand, around the bodies on the
buckboard.

Dawson and the three women waited quietly until
the men stepped back and turned to their horses.
Shaney spoke for the men, saying, "Dawson, Lematte
and his men have to pay for this. We'd be both honored and obliged if you'd join us."

"First things first, said Dawson, nodding at the
bodies as Eldon Furry flipped the corner of the canvas back over the blue, dead faces. "Let's get on out
to the ranch."

The first few hundred yards Carmelita rode double
on Stony, sitting across Dawson's lap. "Are they
really going to ride into Somos Santos and take their
vengeance?" she asked in a secretive tone.

"Yes," said Dawson, "I expect they will."

"And Lematte and his men . . . how dangerous
are they?" she asked, searching Dawson's eyes.

"They're as ruthless and dangerous as any gang of
armed killers, Carmelita," Dawson replied. "There's
one man there that I hadn't expected to see. He'll be
the big problem. I don't think any of these Double
D men are prepared for the kind of gunfight he'll
give them."

"He is the man you will face," Carmelita said with
resolve, as if she already knew without asking.

"Yes, that's how it will play out," said Dawson
with equal resolve.

"There was no way you could reach an under-
standing with the sheriff?" Camelita asked, hoping
against hope.

"I told him to keep his men and himself away
from me, but he won't," said Dawson. "It was all

like talking to the wind. I just did it so I could say I tried."

"If we left this place . . . if we moved somewhere far away, perhaps to my country," Carmelita said, "you would not have to ever cross this man's path."

"Maybe," said Dawson, "but I've done all I can do short of running. And I won't do that."

"I know," said Carmelita, "and I understand. Still I tell myself in my heart that I must try to stop you. It is what a woman must do for someone she cares *strongly* for." She allowed herself a slight smile at her choice of words.

Dawson returned her smile. "I've played it over in my mind too many times to count," he said. "But the fact is, sooner or later Lematte or his men will make a move on me. If I wait, all I'll be doing is giving him the first strike . . . something you never want to give a rattlesnake."

They rode on in silence for a moment, Carmelita with her head against his chest. Finally, as if having run the matter through her mind one last time and finding a way to accept it, she sighed and nodded at the two women in the wagon. "Did he do this to them because of you?" she asked. "Because he knew about you and her?"

"That's probably the biggest part of it," said Dawson. "But when a man does something like that to a woman, there's always more than one reason why he did it. The simple answer is that Lematte is a man who has to crush what he can't control. He has to overpower what scares him."

"And you scare him," Carmelita said with finality.

"Yes, for some reason only he knows about, I scare him something awful," Dawson said.

Carmelita nodded as if having everything in perspective for herself. "Let me go ride with the women," she said. "It will make it easier for all of us to stay together if we can all three talk."

Without commenting on it, Dawson veered the horse over, alongside the wagon, and motioned for Suzzette to stop the team horses while Carmelita climbed down from his lap and got up beside her and Angel Andrews on the wagon seat. Dawson sat still atop Stony and watched the wagon roll forward. Beside him Shaney slowed his horse as he rode past and, nodding toward the three women, said jokingly, "Your luck with the fairer sex has changed a lot since the last time I saw you, Crayton."

Dawson nodded, realizing that Shaney had no idea about him and Rosa Shaw, and what losing her had cost him. "Yep, I'm one lucky fellow," he said, in ironic reflection.

For reasons he could not have explained, Dawson saw himself more clearly than he had for a long time. He stared forward at the soles of the dead men's boots as their bodies rocked and swayed with each turn of the wagon's wheels, moving forward under no power of their own, at the mercy and the whim of a cold dark world.

A reckoning was on its way, he told himself, a gunfight that never should have come about. A gunfight that could have easily been avoided had someone only offered the right word or made the right move, or possessed the right presence of mind to stop it. But now it was too late for words, actions, or deeds. The fight was coming and all he could do was try to come out of it alive. It was as simple as that.

"Take up, Stony," he said quietly to the horse, giving only a slight touch of his boots. He spent the rest of the ride back to the *hacienda* planning what he knew he would have to do when that time came.

Chapter 21

————

The following morning Cray Dawson took Carmelita, Suzzette, and Angel Andrews to the Double D in the buckboard to attend a service for Gains Bouchard and the men who had fallen at his side. With no minister to lead the service, the Double D men stood with their hats against their chests while Shaney read a few lines from a large leather-bound Bible Gains Bouchard kept on a nightstand beside his bed. The imprint of Bouchard's long-barreled Colt showed clearly on the front on the Bible, from years of Bouchard laying the gun there night after night.

When the service had ended Dawson walked away a few steps and looked out from the sloping hillside across a stretch of grasslands where a circle of cattle crowded the sparse shade of a cottonwood tree. "That's Gains's special breeding stock," said Shaney, walking up beside him with the big Bible cradled in his arms. "We could have buried Gains off by himself. But we figured he'd sooner be here on the hillside with his men." He gestured toward the scattering of other worn markers and stones, men who had fallen in the service of the Double D Spread over the years.

"You're right, Shaney," Dawson said quietly. "This

is where he would want to be buried." They stood in silence for a moment feeling a mid-morning breeze on their faces. Then Shaney broke the silence, saying, "The boys are ready to ride to Somos Santos right now, if you are."

"Not yet," said Dawson. "We'll wait a few days out of respect to Gains and the men. Let everybody cool their heads."

"It's going to be hard for me to make these boys do that, Dawson. They all feel like revenge is best served hot, before the dirt settles over these coffins."

"Make them listen to reason, Shaney," said Dawson. "I'm counting on you." He turned to walk back to the buckboard.

"All right, I will," said Shaney, turning beside him and walking a step behind. "But for how long? I've got to give them some kind of idea when we're going."

"Tell them it'll be *soon*, Shaney," said Dawson, offering no more conversation on the matter.

Shaney stood watching him walk to the trail at the top of the hill where the three women sat waiting in the wagon. Dawson stepped up into the buckboard, took up the reins, and sent the horses forward. "Dang it all!" Shaney whispered under his breath.

"What did he tell you?" asked Broken Nose Simms, he and the others gathering around Shaney, putting their hats back atop their heads.

"He said it'll be soon," said Shaney. "Said we ought to get our tempers cooled down first."

When a moment had passed without Shaney offering any more on the matter, Alvin Decker said, "Is that it? That's all he had to say about it?"

"Of course that's all he said!" Shaney looked Decker up and down. "Dawson ain't a big talker! He

says what needs saying then keeps his mouth shut."
He looked all around from one face to the next and
said, "That's a good trait in a man. I'd like to see
more of it around here the next few days."

Barney Woods said impatiently, "Damn it, Shaney,
you can't expect us to stand around here with our
thumbs in our belts, like a bunch of bummers! Lematte and his buzzards have got to pay in blood for
what they've done!"

"They will pay, Barney!" said Shaney. "If we want
Dawson to lead us, then we've got to do like he
says!"

"I don't like it," said Barney Woods.

"Neither do I," said Alven Decker. "I say we send
somebody to tell Dawson he either rides in with us
today, or else we ride in without him!"

"Listen to me, men," said Shaney, "I was asked to
run this bunch temporarily . . . and I'm trying to.
But if you ain't going to listen to me, or Dawson
either one, we should just as well roll up our blankets
and ride away! Let the Double D go to seed!"

The men settled. "Shaney's right," said Max Furry.
"Me and my brother rode into the town with Cray
Dawson. I never seen a man as cool and calm and
in control. He knows what he's doing. I'm waiting
till he's ready. Then I'll do whatever he asks of me.
That's what Gains Bouchard would want me to do.
By thunder, that's what I'll do. What about you,
brother?" He turned to Eldon Furry. "You were there
too. What do you think of Cray Dawson? Is he worth
waiting for?"

"I never seen nothing like the man," said Eldon.
"If he says wait a few days . . . I'll go along with
him on it. He's got my trust, and that's from *now on*."

Shaney looked all around at the cowhands with

his jaw set firmly. "There, now," he said. "That comes from two men who have already looked down their gun barrels at this situation. Anybody got anything more to say about it?" He looked around again. When no one offered anything further, he said, "All right then. Let's get ourselves back to our jobs and wait until Dawson is ready to make a move."

The men nodded and spoke among themselves as they headed up the hill to their horses. Alvin Decker and Barney Woods walked side by side, Woods saying just between the two of them, "I can't stand waiting like this. I've got to do something."

"I'm the same way," said Decker, giving him a look. "What say we talk some more about it later on, without all these ears around us?"

"Suits me," said Barney Woods, glancing back and forth. "With all respect to Crayton Dawson, I don't need nobody's help shooting a crazed wolf, do you?"

"I never did," said Decker. They walked on up to the trail and watched Dawson and the women ride away in the buckboard.

On the way home, Dawson found himself relieved and a bit surprised at the lack of tension between Carmelita and the other two women. While he hadn't expected hostility, he had anticipated a certain amount of tension. Yet, if any tension existed there, Dawson had not detected it on the ride out from Somos Santos, or at any time since. All he noticed was the formal politeness that came from strangers adjusting to one another. Upon arriving back at the *hacienda* after the funeral service, Dawson helped each of the women down from the wagon, then left to attend to the animals.

Inside the *hacienda*, Carmelita had said quietly to Suzzette, "I understand that you and Crayton were together in Eagle Pass."

"We were," said Suzzette, seeing no animosity in Carmelita's eyes or her tone of voice. "But this is not his child I'm carrying."

Carmelita said, "He told me that it was not his child. But whether it was his child or not, I want you to know that it would make no difference. After what happened to you in Somos Santos you would be welcome to stay here anyway."

"Thank you," said Suzzette. "That is kind of you." Her eyes welled slightly, but she touched a fingertip to them and stepped forward, the two women giving one another a hug while Angel Andrews looked on. Seeing the lonely look on Angel's face, Carmelita reached an arm out and drew her into their embrace, saying, "And that goes for you, too. You are both welcome here."

"—I want you to know, Carmelita," said Suzzette, "that I'm not going to be staying here long. In a few days, when I can travel, I'll be taking the stage to Missouri."

"You can stay as long as you like," said Carmelita.

"Yes, and I'm grateful to you. But I have an aunt in St. Louis. I'll be going to stay with her before the baby is born. She thinks I came west to marry a miner." She gave a tired smile. "So I will tell her what she wants to hear when the time comes. It will be all right."

"You decide what is best for you," Carmelita said. The women stepped back from one another. Carmelita offered a smile herself, saying, "Now, if only there was a way for these men to keep from killing one another . . ." She let her words trail, pondering the hopelessness of the matter.

Dawson walked in, and after a few moments of not knowing quite what to say, he excused himself

and went back outside. A few minutes later when
Carmelita joined him she saw that he had gathered
kindling for the *chimnea*. "Will you be doing the
cooking now?" Carmelita asked with a slight smile.

"I figured I'd help out some, give you women
some time to get acquainted."

"I see," said Carmelita. "*Gracias* . . . and now we
are all acquainted. So go away; I will prepare all of
us something to eat."

"Obliged," Dawson said, returning her smile. As
Carmelita walked past him, he grabbed her gently
and pressed her against him in an embrace. "You are
quite a woman, Carmelita. I'm a fortunate man to
have you."

"*Si*," she said, "and I am fortunate to have you."
Then she added playfully, "So do not go and get
yourself killed, not now that things are so good between us."

"I won't," he said, holding her, feeling the warmth
of her. "You have my word on it."

At the edge of the curtains, Angel Andrews
stepped up beside Suzzette and looked out with her.
Then she looked at the hurt in Suzzette's eyes and
said softly as she drew her away from the window,
"Come away from there, Suzzette, it isn't polite to
stare."

"Yes, I know," Suzzette said softly, turning away
from the sight of Dawson and Carmelita embracing.
"Carmelita has been too kind to us. So has Crayton.
I'm going to play straight with them." She looked
away for a second in contemplation, then she said,
"But I can't stay here." She turned back to Angel
Andrews and said, "The stagecoach to Eagle Pass
runs along the Old Spanish Trail every other day this

time of year. I saw it headed north on our way home from the Double D, didn't you?"

"I saw a stagecoach," said Angel, sounding uncertain, "but I don't know where it was headed."

"That's the one, it's the Eagle Pass stagecoach," said Suzzette, being patient with her. "I'm going to rest up tonight and tomorrow. Day after tomorrow I'm going to the Spanish Trail, stop the stage, and get on it. I'll take it to Eagle Pass, then take a cattle train to Missouri if I have to. Do you want to come with me?"

"Will—Will it be all right with your aunt, me coming along with you?"

"Yes," said Suzzette, "don't worry about my aunt. Do you want to come with me or not? It's a chance for you to get out of this kind of life before you get in any deeper."

"Yes, I'll go with you!" Angel added in a tone of desperation, "I'll go anywhere you say. I don't want to be a whore any longer. It's not the way I thought it would be." She swayed forward into Suzzette's arms and began sobbing quietly on her bosom.

"Don't cry. We'll be all right, Angel," Suzzette whispered, comforting her. We'll find work in Missouri . . . you can help me raise this baby. Everything will be fine, you'll see."

The morning the next stagecoach for Eagle Pass left Somos Santos, Sheriff Lematte stood out front of the Silver Seven Saloon puffing his first cigar of the morning. Beside him, Karl Nolly said, "Sheriff, take a look at this."

Lematte looked up and saw Henry Snead walk stiffly from between two buildings with his gun belt hanging over his shoulder and get on the stage. "Yeah, I see him," said Lematte. "The punk has been laid up in a room behind the barbershop, licking his wounds. Hogo learned that he sold his horse, saddle, rifle, and all so he could buy a stage ticket out of town. He was too sore to ride a horse!" He chuckled and added, "The poor, sorry bastard."

"He took one hell of a beating, that's for sure," said Nolly, staring toward the stage intently.

"Hogo spoke to him," said Lematte. "He had the nerve to ask Hogo if he thought I would give him his badge back if he came and talked to me about it?" Lematte shrugged. "Wanted to apologize I suppose."

"What did you tell Hogo to tell him?" Nolly asked.

"You'll love this!" Lematte laughed aloud. "I had Hogo tell him he'd be wasting his time talking to me, unless he brought me Crayton Dawson's head on the end of a stick!"

Nolly laughed. "You're right, Sheriff, that's a good one! I bet this punk would wet himself if he ever ran into Dawson again."

"Yeah, that's what I figure too," said Lematte. "I just said it to let him know he was washed up with me. I wouldn't give him his badge back if he killed Dawson and made him into breakfast sausage!"

Inside the stage, Henry Snead looked out the small window and saw Lematte and Nolly laughing on the boardwalk. He felt the back of his neck burn in humiliation, knowing they were laughing at him. "Sons of bitches," he said to himself, still feeling sore from the beating Dawson had given him. He reached inside his shirt, took out a bottle of rye, and had himself a long drink. Then he gauged the contents of the bottle before capping it and putting it back. Leaning out the opposite window of the stage, he called up to the driver, who sat with one boot raised and resting on the brake handle, "Hey! Driver! How long before we pull out of this shit hole?"

"Watch your language down there, young fellow," the driver said.

"Why?" said Snead. "There's nobody else here! I could curse to the top of my lungs, so what? Nobody would hear it!"

"I'd hear it," said the old driver firmly, "so pipe down and relax."

"How much longer before we leave?" Snead asked.

"I'm waiting for a shotgun rider," said the driver. "If he doesn't get here in a couple more minutes, I'm leaving without him. He's getting over a snakebite. Some days he ain't fit to do his job." The driver spit a stream of tobacco juice, then added, "Not that I need a shotgun driver. Nothing ever happens on the Eagle Pass turnaround."

"Then forget about him, let's go," said Snead.

"You sit still, Mister," the driver said. "We'll leave when I say we leave."

Snead grumbled under his breath and took the bottle from inside his shirt again. He opened it roughly and sloshed the whiskey around. "I can see this is going to be a long, hard trip," he said to himself, raising the bottle to his lips.

Chapter 22

———

Two days of rest and recuperation had Suzzette feeling better than she had in a long time. Before daylight she and Angel Andrews had slipped quietly out of bed and gathered their belongings while Dawson and Carmelita slept in the master bedroom at the other side of the house. Before leaving the house and heading to the barn, Suzzette crept into their room and laid a folded note on a table near the door. She lingered for a moment, looking at the sleeping couple. Then she sighed silently and walked away.

"I don't know why we're having to sneak away," Angel whispered as the two walked out to the barn in a soft circle of light from a lamp Suzzette held above them.

"It's not that we have to *sneak* away, Angel," said Suzzette. "It's just that sometimes it's better to leave this way. I thanked both of them in the note I left. I just don't feel like talking about things anymore, do you?"

"Well, no, I suppose not," said Angel, sticking close beside her as the two of them went inside the barn and readied the team of buckboard horses for the trail.

"Make sure you get these horses rigged on right,"

said Suzzette. "It's ten miles to where we're going to meet the stage."

"I'm not good at this," said Angel, fumbling with the horses' traces and tangling them.

"Here, let me have those," said Suzzette. I'll take care of the horses. You just climb up in the seat and hold the lamp for me."

When the buckboard was ready, Suzzette eased the horses forward as quietly as she could. Once out of the barn and up on the trail, she slapped the traces briskly and soon had the wagon moving along at a quick, steady pace. The rough ride caused Angel to press her hat down on her head and hold on firmly with her other hand. "Suzzette, slow down! If the stage runs all along the Old Spanish Trail, can't we catch it anywhere?"

"Yes," said Suzzette, "but I want to put some distance between me and them."

"But why?" asked Angel, having difficulty hanging on. "I thought everything is all right with Carmelita and Crayton and you."

"It is, Angel," said Suzette, not wanting to explain herself right then. "We'll talk more about it someday . . . but not now, all right?"

"All right," said Angel, "but please slow down! If not for me, then at least think about your baby!"

Suzzette didn't reply, but she did let the horses slow down until the wagon settled a bit. "Well, thank goodness!" Angel remarked.

Suzzette kept the wagon at a slower pace as the horses climbed steadily upward along a switchback trail. When the land flattened onto a higher plateau atop a line of cliffs and deep canyons, Suzzette sped the horses up until they reached a place in the trail where the stagecoach would have to also slow down as it crested the hills. There she stopped the wagon and visored her hand across her forehead, looking out through the morning sunlight for the stagecoach on the stretch of flatland two hundred feet below. Her eyes followed the snaking trail toward Somos Santos and found a dot on the horizon with a rise of dust drifting above it. "Good," she said, gazing out into the distance, "All we've got to do now is wait."

They sat in silence for a few minutes watching the dot until it took on the shape of a stagecoach and six horses pounding along the trail. "Once I get to Missouri, I'm never going to do something like this again," Angel said, as if she'd been in silent contemplation.

"Me neither," said Suzzette, without taking her eyes off the approaching stage.

"Do you want a boy or a girl?" Angel asked.

"What?" Suzzette asked.

"You know . . . your baby," Angel said. "Do you want a boy or a girl?"

"Oh, a boy, of course," said Suzzette. "A girl doesn't stand a chance in this world. Only a fool would want to bring a girl child into this world."

Suzzette's answer silenced Angel. They sat watching the stage until it disappeared beneath them and started its climb upward along the trail. "Let's get ready," said Suzzette, edging the wagon forward until it blocked the trail, giving the stage plenty of time to see it and slow to a stop. "Once he stops for us I'll pull the wagon over beneath those trees and leave it where Crayton and Carmelita will see it when they come for it."

Another ten minutes passed before the stage appeared on the trail, headed toward them. Upon spotting the wagon fifty yards ahead, the driver pulled back on the traces and the brake at the same time, bringing the stage to a gradual halt a few feet away. The driver saw the two women stand up facing him, but he looked all around warily, making sure this wasn't a trick of some sort. From the window beneath the driver's seat, Henry Snead called up to him, his voice a bit thick from whiskey-swollen lips, "What are you stopping for?"

"There's a couple of women up ahead," the driver called down to him. "Just sit still, I'll handle it."

Like hell I'll sit still," Snead mumbled under his breath, rolling up the canvas dust blind. "I'm sick of everybody telling me what to do." He poked his head out the window enough to get a look at Suzzette and Angel standing in the wagon. Then he ducked his head back inside before they had a chance to see him. "Well, ain't this something," he said to himself, his mind already at work inside its whiskey glow.

"Are you having trouble, ladies?" the driver called out, still glancing around for any sign of a trick.

"No trouble," Suzzette replied. "We just want to leave this buckboard here and ride with you to Eagle Pass."

"Well . . ." The driver let his words trail. "As you see I have no shotgun rider today. "Let me pull over and I'll get your luggage aboard."

"We'll bring it to you," said Suzzette, the two of them sitting down long enough for her to rein the horses forward, coming to a stop alongside the stage.

"That's even better," the driver said, grinning through his thick gray mustache. Suzzette and Angel stood up again, Angel lifting the first of their bags up to the driver. But before the driver could take the bag and set it atop the stage behind him, the door swung open and Henry Snead leaned out, hanging onto the stage with his left hand. "Not so fast!" he growled. "Everybody stay like you are!" In his right hand he held his Colt, cocked and pointed into Angel Andrews's face.

"Hey, what's going on here?" the stage driver asked, seeing the gun pointed at the women. "Is this a robbery?"

"No, it's not a robbery, you fool!" said Snead. "So shut your mouth and do like I tell you."

"Are you women with him?" the driver asked.

"Does it look like they're with me?" Snead responded before either woman could answer. "Don't make me tell you again to *shut up*! You meddling old bastard!"

"I'll shut up, but there's no need in that kind of language in front of these ladies," the driver managed to say quickly, still getting the last word in.

"Ladies, ha!" said Snead. "Haven't you ever seen these two before? Haven't you ever been to the Silver Seven in Somos Santos?"

"I don't frequent low places," the driver said.

"If you did," said Snead, "you'd realize that these are no ladies. They've laid down with every man in these parts."

"Except *you*, Snead," Suzzette said boldly. "Does that tell you something about yourself?"

Snead stared coldly at her. "You're Cray Dawson's sweetheart, ain't you?"

"No," said Suzzette, seeing something dark brewing behind Snead's red-rimmed eyes. "I know Dawson . . . but that's all there is to it."

"Bull!" said Snead. "I understand you're carrying his bastard kid in your belly! I expect if I had you under my arm he'd do about whatever I told him to do, wouldn't he?"

"You're drunk, Snead," said Suzzette, noting that all the while he talked he never took the gun away from Angel's face.

"Naw, I'm not drunk," he said. "Not too drunk to see what's just fell into my lap here." He swung up out of the stagecoach and onto the wagon, grunting with the pain from his injuries, but managing not to stagger as he straightened up and steadied himself.

"Get back in this coach!" the driver said, "or I'll take off and leave you!"

Snead looked up at him and laughed, saying, "Now there's an idea, old timer! Why don't you just get this rig on out of here? I'll stay here and ride with these *ladies*!"

"I don't know what you've got in that small mind of yours, Snead," said Suzzette, "but whatever it is—"

"I ain't going nowhere!" the driver said defiantly. "You get that gun down and leave these women-folk alone!"

"I've listened to all I'm going to out of you, fool!" said Snead, turning his gun toward the stage driver.

Suzzette saw Snead's knuckles turn white, saw his grip tighten, saw the killing look in his eyes. "No, wait, Snead! Don't shoot him!" She looked up at the driver and said, "You go on! We'll be all right. Don't worry about us."

"Are you sure, ma'am?" the driver asked. "I don't like the looks of this. I ain't leaving unless you ladies are safe."

Suzzette saw the sawed-off shotgun standing

against the seat beside him and realized that at any
second he might make a grab for it. She knew Snead
would kill him before his hand ever closed around
the shotgun. "Believe me, we'll be all right, Mister,"
said Suzzette, sounding as tough and bold as she
could. "Like he was telling you . . . we're both
whores. We know what he wants from us. Now get
out of here!"

Henry Snead stood watching the stage pull
away, the old driver looking back but making no
attempt to reach for the shotgun. Snead aimed
the pistol back at the two women but let it slump
a little. He grinned, saying to Suzzette, "You're
pretty smart for a whore. I should have come on
up and visited you back in Somos Santos." Then his
grin faded as his memory took hold. "I know you
saw what your boyfriend did to me, in front of the
whole town."

"He's not my boyfriend, Snead," Suzzette insisted.
"Try to get that out of your head, if you can."

"Well then," said Snead, raising the pistol again,
"since he's nothing to you, you won't mind me
shooting a few holes in his belly, will you?"

"I don't want to see anybody get shot, Snead," she
replied firmly. "But when it comes to you shooting
Cray Dawson, I'd say you'd have a better chance
lassoing a wildcat. Dawson is a man, a *real* man.
Don't mistake yourself for one; it'll tangle you up
every time."

"I hate a smart-mouthed *whore*," said Snead,
swinging the pistol toward her, his face telling her it
took all of his control to keep from shooting her.

Suzzette cautioned herself to ease up off of Snead
and see what it was going to take to get rid of him.

"Hey, take it easy, Snead," she said. "I thought we both knew I was teasing you." As she spoke she took off her small feathered hat, pulled a long pin from her hair and shook it out. "Don't you enjoy a little teasing now and then?"

Snead looked her up and down, thinking about her offer, seeing what she had in mind. For a moment he was tempted. But then he shook his head and said, "No, I ain't being sidetracked. I'm going to Dawson's with you riding close up beside me with the Colt tickling your ear. I'm calling Dawson out and killing him, deader than hell." He bit his lip, then added as he remembered Lematte's words, "I'm going to put your boyfriend's head on a stick and take it to Somos Santos."

Suzzette took her time answering, looking him up and down first. "Snead, do you really think I'll take you to Dawson, even if my life depended on it?" She unbuttoned her top buttons and spread her dress open. "So come on, put that out of your mind. Here, take a look at these." She cupped her breasts toward him, caressing them slowly. "Wouldn't it be more fun, the three of us? In this wagon? Naked? Under those big ole shade trees over there?" She smiled seductively. "No charge?"

"God almighty!" said Snead, his breath quickening at the sight of her bare breasts. He shot a glance toward the trees as if considering the possibilities.

"Make up your mind, Henry," Suzzette said softly. "We've got to get busy. We've still got a stage to catch." She gave a slight nod toward the trail ahead.

Seeing Suzzette work on him, Angel joined in, saying, "This is going to really be fun. I'll show everything Lematte taught me to do to him."

Snead almost gasped aloud. "You don't mean . . . ?"

"That's *exactly* what she means, Henry," said Suzzette, cutting in. "I've seen her do it. Whew! I went all crazy inside just watching."

Snead gave another nervous glance toward the trees. But then he seemed to shake the idea off and say, "I've got plenty time for that later."

"No, Henry," said Suzzette. "There is no *later*." She reached a hand around as if ready to pull off her dress. "If you want some of this, let's get to it, before that stage gets too far away for us to catch up to it."

"Uh-uh, there's time," said Snead. "As long as I've got this gun on you . . . I'm the one in charge of time." He stepped over and grabbed Angel by her wrist and shoved her toward the seat. Then he shoved Suzzette into the driver's seat and said, "You drive! And don't forget, I'm right behind you."

Suzzette started to turn the wagon in the opposite direction, away from the *hacienda*. But Snead cocked the pistol and jammed the tip of it against the back of Angel's head. "Don't try playing me for a fool!" he warned Suzzette. "Or I'll blow her head off. I've heard where Dawson is staying. Now turn around and go that way! I'll give you one more chance to do like I tell you. Your next mistake will get your friend a bullet in her head!"

"All right, Henry!" said Suzzette, seeing that he was on the verge of making good his threats. "I'm sorry, *please* settle down! I won't try anything like that again."

Suzzette turned the wagon in the direction of the *hacienda* while her mind raced, wondering what to do. "Henry, you're not really going to kill Dawson over him giving you a beating, are you? I mean, you gave *him* a beating; he didn't come back and kill you."

"That's right," said Snead, taking out his bottle of whiskey as the wagon rocked along the rough trail. "And that was his big mistake. I'm going to kill him, and I'm going to kill him so slow he'll beg me to hurry up and get it over. I want to hear some screaming, and plenty of it." He threw back a drink and said, "Before I kill him, I'll be sure and remind him it was you who brought me to him." He chuckled aloud.

"I see," said Suzzette, as if Snead's words had just made her mind up about something. Angel caught the change in her voice, but Snead didn't. "Hang on, Angel," she said sidelong, quietly between them. Then she said to Snead, "You want to hear some screaming? Then let's get this rig rolling. I'll get you there the quickest way I can."

"Hey, damn it, slow down!" Snead said as the wagon began rolling faster and faster along the high trail.

"Slow down? Suzzette said in a tight voice. "I thought you were in a hurry to do some killing!" She raised a whip from its place beside the seat and swung it out to snap above the horses' backs, speeding them up.

"Cut it out, or I swear," said Snead, "I'll put a bullet in her!"

But as Suzzette glanced over her shoulder she saw Snead's hat blow off his head as he rocked back and forth unsteadily on his knees in the wagon bed. Seeing Snead turn around and watch his hat sail away, Suzzette turned in her seat, raising her right foot, saying, "I'm sorry, Angel! You're getting off here!"

"Suzzette, no!" Angel shouted. But it was too late. Suzzette's kick sent her out of the wagon and tumbling across the rough, rocky ground.

"Stop, you crazy whore!" Snead shouted, bouncing back and forth in the wagon bed. "Stop or I'll shoot!"

"Fire at will, Henry." Suzzette laughed with abandon. "This is one day no *man* is going to make his demands on me. You wanted to hear screaming, start screaming!" she shouted, giving the horses the whip, sending them off the trail and across the rocky ground. The wagon bucked high in the air and slammed down with bone-shattering force. Henry could barely hang onto his pistol, let alone aim and fire it.

Staring forward as the wagon pitched and bucked in its dizzying speed, Henry saw where the broken land ended. He knew that beyond this rocky stretch of land lay nothing but thin air and a drop of over two hundred feet, straight down. "Oh, no!" he screamed. "God, no! Stop it!" But as he screamed he froze, dropping his pistol and clutching the sides of the wagon as if doing so would bring it to a halt.

A hundred yards away Angel Andrews stood in her torn, dirt-streaked dress. Her hand to her bloody head, she watched the wagon sail out off the edge of the earth. For a second the horses appeared to swim in midair. But then gravity took hold and the poor animals went down, their dying screams intermingled with Henry Snead's.

"Suzzette!" Angel screamed, limping as she ran toward the spot where the wagon had left the earth. Among the rocks along the edge of the cliff she saw

Suzzette's dress flutter on a hot Texas breeze. "Oh please, Suzzette!" she cried. "Please be alive!" She raced past strewn luggage that had spilled from the bouncing wagon. Coming to a halt among the broken, jagged boulders lining the cliff, she saw Suzzette lying motionless. "Oh no!" she said, her hands to her face as she moved forward slowly. "Oh, Suzzette. Why did you do this?" She saw Suzzette's eyes turn to her as she kneeled down beside her. "Why, Suzzette?" She sobbed. "The baby!"

"Shhh . . ." Suzzette managed to put a bloody hand on Angel's forearm. "There was . . . no baby, Angel. I made . . . it up. I wanted Crayton so bad . . . I thought maybe . . ." She struggled to find the right words, but couldn't. "Well, you know . . . how it is."

Seeing her friend fade, Angel said, "Suzzette hang on! Please! Don't die!"

Suzzette found the strength to say, "Tell Cray that he *really* missed out on something . . . when a whore loves a man . . . she'll go all out for him, eh?" Her eyes drifted in a weak gesture toward the edge of the cliff and at the luggage strewn everywhere. She offered a thin, dying smile, then said, "No . . . don't tell him anything . . . except that I'm glad . . . for him." She sighed and said, as if she were speaking to him, "Oh, Cray, it hurts so bad . . ."

Angel watched Suzzette's eyes roll slightly upward, then close as if she'd fallen asleep. For a long time she sat as if in a trance with Suzzette's head in her lap, until finally she felt a firm, gloved hand on her shoulder and heard the voice of Alvin Decker say, "Ma'am . . . let's get the young lady up from here and take her home, all right?"

Angel wept as Decker helped her to her feet. "She

and I were going to Missouri," Angel said brokenly.
We were quitting the business, you know?"

"I understand," Alvin Decker said softly, walking
her a few feet away while Barney Woods scooped
Suzzette's pale, limp body into his arms and carried
her back toward their horses.

Chapter 23

"We only saw the tail end of it," said Barney Woods to Cray Dawson back at the *hacienda*. He spoke quietly while Carmelita attended to Angel Andrews's cuts and scrapes with a clean, wet towel. "But it was that snake, Henry Snead. I recognized him right before she kicked this woman out of the wagon. We just couldn't get there in time to do any good. The next thing we saw was her whipping them horses toward the edge of the cliff, then we saw her throw herself off of it at the last second. But it was going awfully fast by then. I don't know why a woman would do something like that. She had to know it was traveling too fast for her to jump off."

Dawson stood over Suzette's body with his head bowed. "This poor, good woman," he whispered. "She did it to keep from bringing Snead to me. She wouldn't take a chance on him killing me." Dawson shook his head slowly.

"Maybe this ain't the best time to bring it up," said Woods, "but the fact is, things ain't going to get no better around here until somebody takes care of Lematte and his bunch. He knows there's vengeance coming for what happened to Bouchard and the boys." He gestured toward Suzette's body. "This sort of thing will keep on happening till we get settled up."

Dawson looked at Woods for a moment, then lowered his eyes back down to Suzzette. He lifted her cold, limp hand and held it in his. "She was put on the wrong side of this thing the minute Lematte saw that she knew me. Any way you cut it, I played a hand in her death."

A silence passed as Woods and Decker looked on. Dawson laid Suzzette's hand gently down at her side and said to the two drovers, "Where were you two headed when you saw them?"

Woods and Decker looked at one another shyly. Then Decker said, "All right, we'll be honest with you, Crayton. We got fed up and was headed to Somos Santos."

"Without Shaney and the rest of the men backing you up?" said Dawson. "You would have gotten yourselves killed."

"We did wrong," said Woods. "Now that we've settled down we realize it. But then, look what happened here." He looked down at Suzzette and shook his head slowly. "We all waited; now this poor woman is dead."

Dawson looked over at Carmelita, then said to Woods and Decker, "You're right. We've waited long enough. Go tell Shaney and the rest of the men that we're going into Somos Santos tomorrow. We'll ride in at noon while the sun is high overhead."

"Now you're talking!" said Woods, getting excited at the prospect. "We'll be here to get you early in the morning and ride in without stopping."

"I'll be ready," said Dawson. As if in afterthought he said to Decker, "Alvin, I need you to do me a favor."

"Just name it, Cray," said Decker.

"I need another horse. Stony has been favoring a hoof. Can you leave your horse here and ride a saddle mule back to the Double D? He's out back in the barn."

"Sure thing," said Decker. "I'll go get him and leave my horse at the rail."

"Much obliged," said Dawson. "Now get on out to the Double D and let Shaney know our plan."

"We're on our way," said Decker, raising his hat and putting it on as the two turned and headed to the door.

No sooner than the two drovers had saddled the red mule and ridden out of sight, Carmelita came over and stood beside Dawson as he stared down at Suzette Sherley's body. "Tomorrow, you and the Double D men are riding into Somos Santos?" she asked in a lowered voice.

"Yes," said Dawson, "tomorrow. You heard those two. They were headed there today on their own. It's got to be settled before anybody else dies."

"I know," said Carmelita. "I only asked so I will know when to light a candle."

"Tomorrow," Dawson said. Still looking down at Suzette he said, "This woman loved me, Carmelita. She loved me, and all loving me did was bring her pain, and get her killed . . . her and her baby."

"Don't think that way," said Angel Andrews, hearing Dawson. She stood up and walked over closer. She started to tell him that there *was* no baby, but at the last second she decided against it. It was not something Suzette would want her to tell him in front of Carmelita, she decided. "I mean . . . it doesn't help to think that way," she said. "What's done is done."

"*Si*," Carmelita said. "Things happen in this life that are out of our control." But as she spoke she saw that there were things Angel needed to say to Cray Dawson. After a second of pause, Carmelita said quietly to Angel as she took her hand off of Dawson's shoulder, "I will go get some fresh water from the well. We will wash her and dress her and bury her this afternoon. I will say the rosary over her."

Angel stood close to Dawson, and when Carmelita had left the room, she told him that there had been no baby. She also told him how Suzzette had called out his name in her dying breath. "Whatever mistakes she made," said Angel when she'd finished, "it wasn't done to bring anyone harm. I suppose she knew that you would want to help her get out of this business if you thought she was carrying a child, even if it wasn't your child."

"She was right," said Dawson. "But I would have helped her get out of the business anyway, Angel. She should have known that. She didn't have to make up a story."

Angel shrugged. "Well, she thought she had to."

"Yes, I suppose she did," said Dawson. They stood in silence until Carmelita came back in with a gourd full of fresh water. Then Dawson turned and left the room as Carmelita and Angel began to unbutton Suzzette's torn dress.

"Carmelita," said Angel, almost in a whisper, once Dawson had left the room. "What happened to Suzzette and me today isn't causing him and the Double D men to go to Somos Santos, is it?"

Carmelita considered it for a moment as the two of them undressed Suzzette. "In some ways perhaps it is, Angel," she said. "But in more ways it is not. I think there must always be more than one reason for men to kill one another. Perhaps tomorrow each man will have in his heart a different reason why someone must die.'' She handed Suzzette's dress to Angel and dipped the clean, soft towel into the water gourd.

When the two women had finished their solemn task, Suzzette lay atop the dining room table with her hair brushed and her bruises covered by a clean dress Carmelita found in her dead sister's closet. Without benefit of a coffin, they wrapped Suzzette in a plain brown wool blanket. After Carmelita said the rosary and Dawson read appropriate lines from a Bible, they buried her beneath the thin shade of a white oak tree behind the *hacienda* and walked back, each silent in their own thoughts, Carmelita carefully avoiding any mention of the following morning and what she knew lay before Cray Dawson and the Double D riders.

In the late evening, after Carmelita and Angel had both gone to their respective bedrooms, Cray Dawson sat in a circling glow of lamplight and took his Colt apart. He cleaned and inspected each moving part, then reassembled the gun piece by piece, carefully wiping each part with a soft white cotton rag. When he'd finished, he raised the gun close to his ear and turned the cylinder slowly, listening to each precision click of metal against metal. Satisfied, he examined each cartridge and loaded the pistol round by round. Having loaded it, he slipped the pistol into his holster lying on the table and slid the pistol in and out a few time, feeling the ease and smoothness of the motion. Then he laid his gun belt aside and cleaned his Winchester repeating rifle in the same meticulous manner.

He stood up quietly and slipped the gun belt up

onto his shoulder. Carrying the lamp he walked to just inside the bedroom where Camelita lay sleeping. For a moment he stood there listening to the faintest sound of her breathing. Then he whispered softly, "Good night, Carmelita." He turned out the lamp, set it on a small table beside the bedroom door, and backed silently out of the room.

In the night Carmelita awakened twice, once as she heard Dawson speaking softly to her from the doorway, then again at the end of a troubled dream when she reached a hand over to his side of the bed and realized he wasn't there. She threw a robe around herself and went from room to room looking for him. Then she slipped on her boots and walked to the barn, but by this time it was only to confirm what she already knew. She sighed, holding the lamp up to the empty stall where Dawson had stabled the horse Decker left for him. Next to that stall Stony stood quietly, only twitching his ears as the lamplight spread upon his stall.

Cray Dawson had no intention of riding into Somos Santos at noon with the Double D men. He was on his way there now. Suddenly it hit her that Dawson had ridden Decker's horse only because he thought he wasn't coming back and he didn't want Stony to fall into the wrong hands. "*Santos nos protegen!*" Carmelita whispered to herself, making a hasty sign of the cross. Then she hung the lamp on a post, grabbed Stony's bridle from a peg, and hurried into his stall.

In the gray hour before dawn, Shaney and the Double D men rode quietly into the front yard and stopped their horses, seeing Carmelita on the front porch with her hands wrapped around a cup of cof-

fee. She was dressed for the road. At the hitch rail
Stony stood saddled and waiting. "I thought Dawson's horse had a bad hoof?" said Decker.

Before Carmelita could answer Decker, Shaney already sensing something amiss, asked, "Where is
Dawson?"

"He left in the night," said Carmelita, "perhaps
two or three hours ago, on the horse Decker left
here."

"Dang it all!" said Shaney, realizing instantly what
Dawson had in mind. "He'll get himself killed going
up against that many guns by himself!" He watched
Carmelita step down from the porch as he spoke to
her. In the front door of the *hacienda* Angel stood
watching, Carmelita having already awakened her
and told her what was going on.

"Godspeed, Carmelita," Angel called out.

"What?" said Shaney. He cocked his head toward
Carmelita as she swung up onto Stony's back.
"Where are you going?" he asked Carmelita gruffly.

"I'm going with you," she said with determination.
"I would have gone already, but I wasn't sure of the
trail in the dark."

"Now listen, Ma'am," said Shaney. "It's going to
be a hard, flat-out ride to get to Somos Santos. We
can't wait up for you."

"You will not have to wait up for me," said Carmelita. "I can ride."

"What do you say, Shaney?" said Broken Nose
Simms, getting anxious. "We best get going! Let her
come along! She'll keep up!"

"All right, Ma'am," said Shaney. "But either keep
up or fall behind . . . we've got some ground to
cover." As he jerked his horse around by its reins,

he spoke in the direction of Somos Santos, "Cray Dawson, you stubborn fool! I ought to bend a skillet over your head!"

From the doorway of the *hacienda*, Angel watched Carmelita and the rest of the riders disappear like smoke into the gray morning mist.

At daybreak Sheriff Martin Lematte stood at the bar in the Silver Seven Saloon with stacks of dollar bills and gold coins piled high before him. Beside him stood Karl Nolly and Mad Albert Ash. Lematte took a drink of hot coffee and lit his first cigar of the morning as Hogo Metacino walked in carrying a telegraph in his hand. "Boss, I've got a peace officer alert for you. You ain't going to believe this!" said Metacino, waving the telegraph before handing it over to Lematte. "We're supposed to keep our eyes peeled for Henry Snead!"

"Henry Snead? For what?" asked Karl Nolly in astonishment.

As Lematte read the telegraph, Metacino laughed and said to Nolly and Ash, "That came in overnight from the Grayson stage depot. A stage driver said that Henry Snead got drunk and forced two women to leave with him in a wagon somewhere along the Old Spanish Trail yesterday! Said Henry is armed with a pistol and has threatened the women's lives!"

"My goodness," Karl Nolly chuckled. "Our Henry, making a fool of himself once again." He raised his coffee as if in a toast to Snead.

"Yes, it's the truth," said Lematte, finishing the telegraph and passing it along to Nolly. "That beating Dawson gave him must've addled his brain." Then Lematte reflected for a moment and said, "According to this it's a couple of *'soiled doves'* from Somos Santos he forced to go with him."

Nolly gave a bemused grin and said to Lematte, "You don't suppose it could be those two whores who left here the other day with Dawson, do you?"

"I suppose that's a possibility. You can never tell where a whore'll turn up." Lematte gave it more thought. But before he could answer any further, a single rifle shot rang out from the street, drawing everyone's attention toward the bat-wing doors and the sound of running boots along the boardwalk. Lematte, Nolly, and Metacino all drew their guns as Joe Poole and Eddie Grafe spilled through the doors and skidded to a halt.

"Don't shoot!" Joe Poole shouted in a shaky voice, his eyes large with fear, seeing the guns pointed at him.

With his Colt still in its holster Mad Albert stood calmly at the bar and sipped his coffee, watching, chuckling under his breath.

"Sheriff! Cray Dawson is out there on the street!" Eddie Grafe said, his breath heaving in his chest. "He tried to kill us on our way here!"

"If Dawson tried to kill you, you'd be dead," said Ash, still holding his coffee cup. He shook his head, set his cup down, and pushed it slowly away from him. He raised his big Colt from his holster and checked it.

"Yeah, Ash is right, so settle down," Lematte said to the two deputies. "Where's Delbert Collins?" As he spoke he took a cautious step toward the bat-wing doors, his pistol in hand, craning his neck for a look out at the street.

"He was headed this way with us," said Joe Poole.

"But he ain't getting around so quick with that bullet wound in his nuts."

"So you ran off and *left* him?" Lematte asked, sounding outraged.

The two looked at one another as if it had just occurred to them what they had done. "But, Sheriff! We thought we better hurry here and tell you about Dawson!" said Poole.

Lematte eased closer up and stood with his back flat against the wall beside the doors for a moment. Ash gave Lematte a dubious look, watching him turn slowly to peep around above the doors, out into the street. Immediately three pistol shots exploded almost as one, sending Lematte jumping backward, his gun falling from his right hand, both hands going to his face as he shouted, "Damn it to hell!"

Splinters from the shattered door frame stuck in Lematte's cheeks like tiny darts. Mad Albert Ash backed away from the bar, taking his time, while the others scurried for firing positions and cover. Outside, Dawson's voice called out above the sound of horses, wagons, and footsteps hurrying to get out of the line of fire, "Lematte! It's time we settled up."

Lematte pulled the splinters from his face and wiped blood from his chin as he replied, "Suit yourself, Dawson! There's six of us in here! You don't stand a chance!"

"Then let's get to it," Dawson said in a firm, even tone of voice, replacing his spent cartridges.

Lematte looked at Ash, stunned. "Is he crazy? He wants to fight all of us?"

"That is what it sounded like to me." Ash grinned. He stood closer to the rear door, his glove off of his right hand and shoved down behind his gun belt.

"Didn't you know it would come to this? He doesn't care how many there are of us. He's got his bark on. Don't you?" He walked the rest of the way to the rear door, shook his head, and stepped outside into the alley. Lematte looked shaken by Ash's unexplained departure.

But he swallowed a knot in his throat and managed to collect himself. "Dawson, we need to talk about this thing!" he called out, scrambling to grab his gun from the floor. Even as he spoke he gave the men a gesture with his hand, letting them know that he meant for all of them to rush the street when he gave them a signal.

"No talking," said Dawson. "I'm here to kill you, nothing else."

"How did things get like this between us, Dawson?" Lematte called out, checking his gun all the while. "Was it Bouchard's death that caused it? Snead giving you that beating? The way I treated those whores? What one thing was it? Huh? I'd like to know before we kill you!"

"I don't know . . . don't care," Dawson said. "You've wanted this showdown ever since I got back to town. *Why* you've wanted it makes no difference now. Get on out here. Bring anybody who wants to join you. I'm taking on all comers today."

"*All comers?*" Joe Poole and Eddie Grafe gave one another a worried look, both of them hunkering down behind an overturned card table.

Lematte spoke to the others in a harsh whisper, looking around as he crouched on the floor, "Is everybody ready?" Seeing the men nod, he called out to Dawson. "I heard what happened, Snead kidnapping them whores. Is that what's brought this to a head? Is there more to it than I know about?"

"Suzzette is dead, Dawson said flatly. "Come on out."

"Suzzette . . . ?" said Lematte. He formed a cruel grin. "Now let me see . . . which one was that?" He waved his men forward in front of him toward the door, saying, "Now! Let's go! *Get him!*"

As Nolly, Grafe, and Poole charged out the front door, Hogo Metacino hurled a heavy poker chair through the large glass window, shattering it, then leaped out onto the boardwalk, his gun blazing.

"Damn you, Sheriff!" screamed Karl Nolly, seeing that Lematte had shoved them forward through the bat-wing doors, but had then ducked back inside at the last second as the shooting started. Nolly fired at Dawson as he cursed Lematte.

Cray Dawson's first shot hit Eddie Grafe dead center, sending him backward into Joe Poole and keeping Poole from getting an aim. Poole never got another chance. Dawson's next shot dropped him dead. Still firing, Dawson sent a shot through Karl Nolly's heart. The impact lifted Nolly backward, spinning him along the front of the Silver Seven Saloon into a bloody spray until he collapsed off of the boardwalk and into the mouth of a littered alleyway.

Standing in the broken window glass, Hogo Metacino shouted loudly as he quickly emptied six shots at Cray Dawson, only one of them grazing Dawson's right forearm. The other shots went wild, one thumping into the boardwalk across the street where Delbert Collins tried hurrying along, with both hands clutching his crotch. "Don't shoot!" Delbert shrieked tearfully. "I'm ruined already!"

Dawson spun toward Delbert Collins and saw no threat there. He swung back toward Hogo Metacino and saw him click his pistol on an empty chamber. "No, don't shoot!" Hogo shouted, repeating Collins's plea. But when Dawson turned his colt from Hogo and back toward the bat-wing doors, Metacino saw his chance and pulled a small, hidden pistol from behind his back. Once again he started firing wildly. This time Dawson's Colt exploded once, decisively, and dropped him dead before he got off his fourth shot.

Dawson had three shots left in his Colt, and one shot chambered and ready in his Winchester. He looked back and forth, through the broken window, and both above and below the bat-wing doors for any sign of Lematte. On the boardwalk where Delbert Collins still stood holding his wounded crotch, sobbing in pain, Councilmen Deavers and Tinsdale appeared from out of a doorway and began shoving him back and forth roughly. "Now let's see how tough you are, *Deputy*!" said Deavers, "you son of a bitch!" He tried to kick Collins in his crotch, but Collins held onto himself.

"Please!" Collins pleaded. "I didn't hurt anybody! Look at the shape I'm in!"

"We don't care," said Tinsdale, speaking loud enough for onlookers to hear him. "We're talking this town back from you vermin!"

Dawson called out to the Silver Seven Saloon, "Lematte. Come out. You're washed up here. Your men are dead. Let's get this thing over with."

"I'm not coming out, Dawson!" Lematte yelled. "If you want me, come in and get me!" Even as he spoke, Lematte made his way along the floor behind the bar, shoving a cringing bartender aside as he tried to get a closer run at the rear door. On his way, Lematte stopped and looked at the butt of a sawed-off shotgun sticking out from a shelf under the bar. "Is this thing loaded?" he whispered.

"Ye—yes!" said the bartender, "of course it is!"

"Good," said Lematte, jerking it out from the shelf and shoving it into the bartender's shaking hands. "Get down there at that end of the bar! When he comes through the doors, stand up and let him have it with both barrels. Do you understand?"

"Sheriff," the frightened bartender said, "I can't do that! I'm no gunfighter!"

"Get down there and do it, or I'll blow a hole through you!" Lematte said, poking his pistol in the bartender's belly.

Outside, Dawson stepped cautiously onto the boardwalk and shoved the bat-wing doors open as quietly as possible. Still, there was a slight creaking sound that caught Lematte's attention. He waited until he heard the doors swing back and forth quietly, realizing that Dawson was now inside, perhaps halfway across the floor. "Now!" he shouted at the bartender as he raised up quickly, his gun going out arms length, cocked and ready.

At the end of the bar the bartender rose up stiffly, pointing the shotgun with his eyes squeezed shut. But it didn't matter. Both the shotgun and Lematte's pistol were pointed at an empty space. Lematte looked dumbfounded. But Dawson called out from across the broken window frame, "Lematte, over here!"

Lematte swung the pistol toward Dawson, shouting at the bartender, "Shoot him!"

A bullet hit Lematte in his chest above the bar top, knocking him back into a shelf of whiskey bottles. The bottles crashed around his feet. The same impact that flung him backward also bounced him forward off of the wall and half onto the bar top. He lay against the bar with his arms spread along the edge, blood pumping out in a thick stream with each beat of his pulse. Dawson stepped in over the window ledge and walked forward, seeing the bartender drop the shotgun and raise his hands high.

"Dawson . . . you bastard!" said Lematte, paying no attention to the flow of blood spreading over the bar top. "I still want to know—" His words stopped in his chest. He started all over. "I still want . . . to know, *why*?" His eyes turned flat and lifeless. He sank until his chin stopped on the edge of the bar top and stayed there, holding him suspended above a reflecting pool of blood. Dawson stood staring at his lifeless face for a moment. Finally, in a quiet tone, giving the only honest answer he could think of, he said, "Beats me, Lematte."

He turned and walked out onto the street, knowing that he had only one shot left in his Colt and knowing that somewhere Mad Albert Ash waited in the shadows. "It was never between you and me, Ash," he said aloud, his eyes searching first in one direction, then another. "We can call it off right here, right now. Both of us can ride away."

"You don't really think that, do you, *Dalton*?" The voice came softly, from every direction, from no direction, the words of some demon apparition, whispered from a lower plane.

Dawson froze, only his eyes moving, searching slowly. He dared not speak. He waited for the next word and wondered if it would come before or *after* the killing shot from Ash's gun.

"I'm the one who killed the young drover," Ash said. "I killed the old rancher, too." There was no face, no direction, only the voice. "You could never forgive all that, could you, *Dalton*? Not after having saved my life. Think about it. Saving my life sort of makes you responsible for everybody I've killed since then, doesn't it?"

"Step out, Ash," said Dawson. "Let's get it done. I know you're not a coward like Lematte. Show yourself!"

"Well spoken!" Ash chuckled. "Tell me, *Dalton*, are you a gunman now?"

"I am," said Dawson. "Now come out, face me!"

"I just repaid you for saving my life, *Dalton*," said Ash, "By not *killing you* when you stepped into my gun sight. Does that make us even now?"

In the distance Dawson saw the rising dust of many horses racing toward Somos Santos. He knew it would be the Double D riders. He wanted to finish this before they rode in. This fight belonged to him, nobody else. "We're even now," said Dawson, "Step out." Blood from the graze on his forearm soaked into his sleeve and dripped from his shirt cuff.

Ash appeared from the corner of the littered alley-way, wiping a hand across his mouth. "Speaking through a drainpipe is an old trick I learned years ago. Have you never heard of it, *Dalton*?"

"No," said Dawson. "And I'm betting you haven't either."

"I hope you do realize that you've only got one shot left in that pistol," said Ash, grinning. "Not that that should make you *nervous*."

"I'm not nervous, Ash," said Dawson, slipping his Colt into his holster, getting ready for a one-on-one showdown. "I'll live or die here today . . . I'm not nervous about it, are *you*?" He reached out to drop his Winchester to the ground.

"Me? Nervous?" said Ash. "Well I hardly think so—"

His words stopped short as his eyes lit in surprise and his right hand went for his Colt.

Dawson had not dropped the Winchester. Instead of turning it loose he had let the stock slide through his hand until his hand reached the trigger, then he swung the barrel up, *fast*, cocking the hammer and letting it fall, in one swift split second.

All of Ash's speed came into play at once, his hand closing and raising his Colt in a streak of gunmetal. But he saw it was too late. The rifle shot nailed him where his ribs met in his chest. His breath left him and he staggered in place, his pistol hanging limply in his hand. He tried to speak but there was no air in him to form his words. He dropped to his knees.

"You should have seen that coming," said Dawson, watching Ash rock back and forth wide-eyed, then pitch face forward in the dirt. He walked in close, took Ash's gun from his hand and shoved it down into his belt. He walked back to the middle of the street and watched the rise of dust grow closer as he punched out his empty cartridges, let them fall to the street, and replaced them.

Along the boardwalk he felt the eyes of the towns-folk on him. But that was something he'd gotten used to now. He walked to the horse he'd ridden in on and shoved his Winchester down into the rifle boot, realizing now that he could have ridden Stony to town after all . . . now that he'd been given this day. Beneath his feet he felt the first low, distant rumble of the horses' pounding hoofs. He took a deep breath and tried to relax. He thought about Suzzette Sherley, and Rosa Shaw, two women whose lives had brushed up against his briefly. Two women who were now dead. One, a woman he loved so much that his insides had ached for her; the other, a woman who loved him so much she had given her life to save him.

As he walked along the dirt street he forced himself not to think about the dead. Instead he thought about the living, about Carmelita and himself. He could see Carmelita's eyes and feel her touch and smell the scent of her on the warm Texas wind. It dawned on him how badly he longed to be with her right then, with her and nobody else . . . at that very moment . . . for no other reason than to live out the rest of this day.